FIC
Dider   Diderot, Denis

        Memoirs of a nun

EVERYMAN,
I WILL GO WITH THEE,
AND BE THY GUIDE,
IN THY MOST NEED
TO GO BY THY SIDE

DENIS DIDEROT

Memoirs of a Nun

Translated from the French by Francis Birrell

EVERYMAN'S LIBRARY

Alfred A. Knopf New York

90

c.1

THIS IS A BORZOI BOOK

PUBLISHED BY ALFRED A. KNOPF, INC.

First included in Everyman's Library, 1992
This translation first published in 1928 by George Routledge &
Sons, Ltd.
Introduction, Bibliography, Chronology, and Notes Copyright ©
1992 by David Campbell Publishers Ltd.

ISBN 0-679-41324-3
LC 91-58702

Library of Congress Cataloging-in-Publication Data
Diderot. Denis, 1713–1784.
[Religieuse.   English]
Memoirs of a nun / Denis Diderot.
p.   cm.—(Everyman's library)
Translation of: La religieuse.
Originally published: London ; Routledge, [1928].
ISBN 0-679-41324-3 : $15.00 ($19.00 Can.)
I. Title.
PQ1979.A76E5   1992   91-58702
843'.5—dc20   CIP

Printed and bound in Germany

CONTENTS

———

INTRODUCTION

Denis Diderot is a writer not too easy to get into focus, partly because of the sheer diversity of his achievements. He laboured for twenty years of his life on the great multi-volume *Encyclopaedia*, famous in its own day as the bible of 'enlightened' opinion. He was a philosopher, and, in *D'Alembert's Dream*, created a quite original form of philosophical fantasy. He was also a dramatist and a theoretician of the drama, and a pioneer art-critic of great brilliance. It was characteristic of him that, in all these activities, he thought it his duty to think them out from first principles; and it was so again when, at the age of forty-five, he embarked on his first novel, *La Religieuse* (*The Nun*).

Actually, 'embarked' is not quite the right word, for the conception of *The Nun* came about, as it were, by accident. The story of this is strange. Among his intimate circle was an elderly and mildly eccentric aristocrat named the Marquis de Croismare. Everyone was fond of the Marquis, who was a most charming, chivalrous and tender-hearted man; thus Diderot, and another friend of his, a German named Melchior Grimm, were most put out when Croismare, who had gone to pay a visit to his country estate near Caen, showed signs of intending to stay there, abandoning his friends in Paris for ever. They therefore, in the early months of 1760, formed a bizarre plot. A year or two before, Croismare had taken a great interest in the fate of a nun who was demanding to be released from her religious vows.* She had managed to have the affair taken out of religious hands and placed before Parlement (the highest legal body in the land); and Croismare had lobbied energetically on her behalf, though to no avail.

---

*She was named Marguerite Delamarre. She was by now in her forties and, it would seem, had received most cruel treatment from her parents, who had forced her to choose between entering a convent or being sent to a house of correction. Her efforts to gain her release having failed, she remained in her convent till the Revolution.

vii

The idea thus came to Diderot and Grimm to forge a fictitious letter to Croismare, as if from this nun, announcing that she had escaped from her convent, and begging the Marquis for help. Their notion was that, knowing Croismare's quixotic nature, it might bring him hurrying back to Paris. How the Marquis was taken in; how further letters were composed and Diderot began to draw up a memoir by the nun, relating the harrowing story of her life; and how the conspiracy took an awkward turn, so that an imaginary death-bed had to be devised for her; all this was related by Grimm ten years later, as was the fact which concerns us most of all – that the 'memoir' of the nun, begun in fun, took hold of Diderot's imagination and developed into a complex work of art.

It so happened that, just about this time, a Jansenist sect known as *convulsionnaires* were in the news, for practising spectacular and macabre acts of self-mortification, including a form of crucifixion. The explorer La Condamine reported one such incident on Good Friday 1760.

Sister Françoise (55 years of age) was fixed to a cross in my presence, with four square nails. She hung there more than three hours. She suffered a good deal, especially in the right hand. I saw her shudder and grind her teeth with pain as they drew the nails out.

These reports were on Diderot's mind, as he began to sketch the 'memoir' of his nun, as were memories of his own younger sister, who had insisted on joining a religious order, against their parents' advice, and had died in a state of religious mania. The whole idea of claustration and religious mortification disturbed him deeply. He was himself an atheist, but not a proselytizing one, and there were aspects of religion he looked on with a certain tenderness; but the monastic idea he found unforgivable. In his first philosophical work, the *Pensées philosophiques*, the lines that most ring in one's memory are this eloquent outburst.

What voices! What outcries! What groans! Who has shut up all these plaintive corpses in these prison-cells? What crimes have these poor wretches committed? Some beat their breast with stones; others tear their body with iron hooks; all have regrets, sorrow and death in their eyes. Who condemns them to these torments? ... *The God whom they*

have offended ... What sort of God is He? *A God full of goodwill* ...
Would a God full of goodwill find pleasure in bathing in tears? Would
such terrors not be a reflection on his clemency? If criminals had to
appease the fury of a tyrant, what more could be expected of them
than this?

What is also significant is that, in the same year – when he
and his friends were gaily devising the nun's death-bed scene –
Diderot made the acquaintance of Richardson's novels and
became an impassioned champion of them. He decided that
Richardson was a moral genius, superior to Montaigne or La
Rochefoucauld because he showed ethics in action; he was
even in danger, he wrote to a friend, of making a liking for
Richardson a condition of his own friendship. But what
amazed and impressed him even more was Richardson's
hypnotic illusionism, which put the reader into the situation of
a child at its first stage play, crying 'Don't trust him! He means
to deceive you!' One day, in a friend's presence, he was
reading the famous death-bed scene in *Clarissa* and, unable to
bear any more, he got to his feet and, to his friend's alarm,
uttered the most piteous outcries against Clarissa's unfeeling
family.

He had once laid it down, in a *Discourse on Dramatic Poetry*,
that a writer ought not to throw a single detail down on paper
until he had completed his plan. His practice with *The Nun*
was just the opposite, and the work seemed to grow unfore-
seen. 'I am at my *Nun*,' he told a friend in August 1760, 'but it
expands under my pen, and I don't know when I shall reach
land.' To another friend, three months or so later, he writes 'I
set to work on *The Nun*, and I was still at it at three o'clock in
the morning. I am going like the wind. It is no longer a letter,
it is a book. There will be things both true and pathetic in it,
and I ought to be able to make them strong but I do not give
myself enough time. I let my thoughts run free; I don't know
how to restrain them.'

*

It is easy to fall into the habit of looking at the early history of
the European novel from the point of view of the direction the

novel eventually took. But to a contemporary of Defoe and Richardson the possibilities of the form are likely to have looked rather different. To a writer of this period, it might have seemed there was a fundamental choice offered: on the one hand a conception of the novel as deception, as falsehood dressed up as truth and leaving a margin of possibility that it might in fact turn out to be truth; and on the other hand a notion of the novel as illusion – illusion unambiguously acknowledged as such. A novel like *Tom Jones*, with its elaborately contrived plot, is bound to belong in the second category, that of 'accepted illusion': it was, and still is, a very fruitful genre and was the one practised by Jane Austen, George Eliot and Dickens. However, the novel as deception, in which the possibility is always left open that the work may turn out to be a genuine document, written by a real-life Pamela or Moll Flanders, or perhaps a piece of 'secret history', is a form which offers, potentially at least, equally rich opportunities. One remembers the extraordinary antics indulged in by Swift to sustain his anonymity at the time of *Gulliver's Travels*. What they signify is not that Swift was interested in hoaxing his readers in any literal sense, but rather a vision of fiction as, in its very fibre, a synonym for fraud, deception and counterfeiting; and it is in the same spirit that Richardson goes to such lengths in his title-pages and prefaces to pretend that his novels are real-life documents. The 'novel as deception' works by never finally severing its connection with real life, including the real life of the reader. Such a novel continually exploits the reader's uncertainty. The author has absconded, as it were, leaving the possibility that there may be no 'author' at all, thus leaving the reader with no certain guide as to the judgments he or she is supposed to pass. (Shall *Roxana* be regarded as a very moral or a very immoral tale?)

But a further consideration arises. The writer who conceives of the novel as falsehood is liable also to be the one tempted to blow the gaff: to frustrate the reader's desire for a 'romance' and remind the reader that a 'narrator' may be a real-life author – perhaps a teasing, bored or angry one. The writer who can throw his or her genius into 'practising' on the reader may equally be tempted to triumph over the reader by showing the whole business up as a fraud and confidence-trick. This was exemplified, famously, by Sterne; and in due course Diderot would discover Sterne and be as overwhelmed by him as he had been by Richardson, writing a novel (*Jacques le fataliste*) in direct imitation of him. (The two main influences on him as a novelist, it is worth noticing, were both English.) But the law I mention proved true with Diderot, even before he had read Sterne; and this novel-as-deception, *The Nun*, born in a hoax, is also very markedly a novel-of-*un*deception.

What one discovers in this first novel of Diderot's – perhaps with a touch of surprise, considering his known character as a 'Man of feeling' – is that it exhibits hardly a trace of sentimentality. The art of fiction evokes in him a salutary and impressive coldness, a detachment somewhat in the manner of Stendhal. The note is struck very early in the novel, in the incident of the nun Suzanne's nosebleed. Having successfully staged a refusal to take her vows, she is returning home with her implacable mother. They face each other in silence in the carriage, and then, writes Suzanne:

I do not know what came over me, but suddenly I threw myself at her feet and bent my head upon her knees. I did not speak, only sobbed and choked. She rebuffed me unfeelingly. I did not get up: blood came to my nose; I seized one of her hands despite her efforts. Then watering her hand with my tears and the blood which was flowing from my nose, and pressing my mouth against this hand, I kissed it and said to her: 'You are still my mother: I am still your child'. She answered (repelling me still more roughly and snatching her hand from mine): 'Get up. wretched girl, get up'. She put so much authority and strength into her voice that I felt I must escape her gaze.

My tears and the blood, streaming from my nose, ran along my arms, and I was quite wet before I noticed it. From something she said I judged that her dress had been soiled and that this displeased her.

The verisimilitude of that nosebleed belongs, one feels, to nineteenth-century rather than to eighteenth-century fiction.

This matter of 'coldness' touches on something central to Diderot's intellectual life. He was very ready to proclaim himself a sentimentalist and believed that virtue tended to be of the party of the sentimentalists. On the other hand, as he could not help telling himself, sentimentality seemed to go hand-in-hand with mediocrity and to be, as it were, the antithesis of 'genius'. The issue was summed up in an encounter of his with the playwright Michel-Jean Sedaine. The success of a performance of Sedaine's *A Philosopher Without Knowing It* greatly excited him, and he rushed halfway across Paris to congratulate the author – arriving, according to Sedaine's account, 'all out of breath, sweating, and exclaiming, with tears in his eyes, "Victory, my friend, victory!"' To this Sedaine's sole reply was, 'M. Diderot, how beautiful you look!' In this, Diderot would say, one saw all the difference between the sentimentalist and the 'observer and man of genius'. It was a favourite story with him and helped to inspire one of his own most influential writings, his *Paradox of the Actor*, where he argues that the actor of genius portrays emotions so powerfully precisely because he feels none of them.

When writing fiction, Diderot seems instinctively to have fallen into a 'genius' tone. Though one needs to add, he was emphatically *not* the actor who feels nothing and he could become, towards his own fiction, the same enthusiastic, naively credulous reader as he was towards Richardson's. He later told a story of how, at the time of writing *The Nun*, a friend of his called on him and found him in floods of tears. 'What on earth is the matter?' asked his visitor. 'I will tell you what is the matter,' replied Diderot. 'I am breaking my heart over a story I am telling myself.' For all this, though, *The Nun* shows that very marked 'coldness' that I have spoken of, a tone which tends to separate his fiction from the rest of his work.

*

Grimm wrote his account of the de Croismare hoax, out of which *The Nun* was born, in 1770, and published it in the pages of a small-circulation manuscript journal which he edited – it never had more than fifteen or twenty subscribers – entitled the *Correspondance littéraire*. The account is entertaining, but it is hard to know in what spirit to take it, for it is full of loose ends and apparent contradictions. Can it really be true, as he asserted, that when the Marquis learned of the monstrous trick played on him, he relished it as a good joke? Was it really true that he was taken in at all, and if so, for how long? Could it have been, as Diderot at one point suspected, that a joke was being played not on the Marquis but on himself? It is plain that Grimm's account, just as much as the forged letters from the nun, must be regarded as some kind of fiction, and this is the conclusion that Diderot came to. He made no attempt to publish *The Nun*, any more than with the rest of his most original works, but near the end of his life he allowed it to appear in the pages of the *Correspondance littéraire*, and when he came to revise the novel for this purpose, he incorporated Grimm's account (somewhat modified), together with the forged letters and Croismare's replies, into the fabric of the novel itself. It was an inspired stroke, for the letters were a brilliant Richardsonian creation, and a compelling novel-of-deception became thereby also a novel-of-undeception.

The Nun, in the form which Diderot finally gave to it, thus falls into four broad sections. First we read of the young Suzanne's family unhappiness, her entry into her first convent, her realization that she has no religious vocation, and her bold public refusal to take vows. Next her more or less forcible despatch to a new convent (Longchamps), the long sequence of her vicissitudes and persecutions there, her unwilling taking of vows, her decision to try to cancel them, and the worse series of persecutions that fall on her in consequence. Thirdly, her removal to the convent at Arpajon and exposure to a quite different form of persecution, at the hands of its lesbian Prioress; leading eventually to her escape in the company of a rascally monk. Finally, a 'Preface to the Preceding Work', containing Grimm's account of the Croismare hoax, and the text of the letters supposedly written after her escape.

When Diderot gave the novel to the *Correspondance littéraire*, he told the then editor, Henri Meister, that he 'did not believe anyone had ever written a more terrifying satire on convents'. The word 'satire' needs a little interpreting, but there is no doubt that the work is a polemic. It is not, however, a polemic against religion as such. It is not even, initially, though it

certainly turns into, a wholesale attack on the conventual
system. The focus of the plot is very precise, it is the crime and
outrage to the human soul in forcing the religious life on
someone with no vocation for it; and neither Diderot, nor his
protagonist Suzanne, a tenacious and inflexible character,
ever lose hold of this issue. To 'crime' and 'outrage', though,
one is asked to add 'danger'. For, by a paradox clearly grasped
by Suzanne herself, whereas she lacks all vocation to the
religious life, she has a real talent for it, which is perilous to
others.

Thus the touching opening episode of the Longchamps
section, dealing with Suzanne's affectionate relationship with
her superior Mother de Moni, is crucial to the novel's strategy.
The humane, far-seeing and truly spiritual Mother de Moni
represents the very best that the conventual life can offer; and
it is shown that, in the convent system, such superior virtues
may be as dangerous, or more so, than the common vices –
worldliness, herd-instinct and lust for cruelty. Mother de
Moni's relationship with her and with all her chosen flock is (it
is Suzanne's word) a 'seduction'. For some of the novices, to
receive consolation from Mother de Moni becomes a craze
and a morbid addiction. 'She did not intend to seduce, but
that is certainly what she did.' Moreover, it is through her
friendship with Mother de Moni that Suzanne discovers that
she has a 'genius' for the spiritual life. It is a rare gift, and
Suzanne is made to reflect what dire use she could have made
of it, what a weapon it would have been to a hypocrite or a
fanatic. The wise Mother de Moni makes a chilling remark,
which Suzanne later has cause to remember. 'Among all these
creatures you see around me – so docile, so innocent, so sweet –
well, my child, there is hardly one, no, not one, whom I could
not make into a wild beast.' Nor is the fatal influence all one
way. If Mother de Moni is fatal to Suzanne, by encouraging
her to take her vows, Suzanne is fatal to Mother de Moni,
dispossessing her of her 'genius' and hastening her end. All
these ironies are directed towards a single conclusion: that the
root of the trouble is not fate or original sin but a profoundly,
irremediably vicious human institution. If these are the fruits
of so mild and enlightened a régime as Mother de Moni's, the

implication is, we are not to be surprised by the horrors and persecutions to come.

As for these horrors, it is to be noticed that they fall into two separate sequences. The *donnée* of the novel, as we know, was the effort of a real-life nun to renounce her vows, and the moment when the same idea occurs to Suzanne forms a turning-point in the novel. In her rebellion against Mother de Moni's successor, she succeeds in destroying her own character, making herself hard, horrible and legalistic. The rebellion is, anyway, bound to be hopeless. The only real possibilities for her in the long run are an unsustainable hypocrisy, madness or suicide. Indeed the only reason for not committing suicide, she reflects with a last flicker of obstinacy, is that everyone seems to *want* her to commit it.

All is changed, though, when she has the idea of repudiating her vows. Her strength of character returns, and what gives such force to all that follows at Longchamps, that crescendo of hardly conceivable malignities, is that they fall on no passive victim but a courageous, resourceful and stubborn woman.

On the day of her arrival at this rich and worldly convent of Longchamps, Suzanne is persuaded to perform at the clavichord, and ('without irony', she tells the Marquis) she finds herself singing Télaire's great air from Rameau's *Castor and Pollux*: 'Sad attire, pale torch-flames, day more terrible than night itself.' It is a telling stroke. Diderot himself, in recommending the novel to Henri Meister, said that it would be a gift to painters, and the nocturnal *tableaux* which follow – the nuns being ordered to step on the prostrate Suzanne's body, their dressing her in a shroud and laying her out on a bier, their leading her to a mock-execution, and so on – make an extraordinary impact.* One especially is most moving. The Grand Vicaire is completing his public inquisition, during which Suzanne has answered every question firmly but laconi-

---

*By a curious chain of circumstances, Diderot's novel inspired the painter Delacroix, whose *L'Amende honorable* illustrates a passage from Maturin's novel *Melmoth the Wanderer*, in which the victimized monk Monçada is dragged from his cell into the presence of a Bishop, a scene which Maturin filched directly from *The Nun*.

cally. He asks her if she wants to accuse anyone in particular, but she replies 'no', and he dismisses her to her cell. Then, on a sudden instinct, she turns back, falls down before him and – displaying her bruised head, her bloodstained feet, her flesh-less arms and filthy and tattered clothes – says simply: 'You see!'

Many strands in the novel come together at this point. Such a charge of emotion and indignation has by now built up in us, that Diderot can enlarge his story into a universal statement. The novel has, so far, been working, implicitly, at three different levels: Suzanne has been telling the story of her wrongs for its own sake, she has been telling it for the special benefit of the Marquis, and she (or Diderot) has been telling it, over the Marquis' head, to the world at large. Now Diderot dares to make this more explicit. He causes Suzanne to raise, to the Marquis, the very question that will have troubled the reader: could a single person have suffered all this gamut of evils of the convent system? Is it not more like some insane fantasy? Her answer is a good one and fits with our sense of something unique and challenging in Suzanne's personality, a sort of lightning-conductor quality.

The more I think over it the surer I am that what happened to me never happened before and will very likely never happen again. Once (and pray to God it was for the first and last time) it pleased Providence, Whose ways are unknown to us, to collect on one unfortunate head the whole mass of cruelties, divided, according to His inscrutable decrees, among the infinite multitude of unfortunate girls who had preceded her in the cloister and who are in turn to succeed her.

Further, the Suzanne who was stoical and laconic to her clerical inquisitor now unlooses her tongue and makes unashamed and imperious appeal to the Marquis' feelings, warning him that if he does not rescue her from the 'abyss' now, his tears and remorse will be in vain later. Finally, gathering strength from the story of her own defeat (she has just learned that her legal suit has failed), she delivers a searing and magnificent tirade against the whole convent system, one in which her voice mingles with Diderot's own.

What need has the Bridegroom of so many foolish virgins? Or the human race of so many victims? Will men never feel the necessity for narrowing the mouths of these gulfs, into which future generations will sink to perdition? Are all the regulation prayers one repeats there worth one obol given in pity to the poor? Does God, Who made man a social animal, approve of his barring himself from the world? ...

*

Suzanne imagines she has suffered all the evils that fate can offer, but in this she is mistaken. For when, all unexpectedly, she is at last released from her sufferings at Longchamps and is transferred to a new convent at Arpajon, she finds that Providence has played her a fresh trick and plunged her into a quite new dilemma. The structure of Diderot's plot here reveals a beautiful balance, for in this Arpajon episode there is not only a shift to a new evil of the cloister, the sexual one, but also a shift in our sympathies. For the real victim in this new episode is not Suzanne but the lesbian Prioress who falls in love with her, a foolish warm-hearted figure driven to tragedy precisely by the convent system. In Diderot's moving portrait of this Prioress one is reminded of a favourite theory of his, which loomed large for him both as an art-theorist and as an amateur physiologist. It was that there is a 'system' in deformity, so that an expert needs only to see a pair of feet to say that they belong to a hunchback, or a woman's throat and shoulders to say that she lost her eyesight in childhood. The theory implied, from an aesthetic point of view, that an artist ought to forget academic rules of 'correctness' and study, rather, the 'secret liaison' and 'necessary concatenation' of natural phenomena. It is along these lines that one is meant to understand Diderot's Prioress. He is treating her, compassionately and scientifically, as a 'system of deformity'. There is a 'skew' running visibly through her whole physical and moral makeup. 'Her head is never still on her shoulders,' writes Suzanne. 'There is always something wrong with her dress. Her face is agreeable rather than the reverse. Her eyes, of which one, the right one, is higher and larger than the other, are full of fire, and yet wandering.' When, later, Suzanne gives the charming picture of the Prioress' *levée*, she notes that her tender, shining black eyes 'are always only half-open' – a neat symbolic suggestion that she does not want to see what she is doing.

Diderot's book has, however, a further surprise for us or trick to play on us. For there was quite a tradition of novels about convents, of a titillating or semi-pornographic kind – *The Nun in Her Shift* and such-like works – and Diderot deliberately plays on the possibility that we shall take his novel for one of these. Suzanne's way of reporting her Superior's erotic advances is erotic in itself. She is caught up in her own innocent amazement and describes it all excitedly and excitingly.

After this, as soon as a nun had done anything wrong I interceded for her and was sure to obtain her pardon by some innocent favour; always a kiss on the forehead, or the neck, or the eyes, or the cheeks, or the lips, or the hands, or the throat, or the arms, but generally on the lips. She discovered my breath was sweet, my teeth white, my lips fresh and scarlet.

In this new episode Suzanne addresses the Marquis less often, nevertheless the reader is soon speculating on the effect of all this on that ardent and impressionable man; and of course all the more so when it comes to the steamy, if semi-comic, scene of the Prioress' first successful seduction of Suzanne. ('Seduction' is perhaps not the right word; at all events the occasion when she first achieves an orgasm in Suzanne's arms.) Too evidently, in Suzanne's present desperate plight, it is all to her advantage to involve the Marquis' feelings, by any means almost; and indeed in a 'postscript' to her narration Suzanne frankly admits that, in telling her story, she may half-consciously have been manipulating him. 'Can it be that we think men less moved by the picture of our sufferings than the image of our charms? Do we say to ourselves that it is easier to attract their fancy than to stir their hearts?"

But this sceptical train of thought, about Suzanne's motives as a story-teller, is intended to reach even further; for it also involves Diderot's relationship with his reader, whose responses to this story are no more beyond suspicion than the

Marquis'. From the beginning, what the Prioress finds excit-
ing in Suzanne is – significantly – not just her beauty but her
story. The great sexual thrill that she promises herself is to
hear Suzanne tell her story; and eventually she stage-manages
this event in the most voluptuous manner imaginable, sitting
with her body enlaced with the story-teller's. It is to be, as she
says herself, a supreme indulgence: the two of them will weep
delicious tears, and 'perhaps we shall be happy amid the
recital of all your sufferings. Who knows how far emotion may
not lead us? . . .' So Suzanne begins; and the reader is treated
to a *louche* and orgiastic parody of the emotions with which he
or she, or any person of goodwill, would have had read the
preceding pages.

> I cannot describe to you the effect it produced on her, the sighs she
> heaved, the tears she shed, the words of indignation she piled on my
> cruel parents and the terrible girls of Saint Mary's and Longchamps.
> I should be sorry to think they ever underwent the smallest part of the
> sufferings she desired for them . . . From time to time she interrupted
> me, got up, walked about and then sat down again: at other times she
> raised her eyes to heaven, then hid her head between my knees.

The story-telling ends in an orgy of kissing, and then, writes
Suzanne:

> I perceived from the trembling that seized her, from her troubled
> speech, the wildness in her eyes and hands, from the warmth with
> which her arms embraced me, that her illness would not be long in
> coming again. I do not know what was happening inside me, but I
> was seized with a terror, a trembling, and a desire to swoon which
> verified my suspicion that her illness was contagious.

This salacious re-enactment of the nun's story, a sort of
ambush for the reader, is an audacious stroke on Diderot's
part; and this subversive passage leads us naturally on to the
final blowing-of-the-gaff about the Croismare hoax, in the
'Preface to the Preceding Work'. The novel is revealed as what
Stanley Fish calls a 'self-consuming artifact' and – for all its
propagandist ardour – it raises doubts about 'innocence' of all

kinds, and especially the innocence of those who tell stories and those who listen to them.

*

Diderot died in 1784, and in the years immediately after his death, there was relative silence about him, nor was his name very prominent in the early days of the Revolution. (The literary hero during this time was Rousseau, and Rousseau-worship rose to extraordinary heights.) Matters changed dramatically, though, near the end of 1796, during the 'Thermidorian' reaction. In July two important texts of Diderot's were published, accompanied by a wild attack on him as the inventor of *sans-culotterie* and the man who had taught the terrorists their contempt for God; and two months later the publisher Buisson issued the first edition of *The Nun* (and also of *Jacques le fataliste*). Diderot's name was, suddenly, enormously in the news.

For the most part the reviews of the two novels were angrily polemical, using them as fodder for the debate about the Revolution. *The Nun* was attacked as 'a masterpiece of implausibility and depraved morality' and was defended, equally polemically, as 'a work kept in reserve by philosophy' to repress any backsliding into 'impious superstition'. The journal *L'Eclair*, itself sympathetic towards Diderot, remarked what a flattering reception his two novels would have received if they had appeared ten years earlier. 'But today what a chorus of imprecations against their author! He is impious! a monster! a corrupter of morals!' Amid all this, however, there were one or two discerning reviews, especially a long one of *The Nun* in the *Décade philosophique*, which spoke of Diderot's portrait of the lesbian Mother Superior as worthy of Racine. 'It is not libertinism, it is the most ardent, the most irresistible love; it is Sappho; it is Phèdre; "C'est Venus toute entière à sa proie attachée." ' Such a defence of the right to depict lesbian passion was not met again till the days of the Third Republic. During the Restauration, *The Nun* was more than once banned; and for many years to come Diderot's remarkable creation, though frequently published and translated, and pillaged by Maturin in his 'Gothic' novel *Melmoth the Wanderer*, was looked on with nervousness, as a 'scrofulous French novel'*: an embarrassment to his admirers and an object of reproach by his enemies.

P. N. Furbank

*'Or, my scrofulous French novel
  On grey paper with blunt type!
  Simply glance at it, you grovel
  Hand and foot in Belial's gripe.'
Browning, 'Soliloquy of the Spanish Cloister'

NOTE ON THE TEXT

The present edition is based on the translation by Francis Birrell, first published by Routledge in 1928 as *Memoirs of a Nun*, adapted in the light of the text established in the Hermann *Oeuvres complètes*, vol. 11, 1975.

SELECT BIBLIOGRAPHY

———

CAPLAN, JAY, *Framed Narratives: Diderot's Genealogy of the Beholder*, University of Minnesota Press, 1985. A stimulating recent study of Diderot's narrative methods.

GREEN, F. C., *French Novelists, Manners and Ideas*, Dent, 1928. See pp. 147–50 for remarks on *La Religieuse*.

MYLNE, V., 'Truth and Illusion in the *Préface-Annexe* to Diderot's *La Religieuse*', *Modern Language Review*, vol. 57, 1962, pp. 350–66. A careful analysis of the complicated problem of the 'Preface'.

PROUST, J., 'Recherches nouvelles sur *La Religieuse*', *Diderot Studies*, vol. 6, 1964, pp. 197–214. A valuable discussion of the sources and composition of *La Religieuse*.

CHRONOLOGY

DATE	AUTHOR'S LIFE	LITERARY CONTEXT
1713	Born (5 October) in Langres, the son of Didier Diderot, a master cutler.	
1715		
1723		
1723–8	Attends Jesuit college in Langres.	
1726	Receives tonsure.	
1728–32	Attends college (probably Collège d'Harcourt) in Paris.	
1732	Is received as Master of Arts at University of Paris.	
1732–42	Lives hand-to-mouth existence in Paris, as law clerk, mathematics tutor, sermon-writer etc., meanwhile reading widely in several languages.	
1733–5		
1733		Pope: *Essay on Man.*
1734		Voltaire: *Philosophical Letters.*
1739		Hume: *Treatise of Human Nature.*
1740–48		
1741	Meets his future wife, Antoinette Champion.	
1742		Prévost's translation of Richardson's *Pamela.*
1742–3	Gets to know Rousseau. Translates Temple Stanyan's *Grecian History.* Visits Langres and reveals his intention to marry; his father has him imprisoned in a monastery, by *lettre de cachet.* Escapes and marries in secret.	
1745	Publishes a translation of Shaftesbury's *Inquiry concerning Virtue, or Merit.*	Crébillon *fils*: *The Sofa.*

Death of Louis XIV.
Death of the Regent: Louis XV assumes power.

War of the Polish Succession.

War of the Austrian Succession.

DATE	AUTHOR'S LIFE	LITERARY CONTEXT
1746	Joins editorial staff of the *Encyclopédie*. Publishes *Philosophical Thoughts*.	Condillac: *Essay on the Origins of Human Knowledge*.
1747	Is appointed co-editor of the *Encyclopédie*, with d'Alembert.	
1748	Publishes libertine novel, *Indiscreet Jewels*, and *Memoirs on Various Mathematical Subjects*.	Montesquieu: *The Spirit of Laws*.
1749	Publishes *Letter on the Blind*. Is arrested and imprisoned in the dungeon of Vincennes. Rousseau, visiting Diderot in prison, conceives his *Discourse on Science and the Arts*.	First three volumes of Buffon's *Natural History*.
1751	Publishes *Letter on the Deaf and Dumb*. The first volume of the *Encyclopédie* appears (November).	Prévost's translation of Richardson's *Clarissa*.
1752	Temporary suppression of the *Encyclopédie*.	
1753	Birth of his daughter Angélique. Publishes *On the Interpretation of Nature*.	
1755	Begins permanent relationship with Sophie Volland.	Rousseau: *Discourse on the Origins of Inequality*. Johnson's *Dictionary*.
1756		
1757	Publishes *The Natural Son* (play). Quarrel and last meeting with Rousseau.	Burke: *Of the Sublime and Beautiful*.
1758		Helvétius: *On Human Intelligence* (*De l'Esprit*).
1759	The *Encyclopédie* is officially suppressed and has to be continued in secret.	Voltaire: *Candide*.
1760	Diderot and his friends hatch playful 'conspiracy' against the Marquis de Croismare, out of which springs Diderot's novel *The Nun* (*La Religieuse*). Charles Palissot's satirical comedy about Diderot and his circle, *The Philosophers*, is staged (2 May) by the Comédie Française.	

HISTORICAL EVENTS

The King disperses the Paris Parlement (May).

Death of Montesquieu. Madame de Pompadour receives proposals for an Austrian alliance.

Beginning of the Seven Years' War. Louis XV compels Parlement to register a decree confirming the Bull 'Unigenitus' as an article of faith. Much talk of the King's sexual misdemeanours and supposed plan to starve the people. Damiens attempts to assassinate the King. Etienne Silhouette, as Controller-general of finance, attempts drastic national retrenchment.

DATE	AUTHOR'S LIFE	LITERARY CONTEXT
1761	Diderot's play *The Father of a Family* is performed.	Rousseau: *La Nouvelle Héloïse*.
1762	Is reading *Tristram Shandy*.	Rousseau: *The Social Contract*. Ossian (Macpherson): *Fingal*.
1762–4	About this time, Diderot writes first draft of *Rameau's Nephew*.	
1764		Beccaria; *On Crimes and Penalties*.
1765	Catherine the Great buys Diderot's library from him and appoints him its 'librarian'.	Marmontel: *Belisarius*.
1766	The remaining volumes of the *Encyclopédie* are published.	Lessing: *Laocöon*.
1769	Writes *D'Alembert's Dream*.	
1770		D'Holbach: *System of Nature*.
1773	Writes *Paradox of the Actor* and (probably) begins *Jacques the Fatalist*. Goes to Russia, arriving in St Petersburg on 8 October.	
1774	Returns (March) from Russia to the Hague. Returns to Paris (September).	Goethe: *The Sorrows of Young Werther*.
1776		Bentham: *Fragment on Government*.
1778	Publishes *Essay on the Life of Seneca*.	Death of Voltaire (May). Death of Rousseau (July).
1781		Schiller: *The Robbers*. Kant: *Critique of Pure Reason*.
1782		Vol. 1 of Rousseau's *Confessions*. Laclos: *Dangerous Acquaintances*.
1783		
1784	Dies (31 July).	Beaumarchais: *The Marriage of Figaro*.

CHRONOLOGY

The Jesuit Society is banned in France.

Marriage of the future Louis XVI to Marie-Antoinette.

American Declaration of Independence.

Death of d'Alembert (October).

MEMOIRS OF A NUN

(LA RELIGIEUSE)

THE answer from the Marquis de Croismare, if indeed he replies to me, will provide the first lines of this story. Even before I wrote to him, I wished to know him. He is a man of the world, grown illustrious in the service; he is elderly and has been married; he has a son and two daughters, whom he loves and by whom he is cherished. He is of good birth, enlightened, intellectual, gay, fond of the fine arts, particularly of anything original. Praises have been sung me of his warm heart, honour, and probity. And I judged by the lively interest he took in my affairs and by all that I have been told of him that I did not compromise myself by applying to him. But he can hardly be expected to change my lot, without knowing all about me; and it is for this reason that I am resolved on overcoming my vanity and repugnance, and that I undertake these Memoirs, in which I describe some part of my misfortunes without art or skill, but with the simplicity of youth and with my natural frankness. Then in case my protector wished me to finish them, or should I possibly desire to do so myself later, when I may perhaps have forgotten incidents which will have become remote, I have concluded with an outline, which ought to be enough to recall everything to my memory, since I shall always remain deeply affected by what I have gone through.

My father was a lawyer. He had married my mother

I

rather late in life and had three daughters. There was more than enough money to settle them all comfortably; but to do that my parents would have had to love all their daughters equally. And I am far from able to accord them such praise. Certainly I was worth more than the others as regards the attractions of mind and appearance, character and talents. And this was apparently a source of affliction to my parents. The advantage nature and study had given me over my sisters became a positive inconvenience to me; and so I desired from my earliest years to resemble them, that I might be loved, cherished, made much of, and excused as they were. If it happened that someone said to my mother: "You have charming children" it was never made to apply to me. I was sometimes handsomely avenged for this injustice, but the praises which I had received cost me so dear when I was alone that I would as lief have been treated with indifference or even insult. For the more predilection strangers showed me the greater was the bad temper exhibited once their backs were turned. How often have I wept at not having been born ugly, silly, stupid, and proud: in a word, with all those faults which my parents found so admirable in my sisters. I asked myself whence came this strangeness of temper in a father and mother otherwise respectable, just and pious. Shall I admit it, my lord? Some observations that escaped my father in his wrath (for he was a violent-tempered man), some incidents collected at different times, the remarks of neighbours, hints of servants, all made me suspect a reason which would in some measure excuse them. Perhaps my father was none too certain about my birth; maybe I recalled to my mother a fault she had committed, or the ingratitude of a man to whom she had too gladly listened. How can I tell? But even if my suspicions were ill-founded, there is no risk in confiding them to you. You will burn this writing and I promise to burn your answers.

As we came into the world in quick succession, we grew up together. Eligible offers were made. A charming young man paid his addresses to my eldest sister but I quickly perceived that it was for me that he really cared, and that she would never be more than the excuse for his presence. I foresaw all the trouble which his preference might bring on me, and I warned my mother. Perhaps this was the only thing I ever did which pleased her, and you will see how I was rewarded. Four days, or at least a few days, later I was told that a place in a convent had been decided upon for me, and the very next day I was taken there. I was so unhappy at home that this did not distress me, and I went off very lightheartedly to my first convent, Saint Mary's.[1] Meanwhile my sister's lover, as he no longer saw me, forgot all about me and married her. He is a solicitor at Corbeil named M.K., and they are as wretched together as possible. My second sister was married to a M. Bauchon, a silk-merchant in Paris, rue Quincampoix, and they are quite reasonably happy.

My two sisters being set up in life, I assumed that my parents would now think of me, and that before long I should leave the convent. I was then sixteen and a half. Fine dowries had been found for my sisters and I promised myself a lot equal to theirs. My head was full of attractive schemes, when I was summoned into the parlour. There I found Father Seraphim, who had been my mother's spiritual director as well as my own. Hence he experienced no embarrassment in explaining the motive of his visit. In fact, I was to take the veil. I protested against this strange proposition, and declared roundly that I felt in no way drawn towards the cloister.

"So much the worse for you," he answered, "for your parents have denuded themselves for your sisters and I cannot at all see what they could do for you in the straitened circumstances to which they are reduced. Think it over. You must either enter this House permanently or go away into some provincial convent at which you will be received for a modest yearly payment, and which you will be able to leave only on the death of your parents; and that may still be a long way off!"

I complained bitterly, and shed a flood of tears. The Superior, who had been informed about everything, was waiting for me as I left the parlour. I was in a state of indescribable distress. She said: "What is the matter, my dear child?" (she understood better even than I did); "what a state you are in! I have never seen anything like it. You quite terrify me. Have you lost your father or mother?" I thought of throwing myself into her arms and answering: "Would to God I had!" But I contented myself with crying out: "Alas! I am a wretched girl, whom everyone hates and wants to bury alive here." She allowed the torrent to pass and awaited the moment of calm. I explained to her more clearly the announcement that had just been made. She seemed sorry for me, and encouraged me

4

not to embrace a state for which I felt no vocation.
She promised to pray, remonstrate, and plead on my
behalf. Oh, my lord, how insincere these Mothers
Superior are! You can have no idea of it. She wrote
indeed, but knew perfectly well beforehand the
answers she would get. She communicated them to me
and only long afterwards did I learn to doubt her
good faith. Meanwhile the time allowed me to make
up my mind was over, and she came to tell me so with
studied grief. First she remained silent and then threw
me out a few words of commiseration, from which I
gathered all the rest. There followed a scene of despair, and indeed I shall have scarcely any other kind
of scene to describe to you. Mothers Superior are past-
mistresses in the art of self-control. But at last she said,
and I really believe she was crying: "So, child, you are
going to leave us and we shall not see you again" and
some other remarks which I did not hear. I had
thrown myself onto a chair, and kept silent or broke
into sobs, remained motionless, or got up, went sometimes to lean against the wall and sometimes to give
way to my grief upon her breast. But after this she
added: "There is one thing you might do. Listen to
me, and never mention a word of the advice I am
going to give you. I count on your absolute discretion,
and for nothing in the world would I lay myself open
to reproach. What are you being asked to do? To
become a novice. But why not do so? You are committed to nothing except to live with us for two years.
One can never tell who will be living and who will
die. Two years is a long time. A lot can happen in two
years." And she joined many caresses, protestations of

5

friendship, and much false sweetness to her insidious proposals.

"I knew where I was; I knew not whither I was being led", and I let myself be persuaded. Then she wrote to my father. Her letter was excellent: indeed it could not have been bettered. My sufferings, my grief, my protests were in no wise passed over, and I assure you that a girl more clear-sighted than myself would have been deceived. And so it ended with my giving my consent. How quickly everything was got ready! The day was fixed, my clothes made, the moment of the ceremony come, without there seeming to-day to have been any interval between these steps.

I forgot to tell you that I saw my father and mother, that I left no stone unturned to soften them, and that I found them inflexible. The Abbé Blin, Doctor of the Sorbonne, gave me the exhortation. The Bishop of Aleppo[2] passed me the habit. The ceremony is not gay in itself, and on this occasion it was as gloomy as could be. Though the nuns pressed round me to support me, I felt my knees giving way a score of times, and I all but fell on to the steps of the altar. I saw and heard nothing and was quite brutish. They led me and I went. They questioned me and answered in my place. At last the cruel ceremony was over; everyone withdrew, and I remained with the flock to which I had just joined myself. My companions surrounded me and embraced me, saying: "Look, sister, how handsome she is! How well the black veil suits the whiteness of her complexion! How nicely it rounds off her head and fills out her cheeks! How beautifully the habit shows off her figure and arms." I scarcely heard them, I was so

unhappy. But I must confess that once alone in my cell
I remembered their flatteries and could not help
looking in my small mirror to judge for myself, and it
seemed to me that they were not entirely undeserved.
There are special honours attached to such an occasion, and they were particularly grand in my case, but
they made scarcely any impression on me. People
pretended to think the opposite and told me so, though
it was obvious nonsense. In the evening, after prayers,
the Superior came into my cell. "Really," she said after
scrutinizing me a little, "I cannot understand your
objection to the habit. It suits you marvellously and
you are quite charming. Sister Susan is a very good-
looking nun. You will be all the more popular on that
account. Come along, let's see; walk a little. You don't
hold yourself sufficiently upright. You mustn't stoop
like that."

She arranged my head, feet, hands, waist, and arms
for me – quite a lesson by Marcel[3] on monastic
elegance. For each state of life has its own brand. Then
she sat down and said: "That's right, but now we must
talk seriously. Two years have been gained. Your
parents may change their plan: you perhaps will want
to remain when they want to take you away."

"Never believe it, Madam."

"You have been long among us, but you do not
know our life. It has its pains no doubt, but also its
consolations."

You can very well imagine all that she added about
the world and the cloister: it is written everywhere and
always in the same way. For, heaven knows, I have had
to read any amount of the rubbish that the monks have

poured forth about their state, which they know well and hate, directed against the world, which they attack, love, and do not know.

I will not go into the details of my novitiate. Were all its rigours observed, no one would survive it. As a matter of fact, it is the pleasantest period of conventual life. A Novice Mistress is the most indulgent Sister imaginable – her mission is to hide from you all the thorns of the profession. As a course of seduction, nothing could be more subtle or refined. She it is who deepens the darkness surrounding you, rocks your cradle, puts you to sleep, imposes on you, and fascinates you. My own was particularly attached to me. I do not believe that any young and inexperienced nature could resist such deadly art. The world has its precipices, but I do not believe that the slope leading down to them can be so gentle. If I sneezed twice I was excused Divine Service, work, and prayer. I went to bed earlier, got up later: the rule ceased for me. Believe me, my lord, there were days when I sighed for a moment of self-sacrifice. Nothing disagreeable happens in the outside world without your hearing of it. True stories are rearranged, false ones invented, while unending praises and thank-offerings are made to God, Who has screened us from such humiliating adventures. But the hour approached, which I had sometimes desired to hasten. Then I became moody, feeling my objections awaken and increase. I went and confided them to the Superior or to our Novice Mistress. These women have their revenge on you for the way you bore them. For you must not suppose that they enjoy the hypocritical part they play and the ridiculous remarks they are compelled to repeat to you. Finally, all this becomes stale and repulsive to them: but they force their natures; and all for the few hundred pounds which come into the house. This is the important object for which they tell lies all their lives and prepare innocent girls for forty or fifty years of despair, and perhaps for eternal misery. For it is certain, my lord, that out of a hundred nuns who die before fifty there are exactly a hundred who are damned, not counting those who go mad, brutish or raving in the process.

One day one of these poor demented creatures escaped from the cell, where she was kept shut up. I saw her. It depends, my lord, on the way you treat me whether I am to date my good fortune or my ruin from that moment. I have never seen anything so horrible. Her hair was in disorder and she was almost naked; she dragged after her her iron chains; her eyes were wild; she tore out her hair; she struck her breast with her fists; she ran about howling; she called down hideous imprecations on herself and others; she looked for a window to hurl herself out of. Terror seized me; I trembled in every limb; I saw my fate in that of the unhappy woman, and immediately I decided in my heart I would die a thousand times over before exposing myself likewise. They foresaw the effect which this sight might have on my mind and thought they must counteract it. I was told any number of ridiculous and self-contradictory lies about this nun; how she was already deranged when she was recieved; how she had had a great fright at a critical time; how she had become subject to visions; how she thought herself in communication with angels; how she had read some pernicious books, which had affected her mind; how she had listened to some extravagant moral reformer, who had so terrified her with God's judgment that her mind had been shaken and then completely unbalanced; how she never saw anything except demons, hell, and a gulf of fire; adding that they were very unhappy about it; that they had never had anything like it before in the house; and anything else you please. But this made no effect on me. Every moment my mad nun came back to mind and I renewed my oath to take no vow.

The moment had, however, come when I must prove that I could keep my word. One morning, after service, I saw the Superior come into my cell. She had a letter in her hand and her expression was one of sadness and discouragement: her arms were hanging down listlessly, and her hand seemed hardly strong enough to hold the letter; she looked at me and tears seemed to be standing in her eyes. She was silent and so was I. She waited for me to speak first, but I restrained myself. She asked me how I felt, said that the Service had been long that day, that I had coughed a little and that she thought I was unwell, to all of which I answered: "No, Mother." She still held the letter hanging from her hand, and in the midst of her questions she put it on my knees, so that her hand still partly held it. Finally, after putting me some questions about my father and mother and having observed that I did not ask what this paper might be, she said: "Here is a letter." I felt my heart beat at the word, and I added in a broken voice, with trembling lips: "From my mother?"

"That is so. Come, read it."

I collected myself a little, took the letter and read it, at first fairly coolly; but as I continued, terror, indignation, anger, fury, different passions succeeded each other in my heart. My tone of voice, my expression changed from moment to moment. Sometimes I hardly held the paper or held it as though about to tear it up; or I clutched it violently as if tempted to crumple it and throw it right away from me.

"Well, my child, and what is your answer?"

"You know quite well."

"No I do not. Times are bad, your family has had losses. Your sisters' affairs are in disorder: both have a large family. Your parents impoverished themselves at the moment of the marriages and have since ruined themselves to support their children. They cannot possibly do anything satisfactory for you. You have taken the habit: the necessary expenses were paid. You held out hopes for the future when you took this step. The rumour of your coming profession has spread abroad. For the rest, count on my help. I have never driven anyone into Religion; it is a state to which God calls us, and it is very dangerous to mingle His voice with one's own. I shall not attempt to speak to your heart if Grace does nothing. Till now, I have not to reproach myself with another's unhappiness. Am I likely to begin, my child, with you who are so dear to me? I have not forgotten how it was at my persuasion that you took the first step, and I will not let people abuse this fact to engage you further than you will. Come, let us concert a plan. Do you wish to make profession?"

"No."

"You feel in no way drawn to the religious state?"

"No."

"What do you want to be then?"

"Anything except a nun. I do not want to be one, and I will not be one."

"Very well. You shall not be one. We will draw up an answer to your mother."

We agreed on the general lines. She wrote a letter which she showed me and which I thought excellent. Meanwhile the Director of the House was despatched to me and also the doctor, who had preached the sermon on my taking the habit. I was recommended to the Novice Mistress and saw the Bishop of Aleppo. I crossed swords with some pious women who meddled in my affairs, though they did not know me. There were continual conferences with monks and priests. My father came; my sisters wrote; my mother appeared last. I resisted everything. Meanwhile the day was chosen for my profession. Nothing was neglected to obtain my assent; but when they saw it was useless to ask for it they decided to get along without it.

From that moment I was confined to my cell; silence was imposed on me; I was separated from everybody and thrown on my own resources. I saw quite plainly that they were resolved to dispose of me without my consent. I was determined not to make any profession. That was definite, and none of the terrors, true or false, with which I was threatened shook my resolution. Still, I was in a deplorable state. I did not know how long it might last – and suppose it stopped, I knew still less what might happen to me. Amid these uncertainties I took a step, my lord, which you will judge as you may. I no longer saw anybody, not the Superior, or the Novice Mistress or my companions. I had the first of these summoned and pretended to fall in with my parents' wishes. But my plan was to end this persecution with a scandal, and publicly to protest against the meditated violence. I told them that they were masters of my fate and could dispose of me as they would; they demanded I should make my profession and I would do so. In a moment joy spread through the House and all was caresses once more, with the old flattery and cajolery. God had spoken to my heart. No one more than myself was made for the state of perfection. It was impossible it should not be so, and it had always been expected. No one who is not really called ever performed their duties with the edification and consistency I had shown. The Novice Mistress had never seen a more evident vocation in any of her pupils. She was surprised at the difficulties I had made, but she had always said to the Mother Superior that they must hold fast and that it would pass; that the best nuns often went through these crises; that they were suggestions of the Evil One, who redoubled his efforts when about to lose his prey; that I was now about to escape from him and henceforth it would be roses all the way: that the obligations of the religious life would be all the easier for my having so much exaggerated them, and that the sudden weighting of the yoke was intended by Heaven to make it seem less heavy afterwards. I thought it curious that the same thing came from God or the Devil, just as one chose to look at it. Religion can provide many cases of the same kind. Some of my consolers said that my thoughts were so many instigations of Satan and others that they were so many inspirations from God. One and the same ill comes either from God who proves or from the Devil who tempts us.

I conducted myself discreetly, and thought I could answer for myself. I saw my father – he spoke to me coldly; my mother, and she kissed me. I received letters of congratulation from my sisters and many others. I knew that a M. Sornin, Vicar of Saint-Roch, would preach the sermon and that M. Thierry, Chancellor of the University, would receive my vows. Everything went well till the evening of the great day, except that having learned that the ceremony was to be secret and that there would be very few present and that the church door would be open only to relations, I invited, by means of the doorkeeper, all my friends of both sexes who lived near. I had permission to write to some acquaintances. All this unexpected concourse presented itself at the door. They could not be excluded, and the congregation was just about what was needed for my plan. How terrible, my lord, was that last night! I did not get into bed, but sat on it and called God to my assistance. I raised my hands to the heavens and called on them as witnesses to the violence done me. I visualized my part at the foot of the altar, a young girl protesting loudly against an action to which she had apparently consented, the shocked feelings of the company, the despair of the nuns, the rage of my parents.

"O Lord! What is to happen to me?"

As I pronounced these words a general weakness overcame me and I fell fainting on my bolster. A shivering fit succeeded the fainting, when my knees beat together and my teeth chattered noisily. This shivering fit was followed by a terrible heat and my mind grew clouded. I do not remember having undressed or having left my cell. But I was found naked but for my shirt, stretched on the ground at the door of the Superior, motionless and almost lifeless. All this I learned subsequently. Next morning I found myself in my cell, my bed surrounded by the Superior, the Novice Mistress, and those who are called assistants. I was much depressed. I was put some questions, and it was clear from my answers that I had no knowledge of what had occurred. Nobody spoke of it. I was asked about my health, if I persisted in my blessed resolution, and if I felt strong enough to support the fatigue of the day. I answered, "Yes," and contrary to their expectation, they did not have to alter their plans.

Everything had been arranged the day before. The bells were rung to announce to everyone that a girl was to be made wretched. My heart still beat. They came to dress me; it was a day for dressing-up. When I now recall all those ceremonies I feel that they contain much that is solemn and very touching to an innocent girl, not led elsewhere by her temperament. I was taken to Church; Holy Mass was celebrated. The good Vicar, who gave me credit for a resignation which I was far from feeling, preached a long sermon, every word of which seemed nonsense to me. There was something preposterous in all his observations about my happiness, my grace, my courage, my zeal, my fervour, and the other fine sentiments which he attributed to me. I was disturbed by the contrast between his praise and the step I was about to take. For a few moments I wavered, but it was not for long. I only felt the more strongly that I lacked all the qualities that go to making a good nun. The terrible moment at length arrived. As I entered the place where I had to make my vows my legs gave way beneath me. Two of my companions held me under the arms. My head sank on to one of them as I dragged myself along. I know not what passed through the minds of those present, but in fact they were watching a young victim being dragged dying to the altar; and there arose everywhere sighs and sobs, among which, I am certain, those of my parents were not to be heard. Everyone was standing up; the young people had clambered on to chairs or were clinging to the bars of the grille, and there was a moment of deep silence as he who presided at my profession said to me: "Mary Susan Simonin, do you promise to tell me the truth?"

"I do."

"Is it of your full pleasure and free will that you are here?"

I replied, "No," but my companions answered for me, "Yes."

"Mary Susan Simonin, do you promise to God chastity, poverty, and obedience?"

I hestitated a moment; the priest waited; and I answered: "No, sir."

He began again.

"Mary Susan Simonin, do you promise to God chastity, poverty, and obedience?"

I answered in a firmer voice:

"No, sir, no."

He stopped and said: "My child, collect yourself and listen."

"Monsignor," I said, "you ask me if I promise to God chastity, poverty, and obedience. I have heard you and I answer 'No'."

Then, turning towards those present, from whom a loud murmur was arising, I made a sign that I wished to speak. The murmur stopped and I said: "Sirs, you, and particularly father and mother, I call you all to witness . . ."

At these words one of the Sisters let down the curtain of the grille, and I saw that it was useless to continue. The nuns surrounded me and overwhelmed me with reproaches. I listened without saying a word. I was led into my cell and shut in under lock and key.

There, abandoned to my own reflections, I began to take courage again; I went over my actions in my mind and saw nothing to repent of. I perceived that, after the scandal I had caused, I could not possibly remain there long, and hoped they might not dare to send me to a convent again. I had no idea what would be done with me, but I could conceive nothing worse than becoming a nun despite oneself. For a long time I was left without any news. Those who used to bring me my food came in, put my dinner on the floor, and went away without a word. After a month had passed I was brought ordinary clothes and gave up those of the House. The Superior came in and told me to follow her. I followed her to the door of the convent. There I got into a carriage in which I found my mother quite alone. I sat down with my back to the horses and the carriage started. We remained opposite each other for some time in complete silence. I lowered my eyes and had not the courage to look at her. I do not know what came over me, but suddenly I threw myself at her feet and bent my head upon her knees. I did not speak, only sobbed and choked. She rebuffed me unfeelingly. I did not get up: blood came to my nose; I seized one of her hands despite her efforts. Then, watering her hand with my tears and the blood which was flowing from my nose, and pressing my mouth against this hand, I kissed it and said to her: "You are still my mother: I am still your child." She answered (repelling me still more roughly and snatching her hand from mine): "Get up, wretched girl, get up." She put so much authority and strength into her voice that I felt I must escape her gaze.

My tears and the blood, streaming from my nose, ran along my arms, and I was quite wet before I noticed it. From something she said I judged that her dress had been soiled and that this displeased her. We arrived home, where I was immediately conducted to a little room that had been prepared for me. On the staircase I once more threw myself at her feet and held her back by her dress. Despite all this she would do no more for me than turn and dart at me an angry look with head, mouth, and eyes, which you may imagine more easily than I can describe.

I entered my new prison, where I remained six months. My food was brought to me, and I had a servant to look after me. I read, worked, wept, and sometimes sang – and so the days passed by. A secret feeling gave me strength – that I was free and that my lot, however hard, might change. But it was decided I should be a nun, and a nun I became.

So much inhumanity and obstinacy on the part of my parents finally confirmed me in my suspicions about my birth. I have never been able to find any other excuse for the way in which I was treated. My mother apparently feared that I should revert to the subject of the division of the property, ask for my part of it, and thus make a natural child share on equal terms with the legitimate offspring. But what had been only a conjecture was soon to become a certainty.

While I was locked up at home I practised but little the external forms of worship, though I was sent to confess on the eve of the great feasts. I told you I had the same Director as my mother. I talked to him and recounted all the hard treatment to which I had been subjected for three years. He knew it already. Of my mother particularly I spoke with bitterness and resentment. This priest had embraced his calling late in life, and was a humane man. He listened to me quietly and said: "Pity your mother, my child, pity her rather than blame her. Her soul is good, and it is despite herself that she uses you thus."

"Despite herself! And what constrains her, pray? Did she not bring me into the world? What difference is there between my sisters and me?"

"A great deal!"

"A great deal? I cannot understand your answer at all. ..."

I was about to enter on a comparison between my sisters and myself when he stopped me, saying: "Come, come, inhumanity is not your parents' failing. Try to be patient with your fate and at least make a virtue of that before God. I will see your mother, and you may be sure that I will use all my influence over her to help you."

That "a great deal" with which he had answered me was a ray of light. I no longer doubted the truth of what I had surmised about my birth.

The following Saturday between five and half-past, as the day was closing in, the servant who waited on me came upstairs to me and said: "Your mother says you are to dress." And an hour later: "Your mother wishes you to come downstairs with me." I found a carriage at the door, into which the servant and I stepped, and I learned that we were going to the Feuillants⁴ to see Father Seraphim. He was waiting for us alone. The servant withdrew while I went into the parlour. I sat down, feeling upset and inquisitive about what he had to say to me. This is what he said:

"I am going to explain the secret of your parents' severity towards you, and have obtained your mother's permission to do so. You are sensible, intelligent, and strong-minded, and have also reached an age when you could be entrusted with a secret even if it did not concern you. A long time ago I exhorted your mother to reveal to you what you are only now to learn. She could never bring herself to do it. It is hard for a mother to confess a grave fault to her child. You know her character. It is not of the kind which makes it easy to admit in this way a sort of humiliation. She hoped to be able to bring you round to her plans without sinking to this last resort. She was mistaken, and now regrets it. To-day she has come round to my opinion, and has charged me with the task of telling you that you are not the daughter of M. Simonin."

I immediately replied: "I suspected as much."

"Well then, consider seriously whether your mother can, without, or even with, the consent of your father, give you a position on an equality with those who are not your sisters, or whether she can admit to your father a fact about which he is already far too suspicious."

"But, sir, who is my father?"

"I am not in her confidence as to that. But it is only too certain that your sisters have been prodigiously favoured and that every possible precaution has been taken by marriage contracts, conversion of real into personal property, stipulations, trusts, and other means to reduce your share to nothing, against the event of your being one day able to apply to the law for restitution. If you lose your parents, you will find there is little for yourself. You refuse the offer of a convent – perhaps one day you will be sorry you are not there."

"That is impossible; I ask for nothing."

"You do not know what pain, labour, and indigence mean."

"I know at least the price of liberty, and the burden of a state for which one has no vocation."

"I have said what I had to say, it is for you to think it over."

He then got up.

"One question more, sir."

"As many as you like."

"Do my sisters know what you have told me?"

"No."

"How could they then bring themselves to rob their sister, for such they think me?"

"Self-interest, self-interest! They would not other-wise have made their present admirable matches. Everyone looks after himself in this world, and I do not advise you to count on them if you come to lose your parents. You may be sure that the small portion you will have to share with them will be disputed down to the last halfpenny. They have large families, which will be an excellent excuse for reducing you to beggary. Besides, they can do nothing of themselves; their husbands do everything. Supposing they had any feelings of pity, the help which they could give you unknown to their husbands would become a source of domestic strife. I am always seeing such things: chil-dren being smuggled away because illegitimate or even when legitimate being assisted at the price of domestic peace. And, then, the bread of charity is very bitter. If you follow my advice, you will make it up with your parents; you will do everything your mother expects of you; you will enter into religion; you will be given a small allowance, with which you will live – if not happily, at any rate tolerably. Besides, I will not hide from you that the open way in which your mother has deserted you, her obstinacy in locking you up, and some other circumstances which I have now forgotten but once knew, have produced exactly the same effect on your father as on you. He was suspicious about your birth before, he is so no longer, and, though no confidences have been made, he is now quite certain you are only his child in as far as the law attributes all children to him who bears the title of husband. You are good and sensible. Think over what you have just learnt."

I got up and began to cry. I saw that he himself was moved. He gently raised his eyes to Heaven and led me back. I picked up the servant who had brought me; we got into the carriage and went home.

It was late. I lay meditating part of the night on what had been revealed to me; I was still meditating on it next day. I had no father. I had lost my mother owing to her scruples; precautions had been taken to prevent my asserting those legal rights to which my birth entitled me; a very cruel domestic captivity; no hope, no resource. Perhaps had everything been explained to me earlier, after my sisters had been established in life, and could I have been kept at home where a good many people called, some one might have been found for whom my character, mind, appearance, and talents would have been a sufficient dowry. This was still not out of the question, but the scandal I had caused at the convent made it harder. It was inconceivable that a girl between seventeen and eighteen years old should have gone such lengths without uncommon strength of character. Men praise this quality, but seem quite happy to do without it in the case of women they propose to marry. This, however, was a course to be attempted before thinking of any other. So I decided to speak about it to my mother. I asked her for an interview, which was granted.

It was winter. She was sitting in an arm-chair before the fire. Her countenance was severe, her gaze fixed, her features motionless. I went up to her, threw myself at her feet, and asked her pardon for all the wrong I had done.

"You can earn my pardon," she replied, "by what

you say to me now. Get up. Your father is away. You have heaps of time to explain yourself. You have seen Father Seraphim; you know who you are and what you can expect of me, unless indeed it be your intention to punish me all my life for a fault I have expiated but too fully. Well, what do you wish with me? What have you decided upon?"

"Mamma," I answered, "I know that I have nothing and can expect nothing. I am far from wishing to add to your sorrows, whatever their nature. Perhaps you would have found me more obedient to your wishes had you informed me earlier of circumstances which I could hardly have suspected. But at last I know; I know who I am, and must conduct myself accordingly. I am no longer surprised at the distinctions made between my sisters and myself. I recognize the justice of them and subscribe to them. But I am still your child. You have carried me in your bosom and I trust you will not forget it."

"May I be well punished," she added keenly, "if I did not confess to you as much as I possibly could."

"Well, Mamma," I said, "restore me your kindness and your presence. Restore me the love of him who thinks himself my father."

"He is almost as certain about your birth as we are," she added. "I never see you with him without hearing his reproaches, which he throws at me by ill-treating you. Do not expect from him the feelings of an affectionate father. And then, I will admit it, you recall to me such treachery, such odious ingratitude on the part of another that I cannot bear the thought of it. This man always comes between yourself and me. The thought of him revolts me, and the hate I owe him flows over on to you."

"What," I replied, "can I not hope that you and M. Simonin will treat me as a stranger, as an unknown girl, taken in out of pity?"

"Neither of us can do so. My child, stop poisoning my life. If you had no sisters, I should know what to do. But you have two, and both have large families. The passion that sustained me is long since dead, and conscience has reclaimed her rights."

"But he to whom I owe my life ..."

"He is no more. He died without giving you two thoughts, and that is the least of his offences."

At this point her expression underwent a violent change, her eyes blazed, indignation seized upon her countenance. She wished to speak, but could no longer articulate owing to the trembling of her lips. She was sitting down, and leant her head upon her hands to hide from me the violent emotions which were seething within her. She remained some time in this state, then got up and walked several times round the room without speaking a word. She stifled her tears till they scarcely flowed, and said:

"The monster. It was none of his doing that he did not smother you in my breast with all the misery he caused me. But God spared us both that the daughter might atone for the mother's sin. Child, you have nothing, and will never have anything; the little I can give you is so much smuggled from your sisters. Such are the consequences of folly. Still I hope I shall have nothing with which to reproach myself at death. I shall have earned your dowry out of my economies. I do not trade on my husband's easy-going nature, but every day I put aside what I from time to time receive from his generosity. I have sold all my jewels and obtained his permission to dispose freely of what I obtained for them. I was fond of cards, but have given them up; of the theatre, and go there no longer; of company, but I have gone into retirement; of luxury, and I have renounced it. If you enter into religion, as M. Simonin and myself desire, your dowry will be the fruit of my daily self-denial."

"But, Mamma," I said, "some well-to-do people still come here. Perhaps one may be found who, being satisfied with my appearance, will not even demand the savings which you intend for my establishment."

"That is no more to be thought of. The scandal you caused at the convent has undone you."

"Is there then no remedy?"

"None."

"But if I do not find a husband, must I be locked up in a convent?"

"Yes, unless you wish to go on making me miserable until my eyes are closed. For I must die at last. At that terrible moment your sisters will be round my bed. How could I bear to see you among them? What would be the effect of your presence on me in those last moments? Daughter, for such you are despite myself, your sisters have obtained by right a name which is yours through crime; do not afflict a dying mother; let her descend peacefully to the tomb. Let her be able to say to herself, when about to appear before the Great Judge, that she has repaid her fault as far as she is able, and that she can flatter herself that after her death you will bring no trouble into her house and will not lay claim to rights that are not your own."

"Mamma," I said, "you can be at rest upon that point. Bring a lawyer to draw up an act of renunciation, and I will subscribe to whatever you like."

"That cannot be. A child cannot disinherit itself. It can only be disinherited as a punishment by justly angered parents. Should God call me to-morrow, to-morrow I should be reduced to the extremity of telling my husband everything, that we might take action in common. Do not expose me to an indiscretion, which would make me odious in his eyes and entail consequences dishonouring to you. If you survive me, you will remain without name, future, or estate. What ideas do you wish me to carry away with me at death? So I shall have to tell your father ... what shall I tell him? That you are not his child! My daughter, if I had merely to throw myself at your feet to obtain from you ... But you feel nothing. You have your father's inflexible soul. ...."

At this moment M. Simonin came in and saw his wife's distress. He loved her and was a violent man. He stopped short, and turning a terrible look on me, said:

"Leave the room."

Had he been my father I should not have obeyed him, but he was not.

He added, speaking to the servant who let me out:

"Tell her not to appear again."

I shut myself up in my little prison and mused on what my mother had told me. I threw myself on my knees and prayed to God for inspiration. I prayed for a long time, and remained with my face glued to the ground. One hardly ever invokes the aid of Heaven save when one cannot steel one's own resolution; and it is very rare then that Heaven does not counsel obedience. Such was my decision. "They want me to be a nun; perhaps also it is the will of God. Very well, I will be one. Since I must be wretched, the scene of my unhappiness can hardly matter." I ordered the servant who waited on me to warn me when my father had gone out. The very next day I asked for an interview with my mother. She sent back word that she had promised M. Simonin not to see me, but that I could write to her with a pencil that was provided me. I wrote then on a piece of paper (this fatal paper has been found again and only too good use of it has been made).

"Mamma, I am sorry for all the sorrow I have caused. I ask your forgiveness and intend never to distress you again. Order me to do whatever you like. If it be your wish that I enter into religion I hope that it is also the will of God."

The servant took this letter and carried it to my mother. She came back a moment later and said to me in a voice of transport:

"If it needed only one word from you to make yourself and your parents happy, why have you put off saying it so long? I have never seen such an expression on the face of my master and mistress since I have been here. They used to quarrel about you unceasingly. Thank Heaven I shall now be spared that. ..."

While she spoke to me I felt that I had just signed my death-warrant, and this foreboding, my lord, will come true if you abandon me. Several days passed without my having any news, when one morning about nine my door suddenly opened, and M. Simonin entered in dressing-gown and nightcap. His presence merely terrified me now that I had learnt he was not my father. I got up and curtsied. I seemed to have two hearts. I could not think of my mother without affection and without wishing to cry. But it was quite different with M. Simonin. Certain it is that a father inspires a kind of feeling one has for no one else but him. One cannot know this, unless like me one finds oneself in the presence of one who has long borne, but has just lost, this august character. Others will never know it. When I passed from his presence into that of my mother, I seemed to myself another being. He said:

"Susan, do you recognize this note?"

"Yes, sir."

"Have you written it of your own free will?"

I could only answer "Yes."

"Are you at least resolved to fulfil the promises contained in it?"

"I am."

"Have you a preference for any particular convent?"

"That is all one to me."

"Very well."

Such were my replies, but unluckily they were not written down. I was told nothing of what was happening for a whole fortnight, during which time they presumably approached various religious houses, who refused to receive me as a postulant owing to the scandal my first step had caused. They were less difficult at Longchamps, doubtless because it was hinted I was musical and had a good voice. The difficulty of the whole matter was greatly exaggerated as well as the favour that was shown me in accepting me into the House. I was even persuaded into writing to the Superior. I did not appreciate the consequences of this written testimony which was asked of me. They were apparently afraid that one day I might revolt against my vows and they wished an attestation in my own hand that these vows had been freely taken. Except for this motive how can this letter, which ought to have remained in the hands of the Superior, have subsequently passed into those of my brothers-in-law? But let us close our eyes to all this, which shows M. Simonin in a light which is disagreeable to me. He is now dead.

I was conducted to Longchamps,[5] in the company of my mother. I did not ask to say good-bye to M. Simonin. I confess the idea only occurred to me when we were half way there. I was expected, as the fame had spread both of my story and my talents; they said nothing about the first, but they were very anxious to see if their new acquisition was worth the trouble. After some conversation on many small matters (for, as you can well imagine, after all that had happened, there was no talk of God, or of vocation, or of the dangers of the world, or of the sweetness of the cloistered life, and no one risked any of these faded pieties, with which the first moments are usually filled), the Superior said to me: "You are a musician and have a voice; we have a harpsichord; if you like, we can go into our parlour." My soul was in anguish, but this was not the moment to manifest the repugnance I felt; my mother went first and I followed her, while the Superior came last, with some nuns attracted by curiosity. It was evening. Candles were brought, and I sat down at the harpsichord. I improvised for some time, as I sought for a piece of music in my head which was usually full of them, but could find nothing. But the Superior was pressing, and I sang without thinking of its aptness, by habit, because I knew the morsel well:

"Tristes apprêts, pâles flambeaux,
Jour plus affreux que les ténèbres."

[Sad preparations, pale torches, day more terrible than darkness.][6]

I do not know what effect it had, but they did not listen long. I was interrupted by their praises, which I was very surprised to have earned so quickly and easily. My mother then placed me in the hands of the Superior, gave me her own hand to kiss, and went off home.

So there I was in another religious house, a postulant, and to all appearances a postulant of my own free will. But you, my lord, who know everything that has happened so far, what will you think of it? For the most part these facts were not produced when I wished to break my vows, some because they were truths, which could not be proved, others because they would have served simply to make me odious. People would have seen in me merely an unnatural child, who blackened the memory of her relations in order to gain her liberty. Everything *against* me could be proved. The case *for* me could be neither produced nor proved. I did not even wish the doubts about my birth to be hinted to the judges. Several people not lawyers urged me to implicate the Director whom I had in common with my mother. This was impossible, and even had it been possible, I should not have allowed it. But while on this point, before I forget it, and in case you wish to make a point of it to help me, I think you might be silent about my music and knowledge of the harpsichord, unless indeed you are strongly of the opposite opinion. This would be enough to reveal who I am. Boasting about my talents does not go with the obscurity and security I seek. People in my position have not these accomplishments and so I must not have them either. If I have to leave the country I will fall back on them. Leave the country! But why, pray, should such a notion terrify me? Because I do not know where to go; because I am young and inexperienced; because I fear want, men, and vice; because I have always lived retired from the world, and because away from Paris I should feel lost. This is perhaps a mistaken view, but it is how I feel. You, my lord, can prevent my being in the position of not knowing where to go or what to do.

The Superiors at Longchamps, as at most religious houses, change every three years. A Madame de Moni was taking up her duties when I was brought into the House. I cannot speak too highly of her, though her kindness it was which ruined me. She was a sensible woman, who knew the human heart, and indulgent, though none had less need to be so: we were all her children. She saw only those faults which she could not help perceiving and which were too important for her not to notice. I am quite disinterested in saying this, as I performed my duties with exactness, and she would do me the justice to say that I was guilty of no fault for which she might have had to punish or pardon me. Any predilection she showed to individuals was the reward of merit, so perhaps I ought not to add that she loved me dearly and that I was not the least among her favourites. I know what a compliment I am paying myself, a compliment greater than you can realize, who never knew her. "Favourite" is the name applied enviously by the other nuns to those whom the Superior loves best. If I have a fault to find with Mme de Moni it is the fact that she was too obviously affected by her love of virtue, piety, frankness, gentleness, talents, and honesty; though she knew perfectly well that those who could not lay claim to these qualities were on that account still further humiliated by her preferences. She had also the gift, perhaps more common in the convent than in the great world, of reading character. It was thus very rare for her to get fond of a nun whom she did not like at first sight. She quickly took a fancy to me, and I had immediately complete confidence in her. Woe to those whose confidence she could not gain without an effort! They had themselves to admit in such cases that they were bad and shiftless characters. She spoke to me of my adventure at Saint Mary's, which I repeated to her, as to you, disguising nothing. I told her everything which I have just told you and forgot nothing which bore on my birth and troubles. She pitied me, comforted me, and bade me hope for a happier future.

Meanwhile my period as a postulant was finishing. The moment for taking the habit arrived and I took it. I went through my novitiate without disgust, and I pass rapidly over these two years as they brought no sorrow to me, save the secret feeling that I was advancing step by step towards entering into a state for which I was not intended. Sometimes this feeling reasserted itself strongly, but at once I had recourse to my good Superior, who kissed me, encouraged my spiritual nature, argued her point of view forcefully, and always ended by saying: "And have not other conditions their thorns as well? We feel only our own. Come, child, let us kneel and pray." Then she would prostrate herself and pray out loud, but with so much eloquence, unction, sweetness, elevation, and strength that one would have said the spirit of God was inspiring her. Her thoughts, expressions, and images penetrated the very depths of the heart. At first one listened, gradually one was swept along and united with her. The soul trembles and one shared her transports. She certainly intended no seduction, but such was certainly the consequence of her actions. One left her with a burning heart and with joy and ecstasy painted on the countenance. How sweet were the tears then shed. She herself for a long time took on the stamp of the impression which she made on us, an impression which did not pass away. This was not my experience alone but that of all the nuns. Some have said that they felt the need of her consolation growing in them like the need for some great pleasure – and I think that I only needed a little more experience of it to have felt the same.

I experienced, however, as the moment of my profession approached, so profound a feeling of melancholy that my Superior was put to a terrible trial. Her talent abandoned her, as she admitted to me frankly.

"I do not know," she said, "what is going on within me; it seems to me that, when you come in, God retires and His spirit is silent. It is in vain that I excite myself, search for ideas, and seek to exalt my soul. I feel myself to be a commonplace and limited woman. I fear to speak. ..."

"Ah! my Mother," said I, "what a presentiment. Suppose it were God who made you mute."

One day when I was feeling more uncertain and depressed than ever, I went into her cell. At first my presence overcame her. Apparently she read in my eyes and my whole appearance that the deep feeling which I carried in my bosom was beyond my control, and she did not wish to struggle without certainty of success. Still she understood the task and gradually warmed to it. As my grief grew weaker her enthusiasm increased. She suddenly threw herself on her knees, and I imitated her. She thought I was going to share her transports, as I hoped too. She pronounced a few words and then was suddenly silent. I waited in vain. She spoke no more, but got up and burst into tears, taking me by the hand and clasping me in her arms.

"Ah, dear child," she cried, "what a cruel effect you produce upon me! See what has happened: I am no longer inspired. I feel it to be so. Go, let God speak to you Himself, since He does not please to do so through my lips."

I cannot with certainty say what had been going on inside her; whether I had inspired in her a distrust of her own strength which could not be overcome, whether I had made her timid, or whether I really had destroyed her communion with Heaven: but the gift of consolation was no longer hers. On the eve of my profession, I went to see her and her melancholy equalled my own. I began to weep, and she also. I threw myself at her feet; she blessed me, raised me, kissed me, and sent me away, saying:

"I am tired of life, I wish to die, I asked God that I might not see this day, but such is not His will. Go, I will speak to your mother: I will pass the night in prayer, and you, pray too. But go to bed; I order it."

"Let me join you in prayer," I answered.

"I will allow it from nine to eleven, no longer. At half-past nine I shall begin to pray, and so will you. But at eleven you will let me pray alone and, yourself, get some sleep. I shall keep watch before God the rest of the night."

She wished to pray, but could not. While I was asleep this saintly woman went along the corridors, knocking at each door, woke the nuns, and made them go down noiselessly into the chapel. They all collected there; and when they were there she bade them address Heaven on my behalf. First they prayed in silence; then she extinguished the lights and all recited the *Miserere* together, except the Superior, who, prostrate at the foot of the altar, whipped herself cruelly, saying: "O God, if You have withdrawn from me through some fault which I have committed, grant me forgiveness. I do not ask You to restore to me the gift which You have taken from me, but that You should address Yourself to this innocent who sleeps, while I invoke You here for her – O God, speak to her, speak to her relatives and forgive me."

Next day she came early into my cell. I did not hear

her, not being yet awake. She sat beside my bed, and lightly placed one of her hands upon my forehead. Distress, agitation, and grief kept passing in turn over her face, and it was in this state that she appeared to me when I opened my eyes. She said nothing of what had passed during the night. She only asked me if I had gone to bed early, and I replied:

"At the hour you told me."

If I had slept.

"Soundly."

"I expected as much. How are you?"

"Very well, Mother."

"Alas," she said to me, "I have never seen anyone enter into religion without being anxious about her. But I have never been so distressed about anyone as about you. I am so desirous that you should be happy."

"If you always love me I shall be."

"Ah! if that were all! You thought of nothing during the night?"

"No."

"And what is passing at this moment through your soul?"

"I am brutish and obey my fate without repugnance and without pleasure. I feel that necessity is dragging me on and I let myself go. Ah, I know none of that soft joy, of that flutter of the spirit, of that melancholy, of that soft anxiety which I have sometimes remarked in those who find themselves in my present state. I feel like an idiot and cannot even weep. They wish it, it must be so. Such is my only thought. But you do not say anything?"

"I did not come to talk to you, but to see you and to listen. I am expecting your mother. Try not to distress me. Let my feelings pile up in my soul. When it can hold no more, I shall leave you. I must be silent. I know myself. My nature has only one jet; still, it is violent, and I must not pour it over you. Lie back a moment yet, while I look at you. Speak only a few words to me, and let me take away what I have come to find. Then I shall go and God will do the rest."

I was silent, lay back on my pillow, and offered her one of my hands, which she took. She seemed to muse and to muse deeply. She kept her eyes with difficulty closed. Sometimes she opened them, lifted them on high, and brought them back to me. She grew agitated: her soul filled with tumult, became calm and then grew agitated again. Truly this woman was born to be a prophetess. She had the appearance and the character of one. She was beautiful – but age, while weakening her features and delving its furrows in them, had in addition given dignity to her countenance. Her eyes were small, but they seemed either to look into herself or to look right through the things round her: and to unravel what was a great distance off, in the past and in the future. From time to time she squeezed my hand silently. She suddenly asked me the time.

"Almost six."

"Good-bye, I am going away. They are coming to dress you. I do not wish to be there as it would distress me. I have now one care only, that in the early stages I may behave with moderation."

She had hardly gone out when the Novice Mistress

and my companions entered. They took off my religious habit and redressed me in the clothes of the world. This is a custom with which you are acquainted.[7] I understood nothing of what was being said around me. I had become practically an automaton. I was aware of nothing, save that from time to time I had a kind of small convulsive fit. They told me what was to be done; and they were often obliged to repeat themselves as I understood nothing the first time. It was not that I was thinking about anything else, but that I was completely wrapt. My head was weary, as when one is overtaxed with thinking. Meanwhile the Superior was closeted with my mother. I never learned what happened at this interview, which was of great length. I was only told that when they separated my mother was so distressed that she could not find the door by which she had come in and that the Superior had gone out with her hands clasped and pressed against her forehead.

Meanwhile the bells were ringing. I came down and found only a small company collected. The sermon may have been good. I did not hear a word of it. They did with me what they would all that morning, which has been erased from my life, for the passage of time has never passed into my consciousness. I do not know what I did or what I said. No doubt I was questioned and no doubt I answered. I pronounced my vows, but cannot remember doing so, and I became a nun as unconsciously as I had become a Christian.

I did not take in the ceremony of my profession any more than that of my baptism – but there is this difference, that one confers grace and the other presupposes

it. Well, my lord, though I did not protest at Longchamps and did at Saint Mary's, do you think me
the more committed for that? I appeal to your judgment; I appeal to the judgment of God. I was so
completely depressed that when some days afterwards
I was told that it was my turn for service in the choir I
did not understand what was being said. I asked if it
was really the case that I had made my profession, and
asked to see the signature to my vows. They had to
support these proofs with the testimony of the whole
community and that of some outsiders who had been
invited to the ceremony. I addressed myself several
times to the Superior and said:

"Is it true then?" and I always expected her to
answer: "No, child, you are mistaken." Her reiterated
assurances did not convince me, as it seemed impossible that I should remember nothing of what had
happened during a whole day, so tumultuous and
varied, so full of singular and striking incidents; not
even the faces of those who had served me, nor that of
the priest who had addressed me, nor of him who had
received my vows. The change from the religious to the
lay habit is the only thing which I remember. From
that moment I was what is called physically alienated.
Months passed before I recovered from this condition,
and I attribute my complete forgetfulness of what
happened to the length of this kind of convalescence.
My case resembled that of people who have had a long
illness, spoken sensibly, and received the sacraments,
but on being restored to health can remember nothing
about it. I have seen several examples of this in the
House, and I have said to myself: "Presumably this is

what happened to me the day I made my profession."
But it remains to be ascertained if such actions are
really done by man, and if, despite appearances, he has
any part in them.

In the same year three important people in my life
passed away – my father, or rather he who passed for
such; he was old, had worked hard, and was snuffed
out; my Mother Superior; and my mother.

The worthy nun felt her last hour approaching from
afar. She condemned herself to silence, and had her
bier carried into her room. Having lost all capacity
for sleep, she passed her days and nights in meditation
and writing. She left behind her fifteen meditations
which seem to me extremely beautiful. I have a copy
of them. If at any time you are curious to see the
notions which our last moments suggest I will show
you them. They are called "The last moments of Sister
de Moni."

At the approach of death she had herself dressed and
was stretched upon her bed. She received the sacraments and held a crucifix in her arms. It was night.
The light of the torches lit up the melancholy scene.
We surrounded her and burst into tears. Her cell was
ringing with cries, when suddenly her eyes lit up with
an unexpected brilliance. She lifted herself suddenly
and spoke. Her voice was almost as strong as it had
been when she was in her usual health. The gift which
she had lost returned to her. She reproached us for our
tears, which made us look as if we envied her her
eternal happiness.

"My children, your grief misleads you. It is there, it
is there," she said, and pointing to heaven, "that I shall

serve you. My eyes will always be looking down upon this House. I shall intercede for you and shall be heard. Come up, all of you, that I may kiss you, and receive my blessing and my last farewell."

While pronouncing these last words this rare woman died, leaving behind her imperishable regrets. My mother died after a short journey which she had made to see one of her daughters later in the autumn. She had had worries, which had weakened her health. I have never found out the name of my father nor the story of my birth. The priest who had been our Director handed me a small parcel from her containing fifty pounds and a letter sewn up in a piece of linen. The letter was as follows:

"My child, it is not much, but my conscience does not let me dispose of a larger sum. It is what remains of the economies I have been able to save out of the little presents M. Simonin used to make me. Live holily, it is best, even for your happiness in this world. Pray for me. Your birth is the one grave sin that I have committed. Help me to expiate it. And may God forgive me for having brought you into the world, out of consideration for the good works you will do there. Above all, do not trouble my family. And although you have not chosen as voluntarily as I could have wished the state you have embraced, shrink from changing it. Why have I not been shut up all my life in a convent? I should not be so troubled by the thought that I must in a moment submit to the terrible judgment of God. Consider, my child, that the fate of your mother in the other world will depend greatly on your conduct in this one. God, Who sees everything, will visit on me in His justice all the good and evil that you will do. Susan, ask nothing from your sisters. They are not in a position to help you. Hope for nothing from your father. He has gone before me; he has seen the great day and is expecting me. My presence will be less terrible for him than his for me. Farewell, once again. O, wretched mother! O, unhappy child! Your sisters have arrived. I am not pleased with them. They pounce on things and carry them off and have distressing quarrels about their rights before the eyes of their dying mother. When they approach my bed, I turn away on my other side. What can I hope to find in them? Two creatures in whom indigence has destroyed all natural feelings. They sigh after the little I am leaving behind me. They put indecent questions to the doctor and nurse, showing with what impatience they await the moment of my departure, which will put them in possession of everything round me. They suspected, I know not how, that I might have some money hidden between my mattresses. They left no stone unturned to make me get up and in this they were successful. Luckily the man to whom I entrusted this packet had come the day before and I had given it to him, as well as this letter, which he has written at my dictation. Burn the letter, and when you learn that I am no more – and that will not be long – have a mass said for me and renew your vows, for I wish you to remain for ever in religion. The idea of you in the world, young, without anyone to support or help you, would be a final anguish in my last moments.''

My father died on the 5th of January, my Superior at the end of the same month, and my mother on Christmas Day (old style).

The succession to Mother de Moni fell upon Sister Christine. But oh, my lord, what a difference there was between the two! You know by now what the first one was like. The second was mean in character, with a narrow intelligence, confused by superstition. She went in for innovating opinions[8] and used to be closeted with Sulpicians and Jesuits. Also she had an aversion for all the favourites of her predecessor. In a moment the House was deep in disturbances, hatred, slanders, accusations, calumnies, and persecutions. We had to explain ourselves on points of theology which meant nothing to us, subscribe to formulas, and give ourselves over to singular practices. Mother de Moni disapproved of all bodily penance. Only twice in her life had she resorted to physical mortification, once on the eve of my profession and once on a like occasion. She said of these penances that they corrected no evil feeling and only ended in puffing people up. She liked her nuns to be well, healthy in body and serene in spirit. Her first step on taking over her duties was to collect all the hair belts and whips, and to prevent the nuns spoiling their food with ashes, or sleeping on the floor. They were to use none of these instruments of penance. Her successor sent each nun back her hair belt and whip and took away the Old and New Testaments. The favourites of the old reign are never the favourites of the new. I meant nothing to the present Superior (to say the least of it) simply because I had been dear to her predecessor. But I quickly made my lot worse by actions which you will call either imprudence or strength of character, according to the way you look at them.

First of all, I gave myself up to all the grief I felt at the loss of our first Superior. Then I praised her on all occasions and instituted between her and our present governor comparisons not favourable to the latter. I painted the state of the House in the old days, and called to memory the peace we then enjoyed, her indulgence towards us, the food, both spiritual and temporal, which was then administered; and I exalted the virtues, the sentiments, and the character of Sister de Moni. Then I threw into the fire my hair belt and got rid of my whip. I lectured my friends on the subject and induced some to follow my example. Thirdly, I procured an Old and New Testament: fourthly, I refused to take sides in religious quarrels, and held on to the title of Christian, refusing to call myself a Jansenist or a Molinist. Fifthly, I held strictly to the rule of the House, neither more nor less. Consequently I would undertake no supererogatory actions, as I found those of obligation quite enough. I would play the organ only on feast days and sing only when I was of the choir. I would no longer permit my good nature and talents to be abused and become a daily drudge. I read and re-read our Constitution till I knew it by heart, and if I was given an order which was either not stated clearly in it or not stated at all, or seemed contrary to it, I refused firmly. I would take up the book and say: "These and these only are the engagements I have undertaken."

My speeches gained me some adherents. The authority of the mistresses became in consequence very limited, and they could no longer dispose of us as though we were their slaves. Hardly a day passed without a scene. In uncertain cases my companions consulted me, and I was always for the rule and against tyranny. I soon had the appearance, and perhaps a little played the part, of a rebel. The Grand Vicars of the Archbishop were being continually called in. I appeared, defended myself, defended my companions; and never once was I condemned, such pains had I taken to have right on my side. It was impossible to attack me on the score of my duties, as I fulfilled them scrupulously. As for those little favours which a Superior can always either grant or refuse, I asked for none. I never appeared in the parlour, and as for visits, as I knew nobody I received none. I had burned my hair belt and thrown away my whip, and advised others to do the same. I never wished to hear another word, good or bad, said of Molinism or Jansenism. When asked if I had submitted to the Constitution, I replied that I had submitted to the Church; if I had accepted the Bull[9] – that I had accepted the Gospel. My cell was visited and my Old and New Testament discovered. Some indiscreet remarks had escaped me as to the suspicious friendships of some of the favourites – the Superior had long private interviews with a young ecclesiastic, and I divined both the real and the pretended reason for them. I overlooked nothing which could make me feared and hated, and so lead to my undoing, and in this I was completely successful. People no longer complained of me to my superiors, but concentrated on making my life difficult. The other nuns were forbidden to come near me, and I soon found myself alone. I had a few friends. It was suspected that these friends would secretly seek some compensations for the constraint imposed upon them, and that, as they could not talk to me by day, they would visit me at night or during the forbidden hours. Spies were set on me, and I was discovered first with one friend, then with another. This imprudence was made an excuse for everything and I was punished in the most barbarous manner: I was condemned for weeks together to assist at divine service on my knees, separated from the rest in the middle of the choir; to live on bread and water; to stay shut up in my cell; and to fulfil the vilest duties in the House. Those called my accomplices were scarcely better treated. When I could not be caught in a fault, faults were imputed to me. I was given incompatible orders and punished for not having carried them out. They put forward the hours of the services and the meals, and altered without telling me all the internal arrangements of the House, so that, with the best will in the world, I was always at fault and always punished. I was brave enough. But no courage can hold out against desertion, solitude and persecution. Things reached such a point that to torment me became a game, the amusement of fifty persons in a league against me. It is impossible to go into their cruelty in every detail. I was prevented from sleeping, watching, or praying. One day several parts of my dress were stolen. Another day it would be my keys or my breviary. My keyhole would be blocked. Either I was prevented from doing anything properly or what I had done properly would be undone. Speeches and actions were attributed to me falsely. I was made responsible for everything and my life was a succession of faults, real or imaginary, with punishments to match.

My health could not hold out against trials so long and severe. I became depressed, gloomy, and melancholic. At first I went to seek strength and resignation at the foot of the altar, and I sometimes found it there. I floated between resignation and despair, sometimes submitting to all the cruelty of my fate, sometimes seeking to free myself by violent means. There was a deep well at the bottom of the garden. How often have I gone there! How often have I gazed into it! There was a stone seat beside it. How often have I sat there, my head leaning against the side of the well! How often, in the tumult of my ideas, have I got up suddenly and resolved to have done with my troubles! What was it held me back? Why did I then prefer to weep, cry out at the top of my voice, trample my veil beneath my feet, pull out my hair, and tear my face with my nails? If it was God Who prevented my destroying myself, why did He not prevent the rest as well?

I am going to tell you something that will very likely seem extraordinary to you, but which is none the less true: namely that I am certain my frequent visits to the well had been observed and that my cruel enemies flattered themselves that one day I should go through with a design which was boiling at the bottom of my heart. When I went in that direction, people affected to go off and be busy somewhere else. Several times I found the door of the garden open at hours when it ought to be shut, and curiously enough on days when I had been specially persecuted. They had strained my violent temperament to breaking point and thought me mad. But the moment I thought I had divined that the means of departing this life were, so to speak, being offered to my despair, that I was being led by the hand to the well and that I should always find it ready to receive me, I thought no more about it. My mind went off in other directions: I hung about the corridors and measured the height of the windows. In the evening, when undressing, I tested vaguely the strength of my garters. Another day I refused to eat anything. I went down into the refectory and stood with my back to the wall, my hands hanging beside me, my eyes shut, and I touched none of the things that were served me. In this attitude I forgot myself so entirely that all the nuns had gone out without my noticing and I was left alone. They made a point of going out noiselessly and leaving me there so that I could be punished for failing to appear at the hour of exercise. How can I put it? I was disgusted with all methods of doing away with myself, because it seemed to me that my enemies, far from opposing me, were encouraging me. Apparently we do not enjoy being pushed out of the world, and perhaps I should no longer be here if they had made a pretence of restraining me. Perhaps by taking our life we try to reduce others to despair, and cling on to it if we think our departure will give pleasure, though naturally such states of mind are very complicated. To tell the truth, as far as I can recall my mentality beside the well, I think I cried out internally at the wretches who were making off so as to help me in my crime: "Come one step towards me, show the slightest wish to save me, come and try to stop me, and you may be sure you will arrive too late." I certainly only lived because they wanted me to die. The passion for doing harm and tormenting other people wears itself out in the world, but not in the cloister.

Such was my state when, going over my past life, I thought of freeing myself from my vows. I mused on it at first quite casually. Alone, deserted, without anyone to assist me, how could I succeed in a project which is so difficult even with the help of friends? However, the idea soothed me: my mind grew more collected: I was more self-controlled. I avoided some punishments and was more patient with those I still received. The alteration was remarked and caused astonishment. Persecution of me stopped at once, as when you are pursued by a cowardly enemy and turn on him unexpectedly. One question, my lord, I should like to put you. Why is it that amid all the desperate thoughts that traverse the head of a desperate nun, that of setting the house on fire never occurs to her? I have never thought of doing so, nor others either, though it is the easiest thing in the world to put into execution. You have only, one day when the wind is high, to carry a flame into a loft, a wood-stack, or a corridor. No convents are ever burnt. Yet in these circumstances the doors fly open and everyone makes for safety. Do you think that perhaps one fears the danger to oneself and those dear to one, and disdains a succour one must share with those one hates? Such a notion is almost too complicated to be true.

If one thinks enough about a thing, one begins to appreciate the justice and even the possibility of it. And this is half the battle. It took me a fortnight, for I make up my mind quickly. And what did I decide to do? Why, to draw up a statement and pass it out for consultation. Neither actions were quite safe. Since the revolution in my mind I was scrutinized more attentively than ever. Eyes followed me everywhere. I did not take a step which was not observed, say a word which was not weighed. People used to come up to me and try to sound me, put me questions and affect pity and friendship. They dwelt on the past, blamed me but mildly or excused me altogether. Better conduct in the future was hoped for, and I was flattered with the prospect of milder treatment ahead. Meanwhile they used to come into my cell every moment of the day and night with every kind of excuse; suddenly and secretly they would half open the curtains and then withdraw. I had formed the habit of going to bed dressed, and adopted another, that of writing my confession. On those days, which are marked down for us, I went and asked my Superior for ink and paper, which were not refused me. So I awaited the day for confessing, and while waiting drew up in my head what I had to put forward. It was a short version of what I have just written to you – but I used borrowed names. However, I made three blunders. The first was to tell my Superior that I had a great deal to write, so as to make this an excuse for asking for more than the usual allowance of paper. The second was to be so concentrated on my report as to forget about the confession. The third was only to remain at the Confessional a moment, as I had made no confession and was quite unprepared for this act of religion. All this was noticed and the deduction made that I had used the paper for reasons different to those given. But if it had not been used for my confession (and this indeed was evident) what had it been used for?

I was not aware that they were alarmed, still I felt that I should not be found with such an important document on me. First I thought of sewing it into my bolster or my mattresses, then of hiding it in my clothes, burying it in the garden, or throwing it into the fire. You can have no idea of what a hurry I was in to write it or how embarrassed I was when it was written. First I sealed it, then thrust it into my bosom and went off to the service, for which the bell was ringing. My movements revealed my anxiety; I was next to a nun who was fond of me. I had more than once seen her look at me with pity and shed tears: she never spoke to me but she certainly suffered for me. I resolved to risk everything and entrust her with my paper. At a moment in the orison, when all the nuns kneel, incline, and are, as it were, buried in their stalls, I gently pulled the paper from my bosom and handed it to her behind my back. She took it and thrust it into hers. This was the most important of all the services she had done me, but she had done me many others. For months together, without compromising herself, she spent her time removing all the little obstacles which they set in the way of my going through with my duties, with the object of providing a reason for punishing me. She went to pull the bell or to answer it when necessary. She was always to be found where I ought to have been and I never knew about it.

I was well advised to do this. As we left the choir the Superior said to me: "Sister Susan, follow me." I followed her, then she stopped in the corridor at another door and said: "This is now your cell. Sister Saint Jerome is going to occupy your former one." I went in and she with me. We had both sat down without speaking, when a nun appeared with my clothes, which she laid on a chair, and the Superior said to me: "Sister Susan, undress and take this garment." I obeyed in her presence, but she watched all my movements attentively. The Sister who had brought my clothes was at the door; she came back, carried away those which I had taken off and went out, followed by the Superior. No reason was given me for this proceeding and I did not ask for any. Meanwhile my cell had been thoroughly searched. My pillow and mattresses had been unsewn; they moved everything that could be or could ever have been moved. They went over my tracks, to the Confessional, to the chapel, in the garden, to the well, to the stone seat. I observed a part of their investigations and suspected the rest. They found nothing, but remained none the less convinced that there was something to be found. They continued to spy on me for several days, went wherever I went, looked everywhere, but all in vain. At last the Superior came to the conclusion that the truth could be learned from me alone. She came one day into my cell and said to me: "Sister Susan, you have your faults but untruthfulness is not one of them. Tell me the truth. What have you done with all that paper I gave you?"

"Madam, I have told you."

"That is impossible, for you asked me for a great quantity and only passed a moment at the Confessional."

"That is so."

"What have you done with it, then?"

"What I told you."

"Come! swear by the Holy Obedience which you have vowed to God that it is so, and in spite of appearances I will believe you."

"You are not allowed to put me on oath for such a trifle nor I to swear one. I could not do so."

"You are mistaken, Sister Susan, and you do not know to what you are exposing yourself. What have you done with all the paper I gave you?"

"I have told you."

"Where is it?"

"I have no longer got it."

"What have you done with it?"

"What one usually does with those sorts of writings which become useless after having served their purpose."

"Swear to me by the Holy Obedience that it has all been used in writing your confession and that you have not got it any longer."

"Madam, I repeat to you that this second thing is no more important than the first; I cannot swear."

"Swear or ..."

"I will *not* swear."

"You will *not* swear?"

"No, Madam."

"Then you are guilty."

"And of what can I be guilty?"

"Of everything. There is nothing of which you are incapable. You have set out to praise my predecessor in order to humiliate me: to despise the usages which she had forbade, the laws which she had abolished and which I thought it right to re-establish: to cause an upheaval in our whole society and to infringe the rules: to divide the Sisters against each other: to neglect your duties: to force me to punish you and those you have seduced, which is what I most detest. I could have used severer methods against you: I have spared you. I thought you would recognize your faults, return to the spirit of your vocation and come back to me. You have not done so. Something wrong is going on in your mind. You have your plans. The interests of the House necessitate my knowing them, and know them I will. I can answer for that. Sister Susan, tell me the truth."

"I have told it you."

"I am going to leave you. Beware of my return. . . . I will take a chair and allow you yet another moment in which to make up your mind. . . . Your papers, if they still exist. . . ."

"I have no longer got them."

"On your oath that they contained nothing but your confession."

"I cannot swear."

She remained silent for a moment, then went out and returned with four of her favourites. Their look was wild and furious. I threw myself at their feet and implored their pity. They all began crying out together:

"Show no pity, Madam; do not let her get round you. Let her give up her papers or go in peace."[10]

I clasped their knees one after the other and said to them, calling them by their names: "Sister Saint Agnes, Sister Saint Julia, what have I done to you? Why do you incite my Superior against me? Did I ever use you so? How often have I intervened on your behalf? You no longer remember? Yet you were in the wrong and I am not."

The Superior, who remained quite motionless, looked at me and said:

"Give up your papers, wretched girl, or tell me what is in them."

"Madam," they said to her, "you have asked her often enough. You are too good. You do not know her. Hers is a disobedient spirit, which can only be tamed by extreme methods. It is her fault, not yours. So much the worse for her."

"Mother," I said, "I have done nothing to offend either God or man, I swear it."

"That is not the oath I want."

"She has written against us, against you, to the Grand Vicar, to the Archbishop. Heaven knows in what colours she may have painted the interior of our House, and people easily believe the worst. Madam, we must crush her if you do not wish her to crush us."

The Superior added: "Sister Susan, see . . ."

I got up suddenly and said:

"Madam, I have seen everything. I see that I am destroying myself. But a moment sooner or later is not worth bothering about. Do what you will with me. Listen to their fury. Go through with your injustice."

At the same moment I stretched out my arms to them. Her companions took hold of them. My veil was torn off and I was stripped without any shame. They found a small portrait of our former Superior on my heart. They seized hold of it. I implored them to let me kiss it once more, but they refused. They threw me a shift, took off my stockings, covered me with sack cloth, and led me down the corridors with my head and feet bare. I shrieked and called for help. But the bell had been rung to warn everyone to stay in. I called on Heaven. I fell on the ground and was dragged along. When I arrived at the foot of the staircase my feet and hands were bleeding and my legs all bruised. My condition would have melted the hardest heart. Meanwhile they opened with some large keys the door of a little dark underground chamber, where I was thrown on to a mat half-rotten with damp. There I found a morsel of black bread and a bowl of water along with a little necessary crockery of coarse manufacture. The mat was rolled up at one end to form a pillow. On a block was a death's head and a wooden crucifix. My first impulse was to kill myself. I put my hands up to my throat. I tore my garment with my teeth. I uttered horrible shrieks. I howled like a wild beast. I was all over blood. I went on trying to kill myself till my strength gave out, which was fairly soon. I spent three days there, and thought I was there for life. Every morning one of my persecutors came and said to me:

"Obey your Superior and you shall leave this place."

"I have done nothing and do not know what is asked of me. Oh! Sister Saint Clement, there is a God."

On the third day, about nine o'clock in the evening, the door was opened by the nuns who had brought me there. After praising the kindness of the Superior they informed me that she had forgiven me and was going to let me go free.

"It is too late," I answered; "let me stay here. I want to die."

Meanwhile they had lifted me up and were dragging me after them. They led me back into my cell, where I found the Superior.

"I have consulted God about your fate: He has touched my heart. He wishes me to have pity on you and I obey Him. Go on your knees and ask His forgiveness."

I knelt down and said: "I ask Your forgiveness for the faults I have committed as You asked for forgiveness on the Cross for me."

"What arrogance!" they cried, "she compares herself to Jesus Christ and us to the Jews who crucified Him."

"Do not think about me," I answered, "but about yourselves and judge."

"That is not everything," said the Superior; "swear by the Holy Obedience that you will never mention what has happened."

"You must have acted very wrongly if you put me on oath not to mention it. No one, except your conscience, shall know anything; I swear it."

"You swear?"

"Yes, I swear."

On this they took off the garments they had given me and let me dress myself again on my own.

I had caught a chill and my condition became critical. My body was a mass of bruises. For several days I had had nothing but a few drops of water and a little bread. I certainly thought that this would be the last persecution I should have to undergo. But the strength which Nature has planted in young people is best gauged from the merely temporary effects of such violent shocks as this one. In a few days I was quite restored, and I discovered, on reappearing, that the whole community was convinced I had been ill. I took up again the observances of the House and my place in chapel. I had not forgotten my paper nor the young Sister to whom I had confided it. I was sure she had not abused the trust I had shown her in leaving it with her, but also that she had been alarmed by having to keep it. Several days after leaving prison, in the choir, at the same moment as when I had given it to her, that is to say as we were kneeling down, and, inclined one towards the other, were disappearing into our stalls, I felt my dress being gently pulled. I stretched out my hand and was given a note containing only these words:

"How much you have alarmed me, and what must I do with this cruel paper?"

After reading it, I rolled it up in my hand and swallowed it. This all happened at the beginning of Lent. The season was approaching when the desire to hear good singing brought to Longchamps all the good (and bad) society of Paris. I had a fine voice, which had hardly deteriorated. Religious houses never neglect anything that can be of the slightest use to them. So I was shown some consideration and enjoyed rather more liberty. The Sisters to whom I gave singing lessons could talk with me without causing remark. She to whom I had confided my report was one of them. During the recreation hours which we passed in the garden I took her aside and made her sing, and while she sang I said to her:

"You know a great number of people, I nobody. I do

not want you to compromise yourself. I would rather die here than expose you to the suspicion of having helped me. You would be lost yourself, I know, without saving me. And could I be saved by your ruin I would not pay such a price."

"Enough of that; what is to be done?"

"Be sure to pass that consultation secretly to some skilful lawyer, without his knowing from what House it comes; to get an answer, and hand it to me in chapel or elsewhere."

"By the way," she said, "what have you done with my note?"

"Do not be frightened, I have swallowed it."

"And do not be frightened yourself, either. I will think over your affairs."

You will observe, my lord, that I was singing while she spoke to me and that she was singing while I answered, and that our conversation was interrupted by snatches of the Chant. This young person, my lord, is still in the House: her happiness is in your hands. If what she has done for me were discovered, there is no torment to which she would not be exposed. I should not like to be the means of opening the dungeon door for her. I would rather go back into it myself. So burn these letters, my lord. Apart from the interest you have been willing to take in my lot, they contain nothing worth keeping.

(That is what I said to you then. But alas! she is no longer alive and I am alone.)

She was not long in fulfilling her promise and in informing me of it in the accustomed way. Holy Week arrived. There was a large congregation for our *tenebrae.* I sang sufficiently well to occasion an outburst of that scandalous applause which you offer to your actors in the theatre, but which should never be heard in the temples of the Lord, especially on those solemn, melancholy days when we celebrate the memory of His Son nailed to the Cross to expiate the sins of the human race. My young pupils were well prepared. Several had good voices, nearly all had expression and taste; it seemed to me that the public had listened to them with pleasure and that the community was satisfied with the result of my labours.

You know, my lord, that on Thursday the Holy Sacrament is removed from Its tabernacle to a special altar of repose, where It remains till Friday morning. This interval of time is passed in successive adoration by the House, who repair to the altar of repose one after the other or two by two. There is a notice which indicates to each nun her hour of adoration. And I was very happy to read on it, "Sister Saint Susan and Sister Saint Ursula, 2 to 3 a.m."

I repaired to the altar of repose at the hour named. My companion was already there, and we took up our positions side by side on the steps of the altar. We prostrated ourselves together and adored God for half an hour. After this my young friend stretched out her hand to me and clasped my own, saying:

"We may never have another chance of talking so long and so freely together. God knows the constraint in which we live and will forgive us for sharing with Him a space of time that should be His entirely. I have not read your report. But it is not difficult to divine what it contains. I shall have the answer immediately.

But suppose this answer justifies you in going on with your idea of breaking your vows, you must see that you will be obliged to confer with the lawyers."

"That is true."

"And that liberty will be essential for that."

"That is also true."

"And that if you perform your duties exactly, you will profit by the present disposition of our Superiors to obtain it?"

"I have thought of that."

"You will perform them, then?"

"I will see."

"One other thing. If your affair goes forward you will remain here, a prey to the fury of the whole community. Have you thought of the persecutions which await you?"

"They will not be greater than those which I have already experienced."

"Of that I know nothing."

"And excuse me, you are mistaken, First of all, they will not dare to tamper with my freedom."

"Why so?"

"Because then I shall be protected by the law. They will have to produce me on occasions. I shall be, so to speak, half way between the world and the cloister. I shall have my mouth open and freedom to lodge complaints. I shall call on you all as witnesses. They will not dare to afford me grounds of legitimate complaint. They will be anxious not to damage their own case. I should ask nothing better than to be ill-treated. But they will not do it. You may be sure that their conduct will be just the opposite. They will appeal to me, they will represent to me all the harm I am doing to myself and to the House. You may be sure that they will only come to threats when they have seen gentleness and seduction are useless, and that they will never employ force."

"But it is incredible that you feel so much aversion for a state, the duties of which you perform so easily and so exactly."

"But indeed I do. I had it at birth and it will never leave me. I shall end by becoming a bad nun. That moment must be forestalled."

"And suppose that you unfortunately fail?"

"I shall ask to change my House or I shall die here."

"One suffers a long time before dying. Ah! my dear friend, what you are doing makes me shudder. I fear for you in either event. If you are relieved of your vows, what will happen to you? What will you do in the world? You have good looks, intelligence, and talents. But I am told that is all useless for a woman who remains virtuous, and virtuous I know you will always be."

"You are fair to me but unfair to virtue. I have confidence in virtue. The rarer she is among men, the more she must be respected."

"Men praise virtue but do nothing for her."

"Still, virtue encourages me and supports me in the plan I have formed. Whatever people say, my morals will be respected. People will not be able to say of me, at any rate, as of most others, that I have left my state through unbridled passion. I see nobody. I know nobody. I ask to be free, because the sacrifice of my liberty has not been voluntary. Have you read my report?"

"No. I opened the packet you gave me because it was unaddressed and I thought it might be for me. But the first lines undeceived me and I did not continue. It was a good idea on your part to hand it over to me. A moment later it would have been found on you. . . . But the time has come when our station finishes. Let us go on our knees. Our successors should find us in the proper attitude. Ask God to enlighten you and guide your steps. I will unite my prayers and sighs with yours."

My soul was somewhat relieved. My companion prayed upright. I prostrated myself, and my forehead was pressed to the bottom step of the altar, my arms were spread over the upper steps. I do not think I ever addressed God with deeper thankfulness and fervour. My heart thumped violently. In an instant I forgot all my surroundings. I do not know how long I remained in that position or how long I might have remained in it. But I must have been a very touching spectacle for my companion and the two nuns who relieved us. When I got up I thought I was alone: I was mistaken, they were all three standing behind me, bathed in tears: they had not dared to interrupt me. They waited till I should emerge of myself from the state of transport and emanation in which they saw me. When I turned towards them my expression was no doubt imposing, if I may judge by the effect it produced on them and by what they also told me, that I resembled at that moment our former Superior when she used to comfort us, and that the sight of me had caused them all the same emotion. Had I had any leaning towards hypocrisy and fanaticism, or had I wished to play a part in the House, I do not doubt that I should have been successful. My soul catches fire, grows exalted, gets touched easily. And the good Superior said to me a hundred times as she kissed me, that no one had my capacity for loving God: that I had a soft heart, others hearts of stone. It was certain that I found it very easy to share her ecstasies and that when she was praying out loud, I could start speaking myself, follow the thread of her ideas, and come, as though by inspiration, on part of what she would have said herself. Others listened silently to her, or followed after her. But I interrupted her, or anticipated her, or spoke along with her. I preserved a very long time the impression I had received, and apparently I must have given something back to her. It was obvious when others had been talking to her: it was obvious when she had been talking to me. But what does all that signify when vocation is lacking? Our station finished, we gave up the place to our successors and before separating my young companion and I kissed each other tenderly.

The scene at the altar of repose made a stir in the House. You can add to that the success of the Good Friday *Tenebrae*. I sang, played the organ, and elicited applause. Oh! you empty-headed nuns! It hardly needed any effort on my part to be reconciled to the whole community. They came half way to meet me, the Superior setting the example. Several people in society came to get to know me. That suited me too well for me to refuse. I saw the First President, Mme de Soubise, and a crowd of decent people; monks, priests, soldiers, magistrates, pious women, and women of the world, and among them that sort of addle-pate you call *red-heels*, and whom I soon sent about their business. I cultivated no acquaintance that anyone could find objectionable. I left such persons to those nuns who were not so particular.

I forgot to tell you that the first mark of favour shown me was to give me back my cell. I had the courage to ask back the little portrait of my former Superior, and they did not dare refuse it me. It returned to its old place on my heart and will remain there as long as I live. Every morning on getting up I first raised my soul to God and then kissed the portrait. When I wish to pray but find that my soul is unresponsive I detach it from my neck, place it in front of me, look at it, and am inspired by it. It is a great pity we never knew the sacred persons whose images are exposed to our veneration. Then they would make a far greater impression on us. They would not leave us, when we are at their feet or opposite them, as cold as they do.

I had an answer to my report. It was from M. Manouri,[11] and was neither favourable nor the reverse. Before pronouncing on the subject a great number of points had to be cleared up, which was difficult without a meeting. So I said who I was and invited M. Manouri to Longchamps. People like him are too busy to get about easily; still, he came. We talked together for a very long time. We agreed on a method of correspondence which would ensure his questions reaching me and by which I should return my answers. For my part I employed all the time he was busy with the affair in disposing people in my favour, interesting them in my fate, and obtaining protectors. I said who I was, told of my conduct in my first House, all my troubles at home, the sufferings inflicted on me in the convent, my protest at Saint Mary's, my stay at Longchamps, my taking the veil, my profession, and the cruelty with which I had been treated since the completion of my vows. People were sorry for me and offered to help me. I accepted all the goodwill shown me against the day when it might be useful without going into further details. Nothing came out in the House. I had obtained from Rome permission to appeal against my vows. The action was due to come on immediately, while everybody was still feeling quite safe about the whole matter. So I can leave you to imagine the surprise of my Superior when whe was presented in the name of Sister Mary Susan Simonin with a protest against the latter's vows, with her request to abandon the religious habit, and to leave the cloister and to dispose of herself as she thought fit.

I had forseen opposition from several quarters: that of the laws, that of the religious House, that of my sisters and brothers-in-law, who would certainly take fright. They had had all the family property, and, once free, there would be large claims which I could make on them. I wrote to my sisters; I implored them to raise no obstacle to my departure. I appealed to their conscience or to my absence of choice when I took my vows. I offered to abandon, by a legal renunciation, all pretensions to any right of inheritance from my father and mother. I spared no effort to persuade them that this step of mine was dictated by neither self-interest nor passion. I made no impression at all on their feelings. Such legal renunciation as I proposed, if made while I was still in religion, became invalid on my changing my state. And they could not be certain that I should ratify it when free. And then, did it suit them to accept my proposals? Can one leave a sister without home or money? Or keep her property? What will the world say? If she comes to ask for bread, can we refuse it her? If she takes it into her head to marry, what sort of man will her husband be? Then suppose she has children? No, we must leave no stone unturned to stop her. It might be most dangerous. So they said and so they acted.

Scarcely had the Superior received the legal form of my appeal when she came running into my cell.

"What! Sister Susan, you want to leave us?"

"Yes, Madam."

"And you are going to appeal against your vows?"

"Yes, Madam."

"You did not take them in all freedom?"

"No, Madam."

"And who put pressure on you?"

"Everybody."

"Your father?"

"Yes."

"Your mother?"

"She too."

"And why did you not appeal from the foot of the altar?"

"I was so little in control of myself that I cannot even remember having been present."

"How can you say that?"

"I am telling the truth."

"What! You did not hear the priest ask you: 'Sister

Saint Susan Simonin, do you promise to God obedience, chastity, and poverty'?"

"I cannot remember it."

"You can only have answered yes."

"I remember nothing about it."

"Do you really imagine people will believe you?"

"Whether they believe me or not, it will be true just
the same."

"Dear child, think of the abuses that would ensue if
excuses like yours were accepted! You have taken a
hasty step: you have let yourself be inveigled by a
feeling of vengeance. You have taken to heart the
chastisement you forced me to inflict on you. You
thought that that would be a sufficient ground for
breaking your vows. You are mistaken, that cannot be,
before either God or man. Remember that perjury is
the greatest of all crimes: that you have already
committed it in your heart and that you are about to
consummate it."

"I shall not be a perjurer, I have sworn nothing."

"Even if you have known bad treatment at the
hands of some people, has it not been repaired?"

"It is not the bad treatment that has determined
me."

"What is it then?"

"Absence of vocation, absence of choice in my
vows."

"If you were not really called, if you acted under
pressure, why did you not say so at the time?"

"And what good would that have done me?"

"Why did you not show the same strength as you
had shown at Saint Mary's?"

"Does our strength depend on ourselves? I was strong the first time. The second time I was out of my mind."

"Why did you not call in a lawyer? Why did you not protest? You had twenty-four hours in which to retract."

"What did I know of all these formalities? And had I known of them, was I in a position to make use of them? Suppose I had been in such a position, had I the power? What, Madam, did you not perceive that I was beside myself? If I call you as a witness you will not swear that I was sane?"

"I shall."

"Very well, Madam. Then you will be the perjurer, not I."

"My child, you are going to make a useless scandal. Return to your senses; I conjure you in the name of your own interests and in the interest of the House. These sort of affairs cannot go through without causing shameful discussion."

"That will not be my fault."

"Society is ill-natured and will make suppositions unfavourable to your mind, your heart, and your morals. They will think ..."

"Whatever they like."

"But talk to me frankly. If you have some secret dissatisfaction, of whatever nature, we will find a remedy."

"I was, I am, and shall be all my life dissatisfied with my state."

"Has the spirit of seduction, which is always round us, and seeking to destroy us, profited from the too great liberty recently allowed you to inspire in you some fatal inclination?"

"No, Madam. You know that I do not take an oath lightly. I call God to witness that my heart is innocent and has never known a shameful thought."

"That is not conceivable."

"And yet nothing can be easier to understand. Everyone has their own character and I have mine. You like the monastic life. I hate it. You have received from God the graces of your vocation. I possess none of them. You would be lost in the world. I am, and ever shall be, a bad nun."

"But why? No one performs their duties better than you do."

"But it is painful and against the grain."

"It is all the more deserving then."

"Nobody can know my deserts better than I do myself, Madam. I am forced to avow that though I submit to everything I deserve nothing. I am sick of being a hypocrite. While I do what saves others, I detest and damn myself. In a word, Madam, I accept no nuns as genuine except those who are kept here by their desire for Retreat and who would remain here though there were neither grilles nor walls about them to restrain them. I am far from being among that number. My body, not my heart, is here. My heart is outside. And had I to choose between death and a perpetual cloister, I should not hesitate for a moment. Such are my feelings."

"What! You will feel no remorse when you leave this veil and habit which have consecrated you to Jesus Christ?"

"No, Madam, because I took them without reflection and without choice."

I answered with considerable self-restraint – for such were not the words which my heart proposed to me. It was saying: "Why am I not at this moment where I can tear them in pieces and throw them far from me?"

My answer, however, overwhelmed her. She grew pale; she wished to speak again, but her lips trembled. She did not know what further to say to me. I paced my cell with long strides and she cried out:

"O Heavens! What will our Sisters say? Oh, Jesus! throw on her a look of pity! Sister Saint Susan!"

"Madam."

"Your mind is made up then? You are going to dishonour us, make us the public butt, and ruin yourself?"

"I want to leave here."

"But if it is only the House which you dislike ..."

"It is the House, it is my condition, it is the Monastic State. I do not wish to be shut up here or anywhere else."

"My child, you are possessed by the Devil. He it is who disturbs you, makes you talk so, and carries you off your feet. It is absolutely true. Consider the state you are in."

When I looked at myself I saw that my dress was in disorder, that my wimple had turned almost completely round, and that my veil had fallen over my shoulders. I was irritated with the words of this ill-natured Superior who used with me only this false and softened tone. I said to her angrily:

"No, Madam. I have no more use for this garment. I have no more use ..."

Meanwhile I tried to readjust my veil. My hands trembled: the more I tried to arrange, the more I deranged it. Losing patience, I seized it violently, tore it, threw it on the ground, and stood opposite my Superior with my forehead encircled by a headband and my hair loose. Meanwhile she walked forward and backwards, uncertain if she ought to stay, saying:

"Jesus, she is possessed! It is the absolute truth. She is possessed."

And the hypocrite signed herself with the cross of her rosary.

I quickly came to myself. I felt the impropriety of my condition and the imprudence of my words. I composed myself as well as I could, picked up my veil and put it on again, and then turning towards her said:

"Madam, I am neither mad nor possessed. I am ashamed of my violent behaviour and ask you to forgive me. But you can judge by it how little I am fitted for the convent life and how right I am to try and leave it, if I can."

She answered without listening, saying:

"What will everyone say? What will the Sisters say?"

"Madam," I answered, "you wish to avoid a scandal. There is a way out. I do not ask for my dowry back; I only ask for liberty. I do not suggest that you open the doors for me; only see to it to-morrow afternoon that they are insecurely watched. You will only notice that I have escaped when to remain longer in ignorance is impossible."

"Wretched girl, what are you daring to propose?"

"A plan that a good and wise Superior would adopt for all those to whom a convent is a prison: and for me a convent is a prison a thousand times more than those in which criminals are locked up. I must leave or perish. Madam," I said in a firm voice and with an assured look, "listen to me. If the laws to which I appeal disappoint me in my expectations; and if pushed on by feelings of despair which I know all too thoroughly ... you have a well ... there are windows in the house ... walls all round ... clothes one can cut up ... hands one can use ..."

"Stop, wretched girl, you make me shudder. What! you could ..."

"I could refuse my food when all other ways of finishing with my sorrow failed. One is free to take one's food and drink, or to go without them. If, after what I have just said, it turned out that I had the courage, and you know I am not without courage, and that it sometimes needs more courage to live than to die ... picture yourself on the Day of Judgment and tell me which will seem to God the more guilty – the Superior or the nun. I do not ask back, and shall never ask back, anything from the House. Spare me from a crime, spare me from long remorse: let us come to an understanding."

"What are you thinking of, Sister Saint Susan; that I should fail in my first duties, lend my hands to crime, take part in sacrilege?"

"The real sacrilege, Madam, is that which I commit daily by profaning with contempt the sacred garments which I wear. Take them from me. I am not worthy of them. Let the rags of the poorest peasant be found for me in the village. Let the cloister-door be left ajar."

"And where will you go to be better off?"

"I do not know where I shall go. But one can only be badly off where God does not wish one to be, and God does not wish me to be here."

"But you possess absolutely nothing."

"That is so. But want is not what I fear the most."

"But fear the disorder want brings in her train."

"The past shall answer for the future to me. Had I been willing to listen to the voice of crime I should now be free. But if it suits me to leave the House, I shall leave it. Either with your consent or by the authority of the law. You can take your choice. ...."

The conversation had been a long one. When I thought over it I blushed for the indiscreet and ridiculous things I had said and done. But it was too late. The Superior was still exclaiming:

"What will the world say? What will the Sisters say?" when the bell summoning us to service separated us. She said to me as she left:

"Sister Saint Susan, you are going to chapel. Pray to God to touch you and restore to you the spirit of your vocation. Question your conscience, and believe what it tells you. It cannot but reproach you. You are dispensed from singing in the choir."

We went down almost together. When the service was over and the Sisters on the point of separating, she tapped on her breviary and stopped them.

"Sisters," she said, "I invite you all to throw yourselves at the step of the altar and implore God's pity for a nun whom He has abandoned, who has lost all taste for, and all the spirit of, religion, and is on the point of performing an act sacrilegious in the eyes of God and disgraceful in those of man."

75

I cannot describe the general surprise. In the twinkling of an eye each one, without moving, had run over her companions and endeavoured to deduce the guilty one from her embarrassment. They all prostrated themselves and obeyed in silence. After a considerable time the Prioress intoned the *Veni Creator* in a low voice, and all continued it in a low voice too. Then, after another moment of silence, the Prioress tapped on her pulpit and all went out.

I leave you to imagine the hum that arose in the community. "Who is it? Who isn't it? What has she done? What does she want to do?" The suspicions did not last long. My request had begun to make a stir in the world: I received countless visits: some brought reproaches, others plans: I was approved by some and blamed by others. I had only one way of justifying myself in the eyes of everyone, which was to tell them of my parents' conduct. You can imagine the discretion I had to observe on this point. Only a few people remained sincerely attached to me besides M. Manouri, who was in charge of my affair, and in whom I could confide everything. When terrified by the tortures with which I was threatened, the dungeon, whither I had once been dragged, fixed itself on my imagination in all its horror. I knew the fury of nuns. I communicated my fears to M. Manouri, who said:

"You cannot avoid all suffering: you will suffer; you must have expected it. You must arm yourself with patience and support with the hope that it will have an end. As for the dungeon, I promise you that you will never return to it. That is my business. ..."

And a few days later he produced an order on the

Superior to produce me whenever she might be called upon to do so.

The next day, after service, I was once more recommended to the public prayers of the community. They all prayed in silence, and repeated in a low voice the hymn of the day before. The same ceremony the third day, with this difference, that I was ordered to place myself upright in the middle of the choir while they recited the prayers for the dying, the litanies of the saints with the refrain *Ora pro ea.* The fourth day was notable for a mummery, which revealed perfectly the strange character of the Superior. At the end of the service I was made to lie down on a bier in the middle of the choir. Candlesticks were placed beside me with a stoup of holy water. I was covered with a handkerchief and the funeral service was recited, after which each nun, as she went out, threw holy water over me, saying, *Requiescat in pace.* You must be familiar with the language of convents to understand the threat contained in these last words.[12] Two nuns lifted off the handkerchief, put out the candles, and left me soaked to the skin by the water with which they had maliciously sprinkled me. My clothes dried on me, and I had nothing into which to change. This piece of mortification was followed by another. The community assembled: I was looked at as though damned: my action was treated as apostasy. And all the nuns, on pain of disobedience, were forbidden to speak to me, to give me assistance, to go near me, or even to touch anything I had used. These orders were rigorously executed. Our corridors are narrow and in some places two people can hardly pass each other. If, while

77

walking along, a nun came in the opposite direction she either retraced her steps or squashed up against the wall, holding on to her veil and dress for fear they should rub against me. If anything had to be handed by me to someone else, I put it on the ground and it was picked up with a cloth. If something had to be given me it was thrown at me. If anyone had the misfortune to touch me she thought herself contaminated and went to the Superior for confession and absolution. Flattery is said to be vile and low, but it becomes very cruel and ingenious when flatterers try to please by inventing means of giving pain. How often have I recalled the words of my heavenly Superior de Moni:

"Among all these creatures whom you see around me, so docile, innocent, and gentle, well, there is not one, no, my child, scarcely one whom I could not turn into a wild beast. Strange metamorphosis to which one is all the more subject the younger one enters into a convent and the less one knows of life. What I say astonishes you. God spare you from learning its truth. Sister Susan, the good nun is she who brings into the cloister some great fault to expiate."

I was deprived of all my occupations. In chapel an empty stall was left on each side of the one I occupied. At refectory I was alone at a table. No one served me, and I was obliged to go into the kitchen to ask for my share. The first time the Sister who did the cooking cried out to me:

"Don't come in, go further off."

I obeyed her.

"What do you want?"

"My food."

"Your food! You're not fit to live."

Sometimes I went away and passed the day without eating anything. Sometimes I insisted, and food was put by the door which they would have been ashamed to give to animals. I used to pick it up weeping, and go away. Sometimes I arrived last at the door of the choir and found it shut. I knelt down and waited till the end of the service. If they were in the garden I went back to my cell. Meanwhile I grew weaker from having taken so little food and from the bad quality of what was provided; still more from the misery caused by so many repeated marks of inhuman treatment. I felt that if I went on suffering without complaining I should never see the end of my case, so I determined to speak to the Superior. I was half dead with fright; still I went and tapped gently on the door. She opened it, and at the sight of me stepped back several yards, crying out:

"Apostate, go further off."

I went further off.

"Further still."

I went further still.

"What do you want?"

"Since neither God nor man have condemned me to death, I want you to give orders that I be allowed to live."

"Live," she said, repeating the words of the cook, "are you worthy to live?"

"Only God can know. But I warn you that if I am refused food I shall be forced to complain to those who have taken me under their protection. I am only here provisionally, till my fate and status are decided."

"Go!" she said. "Do not soil me with your looks. I will see to it."

I went away, and she slammed the door violently. Apparently she did give orders, but I was hardly better treated. The nuns made it a virtue to disobey her. They threw me the coarsest food, which they made still worse by mixing it with ashes and all sorts of filth.

Such was the life I led as long as my case lasted. The parlour was not entirely forbidden me. They could not deprive me of freedom to confer with my judges or my lawyer, though the latter was several times forced to employ threats to get at me. And then a Sister accompanied me. She complained if I spoke in a low voice, lost patience if I stayed too long, interrupted me, gave me the lie, contradicted me, repeated all my remarks to the Superior, changed their sense, filled them with venom, or even denied I had ever said them; anything you like. They went as far as robbing me, taking my things away, removing my chairs, coverlets, and mattresses. They gave me no more clean linen and tore my dress. I had almost to go without stockings and shoes. I had difficulty in obtaining water; I was several times obliged to go and get it myself as the well, the one of which I have spoken. They broke all my jugs and basins, and I was reduced to drinking the water as I drew it, without carrying it away. If I walked under the windows I was obliged to run away or be covered with all the dirt of the cells. Several Sisters spat in my face. I became hideously filthy. As they were alarmed at the complaints I might make to the Director, the confessional was forbidden me.

On a great feast day, Ascension Day I think, they

blocked up my keyhole. I could not go to Mass, and should have probably missed all the other services had it not been for the visit of M. Manouri. They at first told him that they did not know what had become of me, that they no longer saw me, and that I did not perform any of the duties of a Christian. Meanwhile, after endless difficulty, I broke the lock and went to the door of the choir, which I found locked, as was always the case when I was not among the first to arrive. I was lying on the ground, my head and back propped against one of the walls and my arms crossed over my chest, while the rest of my body was stretched out across the passage. The service ended and the nuns arrived to go out. The first stopped dead, and the rest came up behind her. The Superior suspected what the matter was and said:

"Walk over her. She is only a corpse."

Some obeyed, and stamped me under foot; others were less inhuman, but none dared stretch out a hand to lift me. While I was away they took from my cell my praying-desk, the portrait of our founders, my other pious images, and my crucifix. I soon had nothing but what I carried on my rosary, and that was not left me long. So I lived between four walls, in a room without a door or a chair, standing up or lying on a pallet, without the merest necessaries, forced to go out at night to relieve the calls of nature, and be accused the next morning of troubling the sleep of the House, of wandering about, and of losing my reason. As my cell door no longer shut, some nuns used to come in noisily all through the night, pull my bed about, break my windows, and occasion me all sorts of terror. The noise was heard on the floor above and the floor below, and those not in the plot said that something extraordinary was happening in my room: that they had heard melancholy voices, shrieks, the clanking of chains, and that I spoke with ghosts and evil spirits; that I must necessarily have made a pact with Satan, and that they themselves must leave my corridor. There are fools in every community; they are even the majority. They believed all that they were told, did not dare pass before my door, pictured me in their troubled imagination as hideous of feature, made the sign of the Cross in meeting me, and ran away, crying: "Satan, go away from me! O Lord, come to my help!" One of the youngest was at the end of the corridor; I went towards her and she could not avoid me. At first she turned her face towards the wall, muttering with trembling voice: "Oh Lord! Oh Lord! Jesus! Maria!" Meanwhile I advanced towards her. When she felt me near her she covered her face with her hands through fear of seeing me, leapt towards me, hurled herself violently into my arms, and cried: "Pity! Pity! I am lost! Sister Susan, do not do me any harm! Sister Susan, have pity on me!" And as she spoke she fell half dead upon the floor. On hearing her cry, some Sisters ran up and carried her off. I cannot adequately describe how this adventure was travestied. The most criminal story possible was made of it. They said the Demon of impurity had seized hold of me, and attributed to me designs and actions which I dare not name, and strange desires which explained the evident disorder in which they found the young nun. Truly I am not a man, and do not know what two women can conceivably be imagined to do together, still less a single woman. And then as my bed had no curtains and they came at every moment into my room, you can see the absurdity of it for yourself, my lord. These women must certainly have thoroughly corrupt hearts, for all their external deportment, modest looks, and chaste expressions. At any rate, they know that these dishonourable actions can be done all alone, and I do not know it. And I have never understood of what I was being accused, and they expressed themselves so obscurely that I never knew how to answer them.

I should never be finished if I entered into the details of all I was made to suffer. Oh, my lord, if you have children, learn from my fate what you are preparing for them if you allow them to enter into religion without the signs of the strongest and most decided vocation. How unjust the world is! A child is allowed to dispose of its liberty at an age when it may not dispose of a shilling.[13] Kill your daughter rather than imprison her in a cloister despite herself. Yes, I say, kill her! How often have I regretted that I was not stifled by my mother at birth. She would not then have been so cruel! Would you believe it, they took away my breviary and forbade me to say my prayers. You can imagine that I did not obey them. Prayer, alas, was my only consolation. I raised my hands to heaven and cried aloud, and dared hope my prayers were heard by the only Being to see all my suffering. They listened at my door, and one day as I was addressing Him in the misery of my heart and calling on Him for help someone said:

"You appeal to God in vain: there is no more God for you. Die in despair and be damned."

Others added: "Amen on the apostate. Amen on her!"

But here is a trait that will seem to you more strange than any other. I know not if it were wickedness or illusion. It is this. Though I did nothing which pointed to a deranged mind, still less to a mind obsessed by the infernal spirit, they discussed among themselves whether I ought not to be exorcised; it was agreed by a majority vote that I had renounced my chrism and my baptism, that the demon resided in me and kept me away from the services of the Church. Another added that during certain prayers I ground my teeth and shuddered in chapel: that at the Elevation of the Holy Sacrament I twisted my arms about: another that I trampled Christ under foot; that I no longer wore my rosary (which had been stolen from me); that I uttered blasphemies which I dare not repeat to you. All agreed that something unnatural was happening inside me and that the Grand Vicar must be warned. This was done.

This Grand Vicar was a M. Hébert, an experienced old man, rough in manner, but just and enlightened. The disorder of our House had been described to him. Great disorder there certainly was, but if I was responsible for it, it was in all innocence. You can certainly imagine that in the report sent in to him nothing was omitted: my nocturnal wanderings, my absence from the choir, the tumult within me, what one had seen and another had heard, my aversion for holy things, my blasphemies, the obscene actions imputed to me. Everything was good enough for the case of the young nun. They made anything they liked out of it. The accusations were so severe and so numerous that, for all his good sense, M. Hébert could not help being impressed and thinking that there must be a good deal in it. The matter appeared to him sufficiently important for him to look into it himself. His visit was announced, and he arrived sure enough, and accompanied by two young ecclesiastics who were attached to his person and who helped him in his painful duties.

Some little time before, during the night, I heard someone come into my room. I said nothing, and waited till I should be spoken to. I was called in a low, trembling voice.

"Sister Susan, are you asleep?"

"No, who is it?"

"Me."

"Who, you?"

"Your friend, who is dying of terror and risking ruin to give you advice that is perhaps useless. Listen! To-morrow or the day after the Grand Vicar will visit us. You will be accused, so prepare your defence. Farewell. Be brave, and the Lord be with you!"

This said, she withdrew as lightly as a shadow. So you see everywhere, even in religious houses, are to be found compassionate souls that nothing can harden.

Meanwhile my case was followed with warmth. A crowd of people of both sexes, and all callings and conditions, whom I did not know, interested themselves in my fate and worked for me. You were of this number, and very likely the history of my case is better known to you than to myself. For, finally, I could no longer confer with M. Manouri. He was told I was ill, but suspected that he was being deceived, so he addressed himself to the Archbishop's office, where no one deigned to listen to him. It was announced that I was mad, or perhaps worse. Finally he returned to the judges, insisted on the execution of the order, and signified to the Superior that she must produce me alive or dead when summoned to do so. The secular judges applied to the ecclesiastical judges. These no doubt felt the consequences that might result from the incident if the matter was not followed up, and it was apparently this that accelerated the visit of the Grand Vicar, for people in his position, tired by the continual squabbles in convents, are not generally in a hurry to get mixed up in them. They know by experience that their authority is always eluded and compromised.

I profited by my friend's warning to invoke the help of God, reassure my soul, and prepare my defence. I only asked Heaven the happiness to be impartially questioned and heard. I obtained it, but you shall hear at what a price. If it was to my interest to appear innocent and sensible to my judge, it was no less important to my Superior that I should seem to be ill-natured, obsessed by the devil, guilty, and mad. Thus, while I redoubled my fervour and my prayers, they redoubled their wickedness. They only gave me just enough food to prevent my dying of hunger; they wore me out with their persecutions. They multiplied terrors all round me, and took away all possibility of rest at night. They did everything that could destroy my health and distort my mind. Theirs was a refinement of cruelty which you cannot conceive. Judge of the rest by this example:

One day when I was leaving my cell to go to chapel

or elsewhere I saw a pair of pincers on the ground lying across the corridor. I stooped down to pick them up and place them in such a way that the person who had dropped them should easily find them again. The bad light prevented my seeing that they were almost red-hot. I took hold of them, but before I dropped them they had removed all the skin off my hand. At night obstacles were placed at my feet or at the height of my head in places where I had to pass. I was wounded a hundred times and cannot say how I was not killed. I had no light to pick my way, and was obliged to go trembling with my hands out before me. Broken glass was strewn under my feet. I was quite resolved to tell of all this, and more or less kept my word. I found the doors of the closets shut and was forced to go down several flights and run to the bottom of the garden, when indeed the door was open – when it was not ...! Oh! my lord, what cruel creatures cloistered women are when they are sure they are seconding the Superior in her hatred and think they are serving God by driving you to despair. It was quite time the Archdeacon arrived; it was quite time my case was over.

Now comes the most terrible moment in my life. For you must realize, my lord, that I was completely ignorant as to the colours in which I had been painted to this ecclesiastic, and that he was coming in the expectation of seeing a girl possessed or counterfeiting possession. It was thought that only extreme terror could give me an appearance of being possessed, and this was what they devised to effect it.

On the day of his visit, early in the morning, the Superior came into my cell. She was accompanied by three Sisters. One brought a stoup of holy water, the second a crucifix, and the third some ropes. The Superior said to me in a loud and threatening voice:

"Get up ... kneel down and commend your soul to God!"

"Madam," I answered, "before I obey you, may I ask you what is going to happen to me, what you have decided to do to me, and what I must ask God?"

A cold sweat stood out all over my body. I trembled, and felt my knees give under me. I regarded her three inevitable companions with terror. They were standing in a row, with sombre visage, tight lips, and closed eyes. I thought from the silence which was observed that I had not been heard. I repeated the last words of my question, for I had not got the strength to repeat it all: so I said with a feeble, expiring voice:

"What grace must I ask of God?"

"Ask pardon for all the sins of your past life: speak to Him as though you were about to appear before Him."

At these words I thought that they had taken counsel together and had resolved to be rid of me. I had certainly heard that such was the practice in certain religious houses, where they judged, condemned, and tortured. I do not think that this inhuman jurisdiction has been known in any convent. But then I had not believed possible so many things which had come to pass just the same! At this thought of approaching death I wanted to scream, but my mouth was open and no sound came. I held out my pleading arms to the Superior and my fainting body fell back. I fell, but the fall gave me no pain. In these moments of trance, when strength leaves, the limbs escape from control, and fall huddled, so to speak, one upon the other, and Nature being unable to support herself any longer, seems to try and fade softly away. I lost all consciousness and feeling. I only heard all round me the confused and distant voices. I distinguished nothing but a prolonged ringing, and I cannot say whether this was the sound of the voices or merely a ringing in my ears. I do not know how long I remained in this condition, but I was dragged out of it by a sudden coldness which caused me a slight convulsion and drew from me a deep sigh. I was drenched in water, which flowed from my clothes on to the ground. It was the holy water from a large stoup which had been poured over my body. I was lying on the ground stretched in this water, my head propped up against the wall, my mouth partly open, my eyes half dead and shut. I tried to open them and look round, but I seemed enveloped in a thick air, across which I only half saw floating garments and tried vainly to attach myself to them. I made an effort with the arm on which I was not leaning. I wanted to raise it, but found it too heavy. My extreme weakness grew slowly less; I raised myself and propped my back against the wall. I had my two hands in the water and my head bent over my breast. I uttered an inarticulate cry, stifled and feeble. The women looked at me with an expression of doom and inflexibility, which removed from me the courage to appeal to them.

The Superior said: "Put her upright."

They took me under the arms and stood me up. She added: "Since she will not commend herself to God, so much the worse for her. You know what you have to do, go through with it." I thought that the ropes which had been brought were to be used for strangling me. I looked at them, my eyes filled with tears; I asked for the crucifix to kiss and it was refused me. I asked for the ropes to kiss and they were given me. I leant forward, took the scapular of my Superior, kissed it, and said:

"Lord, have pity on me! Lord, have pity on me! Sisters, try not to make me suffer." And I presented my neck. I cannot tell you what happened to me nor what they did to me. Certainly those who are led out to execution (and I thought I was one of them) are dead before being killed. I found myself on the pallet which served for my bed, my arms tied behind my back, and seated with a great iron crucifix on my knees. ...

My lord, I can see from here the suffering I cause you, but you wanted to know if I am a little deserving of the compassion which I expect from you.

Then it was that I felt the superiority of the Christian religion to all the other religions of the world. How profound was the wisdom in what blind philosophy calls the Madness of the Cross. In the state in which I was, what help could I have had from the image of a legislator, happy and acclaimed. I saw Him innocent, with His side pierced, His forehead crowned with thorns, His hands and feet pierced with nails, and expiring in agony. I said to myself: "There is my Lord and yet I dare complain." I clung fast to this notion and felt a rebirth of comfort in my heart. I perceived the vanity of life and how lucky I was to lose it before my faults had had time to multiply. Meanwhile I counted up the years of my life. I discovered I was barely twenty and sighed. I was too weak, too crushed, for my spirit to be able to rise above the terror of death. In good health I could have shown, I think, a braver resolution.

Meanwhile the Superior and her satellites returned, and they perceived that my presence of mind was greater than they had expected or desired. They raised me, a veil was put over my face, two of them took me under the arms, the third pushed me from behind, and the Superior bade me walk. I went, not knowing whither, but thinking it was to my death, and I said: "Lord, have pity upon me! Lord, give me strength! Lord, do not abandon me! Lord, pardon me if I have offended you!"

I arrived inside the chapel. The Grand Vicar had celebrated Mass there. The community was assembled. I forgot to tell you that while I was at the door the three nuns who were leading me squeezed me and pushed me violently forward: they created the effect of having difficulty with me. One dragged me along by the arms while the others held me back from behind, which made me look as if I had resisted and did not wish to go into the chapel, though this was not in the least the case. I was led to the steps of the altar; I could scarce stand up. They pulled me by the knees as if I were refusing to go along with them; they held me there as though I were trying to escape. The *Veni Creator* was sung, the Holy Sacrament exposed, Benediction given. At the moment of Benediction when we bow in veneration those who were holding my arm bent me as though by force while the others held me up by putting their hands on my shoulders. I felt them all acting in this manner but I could not see the point of it: all became clear in the end.

After Benediction the Grand Vicar took off his chasuble, robed himself only in his alb and stole, and advanced towards the steps of the altar where I was kneeling. He was between the ecclesiastics, his back turned towards the altar, on which the Holy Sacrament was exposed, and looking towards me. He came up to me and said:

"Sister Susan, get up."

The Sisters who held me raised me roughly, others surrounded me and hugged me by the middle of the body as if they were afraid I should escape.

He added: "Untie her."

They did not obey him, and affected to see inconvenience or even danger in letting me go free. But I have said that the man was rough. He repeated in a strong, hard voice:

"Untie her."

They obeyed.

My hands were scarcely free when I uttered a melancholy piercing wail, which made him lose colour. The hypocritical nuns, who were coming close to me, withdrew as though in terror.

He pulled himself together; the Sisters returned, pretending to tremble. I remained motionless and he said:

"What is the matter with you?"

I answered merely by showing him my two arms. The rope with which they had garrotted me had sunk almost entirely into the flesh. And it had gone violet with the blood not circulating and being forced from its proper channels.

He realized that my wail was caused by the sudden pain caused by the blood resuming its normal course.

He said: "Let her veil be removed."

It had been sewn in different places without my having perceived it, and much confusion and violence was introduced into the business of removing it, where none would have been necessary had it not been specially intended. The priest must at all cost see me obsessed, possessed, or mad. Meanwhile by dint of pulling, the thread broke in some places, my veil or habit were torn in others, and I could at last be seen.

My face is an interesting one. Deep grief had spoilt its beauty but taken away none of its character. I have an appealing voice: you feel that my expression is a truthful one. This combination of qualities aroused a strong feeling of pity in the young acolytes of the Archdeacon. For his part he was unmoved by such feelings. Fair-minded, but not sensitive, he was one of those who are, rather unhappily for themselves, born to practise virtue without getting any pleasure out of it. They do good, just as they reason, from love of order. He took the sleeve of his stole, and laying it on my head, said:

"Sister Susan, do you believe in God the Father, God the Son, and God the Holy Ghost?"

I answered: "I do."

"Do you believe in our Mother Church?"

"I do."

"Do you renounce Satan and all his works?"

Instead of answering I took a sudden step forward and uttered a loud cry, while the end of his stole slipped from my head. He was distressed and his companions lost colour. Some of the Sisters ran away, while others who were in their stalls left them in the greatest tumult. He made a sign that they should keep quiet. However, he looked at me and expected something extraordinary to happen. I reassured him by saying: "It is nothing, sir. One of the nuns pricked me sharply with something pointed," and, raising my eyes and hands to Heaven, I added, bursting into a flood of tears:

"They wounded me at the moment you asked me if I renounced Satan and all his pomps, and I well see why. . . ."

All protested, by the mouth of the Superior, that I had not been touched.

The Archdeacon put the end of the stole back on my head: the nuns began to come up again, but he signed to them to withdraw. He asked me again if I renounced Satan and his works and I answered firmly: "I renounce them, I renounce them." He had an image of Christ brought and presented it to me to be kissed. I kissed it on the feet, the hands, and the wound in the side. He ordered me to adore it in a loud voice. I laid it on the ground and said on my knees: "Oh, Lord my Saviour, Who died on the Cross for my sins, and for those of the human race, I adore You. Let me profit by all the torments You have suffered. Let a drop of blood that You shed fall on me that I may be purified. Forgive me, O Lord, as I forgive all my enemies."

He then said, "Make an act of faith" . . . and I made one.

"Make an act of love" . . . and I made one.

"Make an act of hope" . . . and I made one.

"Make an act of charity" ... and I made one.

I do not remember in what terms they were conceived, but I think they must have been pathetic, for I called forth sobs from some of the nuns, the two ecclesiastics wept copiously, and the Archdeacon, in astonishment, asked where I had found the prayers I had just recited.

I answered: "In the bottom of my heart. They are my thoughts and feelings. I swear by God, Who hears us everywhere and Who is present on this altar, I am a Christian; I am innocent. If I have committed any sins God alone knows them, and He alone has the right to ask for an account of them and to punish them."

At these words he cast a terrible look at the Superior. The rest of the ceremony drew to an end, a ceremony in which God had been insulted, the most sacred things profaned, and the minister of the Church made ridiculous. The nuns withdrew, save the Superior, who remained with me and the young ecclesiastics.

The Archdeacon seated himself, and taking the hostile report which had been drawn up, read it out loud, and questioned me as to the articles which it contained.

"Why," he said, "do you never confess?"

"Because I am prevented."

"Why do you never draw near the Sacraments?"

"Because I am prevented."

"Why are you never present at the Mass or other divine services?"

"Because I am prevented."

The Superior tried to say something, but he said to her in his rough voice;

95

"Madam, be silent. Why do you leave your cell at night?"

"Because I have been deprived of my water, my jug, and the articles most essential for the calls of Nature."

"Why are people always hearing a noise in your dormitory and cell?"

"Because some nuns spend their time preventing my sleeping."

The Superior again wanted to say something, and he said a second time:

"Madam, I have already told you to be silent. You will answer when I question you. What is this about a nun who was snatched from your arms and discovered stretched across the floor of the corridor?"

"It came from her having been inspired with terror of me."

"Is she a friend of yours?"

"No, sir."

"You have never gone into her cell?"

"Never."

"You have never done anything indecent with her or anyone else?"

"Never."

"Why have they bound you?"

"I do not know."

"Why does your cell not shut?"

"Because I broke the lock."

"Why did you break it?"

"To open the door and go to Divine Service on Ascension Day."

"So you were present in church that day?"

"Yes, sir."

The Superior broke in:

"Sir, it is not true. The whole community ..."

I interrupted her ... "will bear witness that the door of the choir was shut, that they found me prostrated at the door, that you ordered them to walk over my body and that some did so. But I forgive them, Madam, and you as well for giving the order. I am not here to accuse anybody but to defend myself."

"Why have you got neither rosary nor crucifix?"

"They have been taken from me."

"Where is your breviary?"

"It has been taken from me."

"How then do you say your prayers?"

"I say my prayers with my heart and spirit, although I have been forbidden to do so."

"Who forbade you?"

"Madam. ..."

The Superior was going to speak again.

"Madam," he said, "is it true or false that you have forbidden her to say her prayers? Answer Yes or No."

"I thought, and I was right in thinking ..."

"That is not the question. Did you forbid her to say her prayers? Yes or No?"

"Yes, I forbade her, but ..."

She was going to go on.

"But!" riposted the Archdeacon, "but! ... Sister Susan, why are your feet bare?"

"Because I am given neither stockings nor shoes."

"Why are your linen and clothes in this old and filthy condition?"

"Because I have been refused clean linen for more

than three months and am compelled to go to bed in my clothes."

"Why do you go to bed in your clothes?"

"Because I have neither curtains, mattresses, coverlets, sheets, nor night clothes."

"Why have you not got any?"

"They have all been taken from me."

"Are you given food?"

"I ask to be."

"Then you are not?"

I remained silent and he added:

"It is incredible that you would have been so severely treated unless you had done something to deserve it."

"My fault is that I have no call to religion and that I am appealing against vows which were not freely consented."

"That is for the laws to decide, and whatever their decision you must perform the duties of the religious life while you are waiting."

"No one, sir, is more exact than I."

"You must share in the lot of all your companions."

"That is all I ask."

"You lodge no complaint then against anybody?"

"No, sir. I have told you so. I have not come to accuse anybody but to defend myself."

"Go then."

"Where must I go?"

"To your cell."

I took several paces, then returned and prostrated myself at the feet of the Superior and the Archdeacon.

"Well," he said, "what is it?"

I said, as I showed him my head, wounded in several places, my feet bleeding, my arms livid and fleshless, my dress filthy and torn:

"You see!"

I hear you, my lord, and I hear the majority of those who read these Memoirs saying: They are not credible, such multiplied, variegated, and continuous horrors! A succession of such exquisite atrocities conceived in the souls of nuns. I agree; still, it is true, and may Heaven, whom I call to witness, judge me in all its rigour and condemn me to eternal fire if I have allowed calumny to tarnish a single line with the faintest shadow. Though I have for long known how keen a spur to natural perversity can be the aversion of a Superior, above all when perversity can make a virtue of what it does and can applaud and boast of its crimes, anger must not prevent my being just. The more I think over it the surer I am that what happened to me never happened before and will very likely never happen again. Once (and pray to God it was for the first and last time) it pleased Providence, Whose ways are unknown to us, to collect on one unfortunate head the whole mass of cruelties, divided, according to His inscrutable decrees, among the infinite multitude of unfortunate girls who had preceded her in the cloister and who are in turn to succeed her. I have suffered, suffered greatly. But the fate of my persecutors appears, and has always appeared, to me more pitiable than my own. I would rather die, I would always have rather died than surrender my part in order to take up theirs. My ills will come to an end. I hope much from your kindness. Memory, shame, and remorse for their crime will be with them till their last hour. They accuse themselves already, do not doubt it, and they will accuse themselves all their life and terror will go down with them to the tomb. Meanwhile, my lord, my present situation is deplorable, my life is a burden to me! I am a woman with the weak nature of my sex. God may abandon me! I feel I have neither the strength nor the courage to bear what I have borne much longer. My lord, take care lest the fatal moment returns. Though you wore out your eyes to weep over my fate, though you were torn by remorse, that would not rescue me from the abyss in which I should find myself. The abyss would be closed for ever over a desperate girl.

"Go," said the Archdeacon to me.

One of the ecclesiastics gave me his hand to help me up, and the Archdeacon added: "I have questioned you. I shall now question your Superior, and I shall not leave here till order has been re-established."

I withdrew. I found all the rest of the House much alarmed. All the nuns were at the door of their cells talking across the corridor. As soon as I appeared they withdrew and there was a noise of doors slamming one after the other. I went back into my cell and fell on my knees against the wall, praying God to notice the moderation with which I had spoken to the Archdeacon and to make him know my innocence and the truth.

I was at my prayers when the Archdeacon and his two companions appeared in my cell. I told you that I had no carpet, no chair, no praying-desk, no curtains, no mattress, no coverlets, no sheets, no jug and basin, no door which shut, and hardly a pane of glass in the windows. I rose from my knees. The Archdeacon stopped short and, turning his eyes angrily on the Superior, said:

"Well, Madam!"

She answered: "I knew nothing about it."

"You knew nothing about it? You are a liar. Has a single day passed without your coming here, and was it not from here that you came down to me? ... Speak, Sister Susan, has Madam not been here to-day?"

I returned no answer, and he did not insist. But the young ecclesiastics dropped their arms, lowered their heads, and fixed their eyes on the ground, thus sufficiently revealing their pain and surprise. They all went out, and I heard the Archdeacon saying to the Superior in the corridor:

"You are unworthy of your functions. You deserve to be deposed, and I shall complain to Monsignor. All this disorder is to be repaired before I leave." And continuing to walk about and shake his head, he added: "It is horrible! Christians! Nuns! Human beings! It is horrible!"

From that moment I heard no more about the matter. But I was given linen, other clothes, curtains, sheets, coverlets, basin, my breviary, my books of piety, my rosary, my crucifix, panes of glass, in a word everything that made my condition similar to that of the other nuns. The freedom of the parlour was also restored to me, but only for my affairs.

They were going badly. M. Manouri published a first Report which created but little attention. There was too much wit in it, not enough pathos, and hardly any reasoning. Still, it would be wrong to blame this skilful advocate too much. I was insistent that he should not attack the reputation of my parents: I wanted him to spare the state of religion, and above all the reputation of my House. I did not wish him to paint in too odious colours my brothers-in-law and sisters. I had only my first protest in my favour, solemn to be sure, but made in another convent and not renewed since. When one puts such strict limits to one's own defence and has to do with opponents who put no limits to theirs, who crush the just and the unjust under foot, who affirm and deny with equal impudence, and blush neither at imputations, suspicions, slander, nor calumny, it is difficult to carry the day, especially before tribunals whose familiarity and boredom with their work hardly permit them to examine the most important matters thoroughly, and where pleadings like mine are always regarded unfavourably by public men, who are afraid that if one nun petitions successfully against her vows an infinity of others will follow her example. People have a secret feeling that if the doors of these prisons are allowed to fall in favour of one wretched girl, a host of others will rush forward and try to force them. People try to discourage us and to make us all resign ourselves to our lot by making us despair of a change. But it seems to me that in a well-governed state the procedure would be to the contrary. One would enter with difficulty into religion and leave it easily. And why not add this case to a number of others in which the least breach of a formality destroys the whole procedure, though it might be quite a fair one? Are convents then so necessary to the constitution of a state? Did Jesus Christ institute monks and nuns?

Can the Church not possibly get on without them? What need has the Bridegroom of so many foolish virgins? Or the human race of so many victims? Will men never feel the necessity for narrowing the mouths of these gulfs, into which future generations will sink to perdition? Are all the regulation prayers one repeats there worth one obol given in pity to the poor? Does God, Who made man a social animal, approve of his barring himself from the world? Can God, Who made man so inconstant and so fragile, approve the rashness of his vows? Can these vows, which go against the whole grain of our nature, ever be properly observed except by a few ill-constituted creatures in whom the germs of passion are withered and whom we should properly class among the monsters did our knowledge permit us to know as easily or as well the internal as the external structure of man? Can our animal instincts be suspended by the gloomy ceremonies observed at the donning of the habit or at the moment of profession when a man or woman is consecrated to monasticism and misery? Do not they rather make themselves felt in the silent, confined, and lazy life of a convent with a violence unknown to people in the world, who are swept on by a thousand distractions? Where is it that we see imaginations obsessed by impure spectres which follow them about and terrify them? Where is it that we see that profound boredom, that pallor, that thinness, all those symptoms of a languishing and failing nature? Where is it that nights are troubled with wailing and days made wet with causeless tears and preceded by a melancholy to which no reason can be assigned? Where is it that Nature, revolted by a constraint for which she is not intended, breaks down the obstacles that oppose her, goes mad, and throws the whole animal system into a disorder for which there is no remedy? In what place have disappointment and ill-humour crushed all social qualities? Where is it that there is neither father, nor brother, nor sister, nor relative, nor friend? Where is it that man, thinking he is but a momentary and passing being, despises all the softest ties of this world and treats them as a traveller treats the things he meets in his path, attaching to them no significance? Where is the dwelling-place of hatred, nausea, and the vapours? Where is the home of servitude and despotism? Where are the hates that never die? Where are the passions nurtured in silence? Where is the home of cruelty and inquisitiveness?

"No one knows the story of these retreats," M. Manouri stated, "no one knows it."

He added in another place:

"To make a vow of poverty is to swear on oath to be an idler or a thief. To make a vow of chastity is to promise God constantly to infringe the wisest and most important of His laws. To make a vow of obedience is to renounce man's unalienable prerogative, that of liberty. If one keeps one's vows one is a criminal, if one breaks them a perjurer. The cloistered life is fit only for the fanatic and the hypocrite."

A girl asked her parents' permission to join us. Her father said he consented but gave her three years to think it over. The ruling seemed harsh to the young person, who was full of fervour. Still, she had to submit. Her vocation still enduring, she returned to her father and said that the three years had elapsed.

"Very well, my child," he answered, "I have granted you three years to test yourself. You must now allow me as many to come to a resolution myself."

This seemed still harder, and tears were shed. But the father was a strong-minded man who held firm. At the end of six years she made her profession. She was a good nun, simple, pious, and exact in her duties. But it so happened that the Directors took advantage of her frankness to find out at the tribune of penitence what was going on in the House. Our Superiors suspected it, she was shut up, deprived of her religious duties, and lost her wits. How can the mind resist the persecutions of fifty people all intent on the one object of torturing you? They had already laid her mother a trap which well illustrates the avarice of the cloister. They inspired the girl's mother with the wish to come to the House and visit her daughter's cell. She addressed herself to the Grand Vicars, who granted her the permission she sought. She arrived and wen. straight to her daughter's cell. But what was her astonishment at seeing nothing but four bare walls? Everything had been taken away! They were pretty certain that this kind-hearted, sensitive mother would never leave her daughter in such a state. And, sure enough, she refurnished the room and set her up again in clothes and linen, protesting the while that the consequences of inquisitiveness were too expensive to admit of her repeating the experiment and that three or four visits like this one would ruin her brothers and sisters. It is in the cloister that ambition and luxury sacrifice one part of a family to assure the rest a more advantageous lot. It is the gutter where one throws the dregs of humanity. How many mothers like mine expiate one secret crime by another!

M. Manouri published a second Report, which made more impression that the first. People eagerly intervened. I again promised my sisters to leave them in complete and peaceful possession of my parents' estate. There was a moment when my case took a very favourable turn and I had hopes of my liberty. I was all the more cruelly deceived; my case was pleaded in court and lost. The whole commuity was informed of it, except myself. There was a continual stir, tumult, joy, along with small secret conversations, goings and comings in the Superior's rooms and among the nuns themselves. I trembled all over: I could neither stay in my cell nor leave it. I did not have a single friend into whose arms I might throw myself. Oh! what a cruel morning was that on which my case was decided! I wished to pray but could not. I went down on my knees, got up again, began a prayer, but, despite myself, my mind was soon away among my judges. I saw them, I heard the lawyers, addressed myself to them, interrrupted my own and found my cause badly defended. I knew none of the magistrates by sight, but I pictured each of them to myself separately; some favourable, others sinister, others indifferent. I was in an inconceivable agitation and turmoil of ideas. Noise gave way to complete silence; the nuns no longer spoke to each other. Their voices seemed to me more brilliant than usual in the choir – at least those of the choir: the rest did not open their mouths. On going out after the service they silently withdrew. I persuaded myself that the wait disturbed them as much as me. But in the afternoon the noise and moving about suddenly broke out again on all sides. I heard doors opening and shutting, nuns coming and going, and the murmur of people talking low. I put my ear to the keyhole. But they seemed to keep quiet as they passed and walk on tip-toe. I knew I had lost my case. I had not an instant's doubt. I began walking round my cell without speaking. I was suffocating and could not complain: I crossed my arms over my head and propped my forehead, now against one wall, now against another. I wanted to rest on my bed but the thumping of my heart prevented it. It is certain that I heard my heart thumping and that the thumping raised up my dress. Such was my condition when someone came and told me I was wanted. I went down, but dared not go on. The girl who summoned me was herself so cheerful that I felt the news which was brought me could only be very sad. Still, I went. On arriving at the door of the parlour, I stopped short and threw myself into the angle made by the two walls. I could not hold myself up: still, I went in. There was no one there. I waited. They had prevented the man who had had me summoned from appearing before I did. They were pretty sure he came from my lawyer, and wanted to know what might pass between us. They had collected to hear. When he appeared I was seated, my head leaning on my arm, and propped against the bars of the grille.

"I come from M. Manouri," he said.

"To tell me that I have lost my case?" I replied.

"I do not know at all, but he gave me this letter. He looked very unhappy when he charged me with it, and I have come as quickly as possible, as he told me."

"Give it me."

He handed me the letter, which I took without stirring or looking at him. I laid it on my knees and remained in the same attitude. However, he asked me if there was any answer.

"No," I said, "you may go."

He went off and I remained as I was, being unable to move or to make the effort to go away.

In the convent one may neither write nor receive letters without the consent of the Superior. One hands to her both those one receives and those one writes. I had, then, to take her mine. I started off to do so. I thought that I should never arrive. The condemned man who leaves his dungeon to go and hear his sentence does not walk more slowly or wretchedly than I did. But eventually I reached her door. The nuns examined me from a distance. They wished to lose nothing of the sight of my grief and humiliation. I knocked and the door was opened. The Superior was there with some other nuns. I only saw the bottom of their dresses, for I dared not raise my eyes. I gave her my letter with a trembling hand. She took it, read it, and returned it. I went back into my cell, threw myself on my bed, and remained there without reading it, without getting up for dinner, without making a single movement till afternoon service. At half-past three the bell warned me to go down. Some nuns had already arrived: the Superior was at the entrance to the choir. She stopped and bade me kneel outside. The rest of the community came in and the door was shut. After the service they all went out: I let them pass and got up to follow them last. I began from that moment on to resign myself to whatever was wished of me. I had just been forbidden the church. I forbade myself recreation and the refectory. I envisaged my lot from every side, and saw no resource save in submissiveness and the need they might have of me. I could have contented myself with that sort of neglect in which I was left for several days. I had several visitors, but M. Manouri was the only one I was allowed to receive. I found him as I entered the parlour in just the same attitude as I was myself when I received his messenger, his head leaning on his arms and his arms propped against the grille. I recognized him, but said nothing. He dared neither look at me nor address me.

"I have written to you," he said without stirring. "Have you read my letter?"

"I have received but I have not read it."

"You do not know then . . .?"

"Yes, I know everything; I divined my fate and I am resigned to it."

"How are they treating you?"

"As yet they do not think about me at all. But I know from the past what the future has in store for me. I have but one consolation, which is this. Now I am deprived of the hope that supported me it is impossible I should suffer as much as I have suffered already. I shall die. My fault is not one of those which the Convent pardons. I do not ask God to soften the hearts of those to whose discretion He sees good to abandon me, but to give me the strength to suffer, to save me from despair, and to call me to Him promptly."

"Had you been my own sister," he said, weeping, "I could not have done more. . . ."

That man had a warm heart.

"If I can be of any use to you in any way," he added, "dispose of me. I will see the First President: he thinks well of me. I will see the Grand Vicars and the Archbishop."

"See no one, sir; all is over."

"But suppose you could be changed to another House."

"There are too many obstacles."

"What obstacles?"

"Permission difficult to obtain, a new dowry to be found, or the old one to be extracted from this House. And then what shall I find in another House? My own unyielding heart, pitiless Superiors, nuns no better than those here, the same duties, the same griefs. It is better than I should finish my days here. There will be fewer of them."

"But you have interested many people of position in your affairs. Most of them are well-to-do. No one here will want to stop you if you go away empty-handed."

"That I can well believe."

"A nun who goes away or dies increases the property of those who stay behind."

"But these people of position, these well-to-do people, have already forgotten all about me, and you will find them quite cold when it is a matter of finding me a dowry at their own expense. Why should you suppose that it is easier for society to remove a nun without vocation from the cloister than for pious persons to send one there who has a real vocation? Is it easy to find dowries for these last? Ah, sir, everyone has abandoned me since I lost my case. I no longer see anybody."

"Only entrust me with this business: I shall be happier so."

"I ask for nothing, I hope for nothing, I oppose nothing. The only spring I had left is broken. If only I could promise myself that God would change me and that qualities suited to the religious state should replace in my heart the hope, now lost, of leaving it. . . . But that cannot be, this habit has adhered to my skin and to my bones and is all the more intolerable for that. What a fate! To be a nun for ever, to feel I shall never be anything but a bad nun! To pass all my life striking my forehead against my prison bars."

At this point I began to cry aloud. I tried to check myself but it was impossible. M. Manouri, surprised at what I was doing, said:

"May I dare ask you a question?"

"Please do."

"Has a grief so violent as yours no secret explanation?"

"No, sir, I hate the solitary life, I feel here in my heart that I hate it. I feel I shall always hate it, I can never subject myself to the pettinesses which fill up the day of a recluse. It is a tissue of puerilities, which I despise. I should have come round to it by now had I been able. I have tried a hundred times to deceive myself, to break myself in, I cannot. I have envied, I have asked for, my companions' happy imbecility of mind; I have not obtained it; God will not grant it me. I do everything badly, I do everything wrong, my lack of vocation pierces through my every action and leaps to the eye. Every moment I insult the monastic life. They call my inaptitude pride and are intent on humiliating me. My faults and punishments multiply to infinity and I pass my days measuring with my eyes the height of the walls."

"I cannot break them down, but there is something else that I can do."

"Attempt nothing."

"You must change your House. I will see about it. I shall come and see you again. I hope you will not be concealed from me. You shall have news of me at once. Be sure that if you are willing I shall succeed in getting you away from here. If they treat you too badly do not let me remain ignorant of the fact."

It was late before M. Manouri went away. I returned to my cell, and the bell soon sounded for evening service. I was one of the first to arrive. I let the nuns pass and assumed that I should have to stay at the door: and in fact the Superior did shut it on me. In the evening she made me a sign as I came in to sit on the floor in the middle of the refectory. I obeyed, and was only given bread and water. I ate a little bread, which I sprinkled with my tears. Next day a council was held, when the whole community sat in judgment on me. I was condemned to loss of recreation, to hear the service at the door of the choir for a month, to eat on the floor in the middle of the refectory, to confess my crime publicly three days in succession, then repeat the donning of my habit and my vows, to wear a hair-cloth, to fast every other day, and to scourge myself every Friday after evening service. I was on my knees with my veil lowered while this sentence was pronounced on me.

Next day the Superior came into my cell with a nun

who carried on her arm a hair-cloth and the dress of rough material with which I had been clothed when I was led to the dungeon. I knew what that signified. I undressed, or rather my veil was torn off and I was stripped, and I took this dress. My feet and head were bare and my long hair fell over my shoulders. My clothes were limited to this hair-cloth which was given me, a very hard shift, and to the long gown which came down to my feet. It was thus that I was dressed all day and appeared on every occasion.

In the evening, when I had retired to my cell, I heard people approaching and singing litanies. The whole House was drawn up in two rows. They entered and I offered myself. A rope was passed round my neck. In one hand was put a lighted torch, in the other a whip. A nun took the rope by one end and pulled me between the two rows, and the procession made its way towards a little inner oratory, consecrated to Saint Mary. They had come singing low and returned in silence. When I had arrived at the little oratory, which was illuminated by two lights, I was ordered to ask pardon of God and the community for the scandal that I had caused. The nun who led me told me in a low voice what I had to repeat and I repeated it word by word. After that the rope was taken off and I was undressed to the waist, they took my hair which was scattered over my shoulders, threw it on each side of my neck, put in my right hand the whip which I was carrying in my left, and began the *Miserere*. I understood what was expected of me and performed it. The *Miserere* finished, the Superior delivered a short exhortation. The lights were put out, the nuns retired, and I redressed again. When I was back in my cell I felt violent pains in my feet. I looked at them and perceived they were all bleeding from cuts made by broken glass which the nuns had had the wickedness to put in my way.

The next two days I made public confession in the same way, except that on the last day a psalm was added to the *Miserere*. The fourth day my nun's habit was returned to me with almost the same ceremony as that employed for this solemnity when it is public.

The fifth day I renewed my vows. For a month I went through the rest of the penitence imposed on me, after which I returned more or less into the common order of the community, and I took my turn in the choir, and at the refectory, and performed in turn the various duties of the House. But what was my surprise when my eyes lit on that young friend who had interested herself on my behalf. She appeared almost as changed as I was. She was terribly thin, and her face was as pale as death, her lips were white, and her eyes almost lifeless.

"Sister Ursula," I said in a low voice, "what is the matter with you?"

"What is the matter with me?" she answered; "I love you and you ask me that? It was time your torture finished – I should have died of it."

The last two days of my public confession I had not had my feet wounded for the sole reason that she had had the forethought to sweep the pieces of glass to right and left. The days I was condemned to fast on bread and water she went without part of her portion, which she put into a white napkin and threw into my cell.

The nun who was to lead me by the rope had been chosen by lot and the lot fell upon her. She had the strength of mind to go the Superior and protest that she was resolved to die rather than go through with such a cruel and infamous performance. The girl was happily of good family, and in possession of a handsome allowance, which was spent according to the Superior's good pleasure. And she found a nun to replace her for a few pounds of sugar and coffee. I dare not think that the hand of God has fallen on this unworthy nun. Certainly she has lost her wits and is shut up, but then the Superior lives, rules her House, torments everybody, and is in perfect health.

My health could not possibly resist such long and cruel attempts upon it. I fell ill, and in these circumstances Sister Ursula was able to show all the friendship she had for me. I owe her my life. Not that there was any advantage in that, as she sometimes said herself. However, there was no sort of service she did not do me every day that she was at the infirmary. And the other days I was not neglected, thanks to the interest she took and to the small rewards she distributed to those who were looking after me, according as I had been more or less satisfied with them. She had asked to look after me at night but the Superior had refused permission, alleging that she was too delicate for such fatiguing work. This was a real disappointment to her. But all her cares could not prevent my illness developing. I was reduced to the utmost extremity. I received the last sacraments. A few moments before I asked to see the whole community assembled, and my wish was granted. The nuns surrounded my bed, with the Superior in the middle of them. My young friend sat by my pillow and held my hand, which she bathed with her tears. It was presumed that I had something to say. I was lifted up and supported in a sitting posture by two pillows. Then, addressing my Superior, I asked her to grant me her benediction and to forget the faults I had committed. I then asked pardon of all my companions for the scandal which I had brought on them. I had a large number of trifles brought to my bedside which either decorated my cell or were for my private use, and I requested the Superior to let me dispose of them. She agreed, and I gave them to those who had served her as satellites when I was thrown into the dungeon. I made the nun who led me with the rope the day of my public confession come up to me, and I said as I kissed her and gave her my rosary and crucifix:

"Sister, remember me in your prayers and be sure that I will not forget you when I am before God."

And why did not God take me then? I was going to Him so calmly. And that is so great a happiness, and one which no man can promise himself twice: who knows in what state I shall be at my last hour? But still I must needs pass through it. May God renew all my sufferings if He will make me at the end as peaceful as I then was! I saw the heavens open, and they doubtless did. For Conscience does not deceive, and it promised me eternal felicity.

After taking the sacraments I fell into a kind of lethargy and I was despaired of all that night. They came and took my pulse from time to time. I felt hands moving over my face and heard different voices

saying as if from a distance: "It is going up again. ...
Her nose is cold. ... She will not last till to-morrow.
... You will keep your crucifix and rosary." ... And
another angry voice which said: "Go away, go away.
Let her die in peace! Have you not tortured her
enough?" It was a very sweet moment for me when I
emerged from this crisis and opened my eyes again to
find the arms of my friend round me. She had never
left me. She had passed the night in attending to me,
in repeating the prayers for the dying, in making me
kiss the crucifix, and in putting it to her own lips after
withdrawing it from mine. She thought when she saw
me open my large eyes and utter a deep sigh that it
was my last. She began to cry out and call me her
friend, saying: "Lord, receive her soul. When you are
with God remember Sister Ursula!" I looked at her
with a sad smile, shedding a tear and clasping her by
the hand. At this moment M. B—— arrived. He
was the House doctor, a clever man by report, but
tyrannical, proud, and hard. He pushed my friend
away violently, took my pulse, and felt my skin. He
was accompanied by the Superior and her favourites.
He put some monosyllabic questions on what had
passed, and answered:

"She will get over it."

Then looking at the Superior, who was not best
pleased with this:

"Yes, Madam, she will get over it. The skin is good,
the fever has fallen, and life is beginning to grow in the
eyes."

At each of these words happiness spread over the
face of my friend, but over that of my Superior and her

companions some sort of disappointment, but poorly disguised by the decencies.

"Sir," I said to him, "I do not ask to live."

"So much the worse," he answered.

Then he ordered something and went away. I was told that during my lethargy I had several times said: "Mother, so I am going to join you! I will tell you everything." Apparently I was addressing my former Superior, I have no doubt of it. I did not give her portrait to anybody, and wished to carry it with me to the tomb.

The prognosis of M. B—— was realized. The fever diminished, and at length abundant perspiration enabled me to throw it off completely. My recovery was no longer doubted, and cured I was, but my convalescence was a long one. It was ordained that I should suffer in this House every pain it is possible to experience. My illness was in some way infectious. Sister Ursula had scarcely left me the whole time. As my strength began to return, she lost hers; she suffered from indigestion, and was attacked in the afternoon with fainting fits which sometimes lasted a quarter of an hour. When in this state she might have been dead. Her eyesight failed, a cold sweat covered her forehead and collected in drops which ran along her cheeks. Her arms hung motionless at her sides. She gained a little relief only when she was unlaced and her garments loosened. On returning to herself her first idea was always to look for me at her side, and she always found me there. Sometimes even, when she kept a little sense of feeling and consciousness, she moved her hand round her without opening her eyes. This action was so

clear that some nuns who had offered themselves to this
wandering hand and were not recognized, because
then she was falling back motionless, said to me:

"Sister Susan, you are the one she wants; stand by
her."

I dropped at her knees and put my hand on her
forehead and kept it there till the end of her swoon.
When it was over she said to me:

"Well, Sister Susan, so it is I who am to go and you
who are to stay. I shall be the first to see her; I shall talk
to her of you, and she will not listen to me without a
tear. There are bitter tears, but there are also sweet
ones, and if there is Love in Heaven, why should there
not be tears as well?"

She then put her hand over my neck, wept abundantly, and added:

"Good-bye, Sister Susan, good-bye, darling! Who
will share your sorrows when I can no more? Who will
it be? Oh, how I pity you! I am going away, I feel it, I
am going away. If you were happy how sad I should be
to die!"

Her condition terrified me. I spoke to the Superior: I
wished her to be put in the infirmary, relieved of the
services and other painful duties of the House, and for
a doctor to be called in. But I was always told that it
was nothing, that these fainting fits would pass of
themselves, and that Sister Ursula asked nothing better than to go through with her duties and lead the
communal life. One day after matins, which she had
attended, she did not put in an appearance. I thought
she must be very ill. Morning service over, I flew to her
and found her stretched out in her clothes on her bed.

"There you are, dear one, I thought you would not be long in coming, and I was expecting you. Listen. How impatient I was for you to come. I was in such a dead faint and for so long a time that I thought I should remain in that condition and never see you again. Look! there is the key of my oratory, open the cupboard of it and remove the plank in the middle which divides the drawer into two halves. Behind this plank you will find a packet of papers. I have never been able to bring myself to part with them, however great the danger of keeping them! My tears have made them nearly illegible. When I am no more, burn them."

She was so weak and oppressed that she could not pronounce two words of this speech in succession. She hesitated over almost every syllable, and then spoke so low that I could hardly hear, though my ear was almost pressed against her mouth. I took the key and pointed to the oratory with my finger. She made a sign to say "Yes." Then, perceiving that I was going to lose her, and persuaded that her illness was either caught from me or the result of the unhappiness it had caused her and the care she had bestowed on me, I began to weep and lament with all my strength. I kissed her forehead, her eyes, her face, her hands. I asked her pardon, but she was as one distraught and did not hear me. One of her hands lay on my face and caressed me. I think she did not see me any longer, perhaps even thought I had gone away, for she called me:

"Sister Susan?"

"Here I am."

"What time is it?"

"Half-past eleven."

"Half-past eleven. Go to your dinner. Be off, you can come back immediately afterwards."

The dinner-bell rang and I had to leave her. When I had reached the door she called me back. I returned; she made an effort to offer me her cheeks to kiss. I kissed them. She took my hand and held it clasped. It seemed that she could not, that she would not, leave me.

"However, I must," she said, letting me go; "God wills it. Good-bye, Sister Susan. Give me my crucifix."

I put it between her hands and went out.

The company was on the point of leaving the table. I spoke to the Superior, before all the nuns, of the dangerous state of Sister Ursula, and I urged her to judge for herself.

"Well, well," she said, "I will have a look."

She went up to Sister Ursula's room, accompanied by a few others. I followed them. They went into the cell. The Sister was no more. She was stretched on her bed, fully dressed, her head inclined on her pillow, her mouth half open, her eyes shut, and the crucifix in her hands. The Superior looked at her coldly and said:

"She is dead. Who would have thought her end so near? She was an excellent child. Let the knell be tolled for her, and let her be buried."

I remained alone by her bedside. I cannot describe to you my grief, yet I envied her. I came up to her, offered her the tribute of my tears, kissed her several times, and drew the sheet over her face, for her features were beginning to show the signs of death. Then I saw to executing her orders. So as not to be interrupted in this occupation I waited till everyone was at service. I opened the door, knocked down the plank, and found quite a large roll of papers which I burned during the evening. She had always been a melancholy girl, and I never remember having seen her smile, except once during her illness. So now I was alone in the House, alone in the world. For I knew of no one who took any interest in me. I had heard no more about the lawyer Manouri. I assumed he had either been discouraged by the difficulties with which he met or that, distracted by pleasure and work, the offers of help which he had made were now far from his mind. I did not blame him much. I tend to be by nature indulgent and can forgive everything except injustice, ingratitude, and inhumanity. So I excused M. Manouri as much as possible and all those society people who had shown such vivacity while my case lasted and for whom I no longer counted, among them even yourself, my lord. And then our Ecclesiastical Superiors visited the House. It is the visitors' duty to come in, inspect the cells, question the nuns, observe for themselves the spiritual and temporal administration, and according to the spirit they bring to the work disorders are lessened or increased. I saw once more the honest and severe M. Hébert with his two young sympathetic acolytes. Apparently they remembered the deplorable state in which I formerly appeared before them. Tears stood in their eyes, and I observed tenderness and delight upon their countenances. M. Hébert sat down and made me sit beside him. His two companions stood behind his chair, and their looks turned on me. M. Hébert said to me:

"Well, Susan, how are they treating you at present?"

"They take no notice of me, sir."

"So much the better."

"That, too, is all I ask. But I have an important favour to ask of you, to call my Mother Superior here."

"And why?"

"Because if anyone happens to lay a complaint before you, she will not fail to accuse me of having done it."

"I see. But still, tell me what you know."

"I implore you, sir, to have her called that she may hear for herself your questions and my replies."

"Still tell me."

"Sir, you will be my ruin."

"Be afraid of nothing. From this day on you are no more under her authority. Before the end of the week you will be transferred to Saint Eutropia's,[14] near Arpajon. You have a good friend."

"A good friend, sir; I know of none."

"Your lawyer."

"M. Manouri?"

"Yes."

"I thought that he had forgotten all about me."

"He has seen your sisters, he has seen the Archbishop, the First President, and all the leading religious people. He has provided a dowry for you in the House just named. You have only an instant to remain here. Thus, if you know of any disorder, you can tell me of it without compromising yourself, and I order you by the Holy Obedience."

"I know of none."

"What! They have shown restraint in their treatment of you since you lost your case?"

"They thought, they had to think, that I had committed a fault in appealing against my vows. And they made me ask pardon of God."

"But it is just the circumstances attending this pardon that I should like to know."

As he said this he shook his head and frowned, and I saw that it rested with me to repay my Superior some of the blows she had made me receive. But this was not my plan. The Archdeacon saw clearly he would get nothing out of me and went away, recommending me to be silent about my translation to Saint Eutropia's at Arpajon.

While the worthy M. Hébert was walking by himself in the corridor, his two companions returned and saluted me very affectionately and tenderly. I do not know who they are, but may God preserve in them their tender and pitiful natures, which are so rare in men of their calling and which are so proper to those in whom human feebleness confides and who intercede for the pity of God. I thought that M. Hébert was busy consoling, interrogating, and reprimanding some other nun, when he came back to my cell and said:

"How do you come to know M. Manouri?"

"Through my case."

"Who found him for you?"

"The wife of the President."

"You had frequently to confer with him in the course of your affair?"

"No, sir, I have rarely seen him."

"How then did you give him the information?"

"By statements drawn up in my own hand."

"You have copies of these statements?"

"No, sir."

"Who passed him on these papers?"

"The wife of the President."

"And how did you know her?"

"Through Sister Ursula, my friend and a relation of hers."

"Have you seen M. Manouri since you lost your case?"

"Once."

"That is not much. He has not written to you at all?"

"No, sir."

"And you have not written to him?"

"No, sir."

"He will inform you no doubt of what he has done for you. I command you not to see him at all in the parlour, and if he writes to you, either directly or indirectly, to send me the letter without opening it. You understand me, without opening it."

"Yes, sir, and you will be obeyed."

M. Hébert's distrust was equally wounding to me, whether it had reference to M. Manouri or to myself.

M. Manouri came to Longchamps the same evening. I kept my word to the Archdeacon and refused to see him. The next day he wrote to me by his emissary. I received his letter and sent it unopened to M. Hébert. It was a Tuesday, as far as I can remember. I awaited with continual impatience the effect of the Archdeacon's promise and M. Manouri's activities. Wednesday, Thursday, and Friday passed without my hearing a word of anything. How long the days seemed! I trembled lest some obstacle had arisen and upset everything. I was not regaining my liberty but I was changing my prison, and that is something. One happy event sows in us hopes for another, and that perhaps is the origin of the proverb: "*Bits of good luck never come singly*".

I knew the companions whom I was leaving and had little difficulty in supposing I should be better off by living with other prisoners. Whatever they might be they could not be more ill-natured or more evilly disposed towards me.

Saturday morning about nine there was a great stir in the House and little was needed to go to the heads of the nuns. They came and went and whispered. The dormitory doors opened and shut. Such, as you may have already observed, are the signs of monastic revolutions. I was alone in my cell. My heart was beating. I listened at the door, looked out of the window, and bustled about without knowing what I was doing. And I said to myself, trembling with joy: "It is me they have come to look for. In a moment I shall no longer be here" ... and I was not mistaken.

Two unknown persons introduced themselves to me. They were a nun and the door-keeper from Arpajon. They informed me briefly of the reason for their visit. I seized tumultuously on my few treasures and threw them anyhow into the apron of the warder, who made them up into parcels. I did not ask to see the Superior. Sister Ursula was no more; I was leaving nobody.

I go down; the doors are open. After what I am

taking with me has been examined, I get into a carriage and am off.

The Archdeacon and his two young ecclesiastics, the wife of the President, and M. Manouri, who were with the Superior, were warned of my departure. On the way the nun informed me about the House. The doorkeeper added as a refrain to each word of praise which was bestowed on it, "It's simple truth." ... She congratulated herself on the fact that she had been chosen to come and fetch me, and wished to be my friend. In consequence she let me into a few secrets and gave me some advice as to my conduct. This advice no doubt met her case but could be of no use to me. I do not know whether you have seen the convent of Arpajon, one side of which looks out on the high road, the other on the gardens and the country. At each window of the side giving on the road were one, two, or three nuns. This circumstance told me more about the order that reigned in the House than everything the nun and her companion had said to me. They apparently recognized our carriage, for in the twinkling of an eye all these veiled heads disappeared and I arrived at the door of my new prison. The Superior came to meet me with open arms, kissed me, took me by the hand, and led me to the communal hall, where some nuns had already arrived, while others came running up.

The Superior is called Madame ——, and I cannot resist the temptation of describing her before going any further. She is a quite round little woman, but quick and lively in her movements, her head is never still on her shoulders; there is always something wrong with her dress. Her face is agreeable rather than the reverse.

Her eyes, of which one, the right one, is higher and larger than the other, are full of fire, and yet wandering. When she walks she throws her arms backwards and forwards: if she wants to say something she opens her mouth before she has planned out her ideas and so she stammers a little. When seated, she fidgets on her chair as though something were making her uncomfortable. She forgets the conventions and decencies and lifts up her wimple to scratch. She crosses her legs, puts you questions, you answer and she does not listen. She talks to you and gets lost, stops short, does not know where she is, loses her temper and calls you a silly creature, a fool and imbecile if you do not put her straight. She is sometimes familiar to the point of intimacy, sometimes imperious and haughtily proud, but her dignified moments are short. She is alternately soft-hearted and hard. Her features, which have lost their shape, reflect her scatterbrained intelligence and unreliable temperament. In consequence order and disorder reigned alternately in the House. There were days when all was in confusion, pensioners with novices, novices with nuns. Everyone ran in and out of each other's rooms, where tea, coffee, chocolate, and liqueurs were drunk together, and service was despatched with the most indecent haste. Amid all this din and disturbance the face of the Superior suddenly changes, the bell sounds; everyone becomes quiet and withdraws. The deepest silence follows on the noise, and you might think everyone suddenly dead. Suppose a nun neglects the smallest detail, she is made to come in to her cell, sternly treated, ordered to undress and give herself twenty strokes with the whip. The nun obeys, undresses, takes her whip and scourges herself. But hardly has she given herself a few strokes when the Superior, once more all softness, snatches from her her instrument of penitence, begins to weep, says how much she hates punishing anyone, kisses her forehead, her eyes, her mouth, her shoulders, caresses her, and compliments her. "What a charming white skin! How deliciously plump you are! What a lovely neck! What fine hair! Sister Saint Augusta, you are ridiculous to be so shy. Let down your underclothing! I am a woman and your Superior. What a splendid bosom! How firm it is! Am I to allow it to be torn by the nails of that whip? Certainly not." . . . And she kisses her again, lifts her up, dresses her herself, says the softest things to her, dispenses her from services, and sends her back to her cell. Women like this are very difficult to live with. One never knows what they will like or dislike, what you must do or not do. Nothing is regulated. There is either too much to eat or one dies of hunger. Domestic arrangements are upset, remonstrances ill-received or disregarded. One is either too intimate or not intimate enough with Superiors of this kind. There is no real distance between them and us, no measure. One passes from disgrace to favour, from favour to disgrace, without knowing why. Would you like me to tell you of a detail, which is typical of her administration? Twice a year she ran round from cell to cell and had all the bottles of liqueur she found thrown out of the window, and four days later she herself sent other bottles back to most of the nuns. Such was the woman to whom I had made the solemn vow of obedience, for we carry on the vows made in one House to the next.

I went in with her; she led me, holding me round the waist. A collection of fruit, marzipan, and jam was served. The grave Archdeacon began to praise me, but she interrupted, saying: "She has been badly treated, badly treated, I know." The grave Archdeacon wished to continue, but he was interrupted with: "However did they part with her? Why, she is modesty and gentleness itself, and, I am told, extremely talented." The grave Archdeacon wished to take up his last remarks, but the Superior interrupted again, whispering in my ear: "I love you to madness. When these heavy fellows are gone I will make our Sisters come and you will sing us a little song, won't you?" I wanted to burst out laughing. The grave M. Hébert was a little disconcerted, and his two young companions smiled at his embarrassment and my own. Meanwhile M. Hébert readopted his ordinary character and manners, ordered her roughly to sit down, and imposed silence on her. She sat down but was not at her ease. She twisted about in her place, scratched her head, rearranged her dress where it was not disordered, and yawned. Meanwhile the Archdeacon held forth sensibly on the House which I had left, the sufferings I had experienced, on the House into which I was entering, and on the obligations which I owed to those who had helped me. At this point I looked at M. Manouri, who lowered his eyes. Then the conversation became more general, and the painful silence imposed on the Superior ceased. I went up to M. Manouri and thanked him for the service he had rendered me. I trembled and stammered and did not know what sort of return for his kindness to promise him.

My distress, my embarrassment, my real feeling (for I was genuinely touched), a mixture of tears and joy, all my actions spoke to him much better than anything I could have done. His answer was no better planned than my speech, he was just as distressed as I. I do not know what he said, but I gathered that he would be adequately recompensed if he had softened the rigour of my fate; that he looked back upon what he had done with even more pleasure than I could; that he was very sorry his duties which tied him to the Paris Courts of Justice would prevent his often visiting the cloister at Arpajon; but he hoped the Archdeacon and the Superior would permit him to inquire after my health and situation.

The Archdeacon did not intend it, but the Superior answered: "My dear sir, as much as you please. She must do whatever she wants. We must try to repair here the miseries inflicted on her." Then in a low voice to me: "My child, so you really suffered a great deal. But how could those creatures at Longchamps have the courage to maltreat you? I knew your Superior. We were pensioners together at Port Royal[15] and everyone detested her. We shall have plenty of time together and you shall tell me all about it." As she said this she took one of my hands and tapped it gently with her own. The young ecclesiastics also paid me their compliments. It was growing late: M. Manouri took leave of us. The Archdeacon and his companions went to the house of M. ——, the lord of the manor of Arpajon, where they had been invited, and I remained alone with the Superior. But not for long. All the nuns, all the novices, all the pensioners came running headlong in. In a moment I saw myself surrounded by a hundred persons. I did not know to whom I ought to listen or what I ought to answer. There were faces of every kind and remarks of every complexion. But I perceived they were dissatisfied neither with my answers nor my appearance.

When this importunate conference had lasted some time and the first pangs of curiosity were allayed, the crowd grew less. The Superior sent off the rest and came and settled herself in my cell. She did me the honours in her own manner. She showed me the oratory and said: "There my little friend will pray to God. I want her to have a cushion on the step so that her little knees will not be hurt. There is no holy water in the stoup. Dear Sister Dorothy always forgets something. Try this chair; see if it suits you."

So saying she sat me down, my head over the head of the bed and kissed me on the forehead. Then she went to the windows to make sure that the sashes slid easily; then to my bed, where she pulled and repulled the curtains to see if they shut properly. She examined the coverlets.

"They are all right," she said, and took the bolster and making it billow, said: "Our dear little head will be all right on that. The sheets are not very delicate, but they are those of the community. The mattresses are good."

That done, she comes up to me, kisses me, and goes off. During all this scene I said internally: "What a silly creature!" and looked forward to both fair weather and foul.

I settled myself into my cell. I was present at evening

service, at supper, and at recreation which followed.
Some nuns came up and talked: others kept their
distance. The first counted on my defending them to
the Superior; the second were already alarmed at the
predilection shown me. The first moments passed in
reciprocal compliments, questions on the House I had
left, trials of my character, my inclinations, my tastes,
and my mind. They test you everywhere. They lay a
succession of little traps for you, and deduce the most
exact conclusions. For example, they throw out a
spiteful word and look at you. They start a story and
wait for you to ask how it goes on or to let it drop. If
you say something commonplace they find it charming, though they know it is nothing of the sort. They
praise and blame you according to plan, and try to
scrutinize your most secret thoughts. You are questioned about your reading, offered both sacred and
profane books and your choice is noted. They propose
slight infractions of the Rule. Confidences are made
you and words thrown out about the failings of the
Superior. Everything is stored up and repeated. They
leave you and take you up again. They sound your
feelings about morals, devoutness, the world, religion,
the monastic life, and everything, and there grows
from out of these repeated experiments an epithet
which sums you up and is attached as a surname to the
one you bear. Thus I was called Saint Susan the
Reserved. The first evening I was visited by the
Superior. She came in to see me undress. She it was
who took off my veil and wimple and put on my nightcap. She it was who undressed me. She said a hundred
pretty things to me and caressed me a thousand times,

all of which embarrassed me a little, I don't know why, for it meant nothing to me or to her either. Even now when I think over it, what could it have meant to us? However, I spoke about it to my Director, who treated this familiarity, which seemed to me quite innocent and still does, in a very serious tone, and forbade me in a grave voice to lend myself to it any more. She kissed my neck, my shoulders, my arms, praised my plumpness, my figure, and put me to bed, raised the coverlets on each side, kissed my eyes, pulled my curtains, and went off. I forgot to say that she presumed I was tired and allowed me to remain in bed as long as I liked. I profited by this permission. This was, I think, the only good night I have passed in the cloister, and I have spent almost all my life there. Next day, about nine, I heard a gentle tapping at my door. I was still in bed. I answered, and the person entered. She was a nun, who said in a pretty bad-tempered way, that it was late and that the Mother Superior was asking for me. I got up, dressed hurriedly, and went to her.

"Good morning, child," she said. "Have you had a good night? Here is your coffee, which has been ready for you for an hour. I hope it will be good. Drink it up quickly and then we will talk."

While saying this she stretched out one handkerchief on the table, put another on me, poured out the coffee and put in the sugar. The other nuns did the same for each other. While I took my breakfast she talked to me of my companions, painted them according to her aversion or fancy for them, did a thousand little friendly acts for me, put me a thousand questions about the House I had left, about my parents, and my disagreeable experiences; she praised and blamed as whim directed and never listened my answer out. I did not contradict her. She was satisfied with my mind, my judgment, and my discretion. Meanwhile a nun joined us, then another, then a third, a fourth, and a fifth. They talked about the Superior's birds; this one about the twitches of one Sister, that one about the absurdities of those who were absent, and they were all in very good spirits. There was a spinet in a corner of the cell and I laid my fingers on it absent-mindedly, for, being newly arrived in the House and not knowing the subjects of their pleasantry, I did not find the conversation very amusing, and, even had I been better informed, I should not have been more amused. It needs too much intelligence to be really amusing, and does not everyone have his absurdities? While they laughed I played some chords. Little by little I attracted attention. The Superior came up to me, and, tapping me on the shoulder, said: "Now, Saint Susan, entertain us: play first, and then you shall sing." I did what she told me and executed a few pieces which I knew by heart. I improvised at whim, and then I sang some verses from the psalms of Mondonville.

"That is excellent," said the Superior to me, "but we have as much holiness as we please in chapel: we are alone; these are my friends and they will also be yours. Sing us something gayer."

Some of the nuns said: "But perhaps that is all she knows; she is tired by her journey, we must let her off lightly. That is quite enough for once."

"No, no," said the Superior, "she is a marvellous accompanist and has the loveliest voice in the world."

(And to tell the truth, it is not ugly, but has more exactness, softness, and flexibility than strength and breadth.) "I shall not let her go till she has given us something else."

I was somewhat annoyed by the remarks of the nuns, and so I answered the Superior that the Sisters were no longer enjoying it.

"But I am."

I suspected that this would be the answer. So I sang a very delicate chansonette, and they all clapped, praised me, kissed me, caressed me, and asked me for another song – false little affectations dictated by the answer of the Superior. There was hardly a girl there who would not have ruined my voice or broken my fingers if she could. Though they had perhaps never heard a note of music in their lives, they tried to throw at my singing epithets as ridiculous as they were disagreeable, but these had no success with the Superior.

"Be quiet," she said. "She sings and plays like an angel, and I wish her to come here every day. I played the harpsichord a little in the old days, and I want her to teach me again."

"Ah, Madam," I said, "once one has learnt one does not completely forget . . ."

"Very willingly – give me your seat."

She improvised, and played some things, foolish, strange, disconnected, like her ideas. But I perceived across her faults of execution that her touch was infinitely lighter than mine. I told her so, for I like praising people and rarely lose an opportunity when I can do so truthfully. It is so pleasant. The nuns withdrew one after the other and I was left almost alone with the Superior, talking about music. She was seated, I was standing. She took me by the hands and said to me as she squeezed them: "But besides playing well she has the prettiest fingers in the world. Look, Sister Theresa." Sister Theresa lowered her eyes, blushed, and stammered. But whether my fingers were pretty or not, whether the Superior was right or wrong to observe it, what could it matter to Sister Theresa? The Superior clasped me round the waist and decided that I had the prettiest possible figure. She pulled me to her and made me sit on her knee. She raised my head with her hands and asked me to look at her. She praised my eyes, my mouth, my cheeks, my complexion. I made no answer, my eyes were lowered, and I lent myself to all her caresses as though I were idiotic. Sister Theresa was distracted and agitated; she walked from right to left, touched everything without wanting anything, did not know what to do with herself, looked out of the window, or thought she heard somebody knocking at the door – till the Superior said: "Sister Theresa, you can go away if you are bored."

"No, Madam, I am not bored."

"You see I have a thousand things to ask this child."

"I can well believe it."

"I want to know her whole story. How can I repair the wrongs done her if I do not know what they are? I want her to tell me them all without omitting anything. I am sure my heart will be lacerated and that I shall weep; but that does not matter. Sister Susan, when shall I be told everything?"

"Whenever you order it, Madam."

"I should ask you to tell me at once if there were time. What time is it?"

Sister Theresa answered. "It is five o'clock, Madam. The bells will ring for vespers in an instant."

"Still, she can begin."

"But, Madam, you promised to give me a moment's comfort before vespers. I am disturbed in mind and should like to open my heart to Mamma. If I go to chapel without doing so I shall be unable to pray; my mind will wander."

"No, no," said the Superior; "you are becoming ridiculous with your notions. I swear I know what the matter is. We will talk of it to-morrow."

"Madam," said I to the Superior, getting up from her knees on which I had remained sitting, "grant my Sister what she asks of you. Do not lengthen her unhappiness: I am going to retire. I shall have sufficient opportunity to satisfy the interest which you are good enough to take in me. And when you have heard my Sister Theresa she will no longer be unhappy."

I made a move towards the door to go out. The Superior retained me with one hand. Sister Theresa, on her knees, had seized the other, which she kissed as she wept, and the Superior said to her:

"Really, Saint Theresa, you are very tiresome with all your worries. I have already told you that it displeases and embarrasses me. I do not like being embarrassed."

"I know, but I am not mistress of my feelings. Much as I should like it, I cannot ..."

Meanwhile I had withdrawn and left the young Sister alone with the Superior. I could not help looking

138

at her in chapel. She was still depressed and melancholy. Our eyes met several times. And she seemed
hardly able to meet my gaze. As for the Superior, she
had gone to sleep in her stall.

The service was over in the twinkling of an eye. The
choir was not, it seemed to me, the part of the House in
which the inmates most liked to be. They went out
with the lively chatter of a flock of birds escaping from
their cage: they scattered to each other's rooms, running, laughing, and talking. The Superior shut herself
into her cell, and Sister Theresa stopped at the door of
her own to spy on me as if anxious to know what I was
going to do. I went into my own room and the door of
Sister Theresa's cell only shut some time after, and
then softly. The idea crossed my mind that the girl was
jealous of me and was afraid I might take her place in
the good graces and intimacy of the Superior. I
observed her several days running, and when I
thought my suspicions sufficiently confirmed by her
little outbursts of bad temper, childish alarms, perse-
verance in tracking me everywhere, studying me,
always putting herself between the Superior and
myself, interrupting our talks, pouring cold water on
my good qualities in order to make my faults stand out:
– still more by her loss of colour, tears, the decline of
her health, and even of her intelligence, I went to find
her and said:

"What is the matter, my friend?"

She did not know how to answer. My visit surprised
and embarrassed her. She did not know what to say or
do.

"You are unjust to me. Be frank. You are frightened

that I may abuse the affection I have inspired in the Superior to chill her love for you. Be reassured. Such is not my character. If ever I were sufficiently lucky to gain any influence over her mind ..."

"You will have everything you want; she loves you; she is doing for you to-day exactly what she did for me at first."

"Very well, you may be sure that I shall only use the confidence she grants me to make her fonder of you."

"And will that depend on you?"

"Why should it not depend on me?"

Instead of answering me, she threw herself on my neck and said to me with a sigh: "It is not your fault, I know very well. I tell myself so constantly. But promise me ..."

"What do you want me to promise?"

"That ..."

"Go on. I will do everything I can."

She hesitated, covered her face in her hands, and said to me in such a low voice that I hardly heard what she said:

"That you will see her as rarely as possible."

The request appeared so strange to me that I could not help answering: "What can it matter to you how often I see our Superior? It does not annoy me that you see her incessantly. You must not be angry if I see her just as much. Is it not sufficient that I swear that I shall do no harm to you or anybody else?"

She only answered with the following words, which she pronounced in a melancholy tone as she left me and threw herself on her bed: "I am ruined."

"Why ruined? You must think I am the wickedest creature in the world."

That was how we were when the Superior came in. She had passed my cell: she had not found me there, and had been over nearly the whole House uselessly. It had not occurred to her that I was with Sister Theresa. When she found it out from the girl she had sent to find me, she ran up to join us. By her look and expression she seemed a little upset. But then her general bearing was rarely consistent with itself. Saint Theresa was sitting silently on the bed, I was standing up. I said to her: "Mother, I ask your forgiveness for having come here without your permission."

"Certainly," she said, "it would have been better to have asked."

"But I felt so sorry for our Sister. I saw how unhappy she was."

"And why?"

"Can I tell you? And, after all, why not? Her delicacy does so much honour to herself and proves so clearly her attachment to you. The marks of goodwill which you have bestowed on me have disturbed her in her feelings of affection for you. She was afraid I should obtain a preference over her in your heart. This feeling of jealousy, which is after all so respectable, so natural, and so flattering for you, Mother, was apparently torturing my Sister and I reassured her."

The Superior, after listening to me, adopted a severe and imposing air and said to her:

"Saint Theresa, I have loved you and I love you still. I shall never have to complain of you and you will never have to complain of me. But I cannot tolerate these pretentions to exclusiveness. You must dismiss them from your mind if you do not want to lose what remains of my attachment for you, and remember what happened to Sister Agatha." Then turning to me she said: "The tall dark girl you saw opposite me in the choir." For I had talked to so few people: I had been such a short time in the House: I was so new that I did not yet know the names of my companions. She added: "I loved her, when Sister Theresa came, and I began to be fond of her. She was alarmed in the same way and had the same silly ideas. I warned her of it, she failed to correct herself, and I was obliged to take severe measures, which have lasted longer than I like and are contrary to my disposition. For everyone will tell you that I am kind-hearted and always hate punishing people ..." Then, turning to Sister Theresa, she added: "My child, I do not wish to be upset. I have already told you so. You know me. Don't make me go against my natural disposition." Then she said to me, leaning on my shoulder: "Come, Sister Susan, take me back."

We went out. Sister Theresa wanted to follow us. But the Superior, turning her head negligently over my shoulders, said in a tyrannical tone: "Go back to your cell and do not leave it without my permission" ... She obeyed, slamming the door violently, while some remarks escaped her which made the Superior tremble, I do not know why, for they were quite meaningless. I saw how angry she was and said: "Mother, if you have any feeling for me, forgive Sister Theresa. She has lost her head and does not know what she is saying or doing."

"Forgive her? Gladly. But what will you give me in return?"

"Can I be lucky enough to have something to give which may please or appease you, Mother?"

She lowered her eyes, blushed, and sighed. Really she might have been in love with me. Then she said, throwing herself nonchalantly on me as though she were swooning: "Give me your forehead to kiss." I bent down, and she kissed my forehead. From then onwards as soon as a nun had done anything wrong I interceded for her and was sure to obtain her pardon by some innocent favour; always a kiss on the forehead, or the neck, or the eyes, or the cheeks or the lips, or the hands, or the throat, or the arms, but generally on the lips. She discovered my breath was sweet, my teeth white, my lips fresh and scarlet.

I must certainly have been very beautiful if I deserved the least part of the praise she showered on me. My forehead was white, regular, and charmingly shaped; my eyes were brilliant; my cheeks scarlet and soft; my hands small and plump; my bosom firm as marble and admirably shaped; as for my arms, they could not possibly be better shaped or rounder. No Sister had such a well-made neck or of a more exquisite beauty. I don't know all she said. There was an element of truth in all her compliments. I discounted a great deal of it but not everything. Sometimes she used to scan me from head to foot with a look of satisfaction that I have never seen on any other woman, and said: "It is most fortunate that God called her into this retreat. In the world, with a face like that, she would have damned every man she met and herself into the bargain. But then, God is always right."

We were walking towards her cell as we talked. I prepared to leave her, but she took me by the hand and said: "It is too late now to begin your story of Saint Mary's and Longchamps. But come in, you shall give me a short harpsichord lesson."

I followed her. In a moment she had opened the harpsichord, put the music-book in position, and drawn up a chair, for she was quick in her movements. I sat down. She was frightened I might take cold. She took a cushion from one of the chairs and put it in front of me, leant down, took my two feet and put them on it. Then I played some pieces by Couperin, Rameau, and Scarlatti.

Meanwhile she had lifted a corner of my neckerchief, her hand was placed on my bare shoulder, and the end of her fingers rested on my breast. She sighed and seemed oppressed; her breathing became irregular, the hand, which she kept on my shoulder, first pressed it hard and then not at all, as though she were without force or life, and her head fell on mine. Really the silly woman seemed to display incredible sensibility and the most lively appreciation of music. I have never known anyone on whom it produced such a curious effect.

We were thus amusing ourselves in a manner as simple as it was pleasant, when all of a sudden the door opened violently. I was in terror and the Superior too. It was that preposterous Sister Theresa. Her clothes were in disorder, her eyes were troubled and travelled from one to the other of us with the most extraordinary attention, her lips trembled, she could not speak. Still, she came to herself again and threw herself at the feet of the Superior. I joined my prayer to hers and again obtained her forgiveness. But the Superior protested to her in the most formal manner that this would be the last time, at least for faults of this kind, and we both went out together.

As we were going back to our cells I said: "My dear Sister, take care or you will turn our Mother against you. I will never desert you, but will use my credit with her on your behalf, and I shall be in despair if I can do nothing for you or anyone else. But what are you thinking about?"

No answer.

"Why are you afraid of me?"

No answer.

"Cannot our Mother love us both equally?"

"No," she answered violently, "that is impossible; I shall soon be disgusting to her and that will kill me. Why did you come here? You will not be happy long, I am sure, and I shall be wretched for ever."

"Certainly," I said, "I know it is a great misfortune to have lost the good graces of one's Superior, but I know a greater one, which is to have deserved it. You have nothing with which to reproach yourself."

"Would to God it were so!"

"If you have something with which to reproach yourself you must repair it, and the surest method is to bear the punishment patiently."

"I cannot! I cannot!" And then: "Is she the person to punish me?"

"She, Sister Theresa, she! Do you talk thus of your

Superior? That is not right. You forget yourself. I am sure that this is a graver error than those with which you reproach yourself."

"Would to God it were so," she repeated. "Would to God it were so"; and we parted, she to go and wait in her cell, I to reflect on the strangeness of the female mind.

Such is the effect of retiring from the world. Man is born for society. Separate him, isolate him, his ideas grow disconnected, his character becomes twisted, and a thousand ridiculous affections grow in his mind, like roots in uncultivated ground. Put a man in a forest and he becomes ferocious; in a cloister where the notion of inevitability is joined to the notion of slavery and it is still worse. You can leave a forest, you cannot leave a cloister. Perhaps more force of soul is necessary to resist solitude than want. Want lowers a man, retirement depraves his mind. It is better to live in abjection than in madness? That I dare not decide, but both are to be avoided.

I saw that the affection my Superior had conceived for me grew from day to day. I was continually in her cell or she in mine. If I was in the smallest degree unwell I was sent into the infirmary, released from going to chapel, sent early to bed, or forbidden to get up for Morning Prayers. In the choir, in the refectory, at recreation she found means to show the marks of her affection. In the choir, if she came on some verse manifesting an affectionate or tender sentiment she would sing it herself, addressing me at the same time, or looked at me if it were sung by another. In the refectory she always sent me some dainty which had been served her. At recreation she hugged me round

146

the waist and said the softest and most obliging things.
She was given no present which she did not share with
me. Chocolate, sugar, coffee, liqueurs, snuff, handkerchiefs, or anything: she bared her cell of engravings,
domestic utensils, linen, furniture, and an infinity of
pleasant things that they might adorn mine. I could
hardly be absent a moment without finding myself on
my return enriched by some presents. I used to go and
thank her in her room and she would manifest an
inexpressible delight. She would embrace me, caress
me, take me on her knees, talk to me about the most
secret details of the House, and would promise herself,
if I loved her, a life a thousand times more agreeable
than that which she would have passed in the world.
After that she would stop and look at me with melting
eyes and say:

"Sister Susan, do you love me?"

"How could I not love you? I should have to be very
ungrateful."

"That is true."

"You are so full of kindness ..."

"Say, rather, of affection for you."

As she uttered these words she lowered her eyes; the
hand with which she was embracing me clasped me
more tightly ... She drew me to her: her face was near
my own. She sighed, fell back on the chair, and
trembled. One would have said she wished to tell me
something and did not dare; she shed tears, and then
said:

"Ah! Sister Susan, you do not love me."

"What! Not love you, Mother!"

"No!"

"Then tell me, what must I do to prove it?"

"That you must guess."

"I try to and cannot."

Meanwhile she had raised her neckerchief and placed one of my hands on her breast. She was silent and so was I. She appeared to experience the greatest rapture. She asked me to kiss her forehead, her cheeks, her eyes, and her lips. I obeyed her. I do not think there can have been any harm in that. Meanwhile her pleasure increased, and as I asked nothing better than to add to her pleasure in any innocent way, I kissed her again on her forehead, her cheeks, her eyes, and her lips ... She exhorted me stammering and in a low and strange voice to redouble my caresses, and I did so. Then came a moment, I know not if it was pleasure or pain, when she turned pale as death: her eyes closed, all her body stiffened violently, her lips first were tightened and then wet as if with a light froth; then her mouth opened slightly and she seemed to me to die, as she uttered a deep sigh. I got up quickly: I thought she was ill. I wished to go out and call for help. She opened her eyes fully and said in a dying voice: "My innocent, it is nothing. What are you going to do? It is nothing." I looked at her with puzzled eyes, uncertain if I should go or stay. She opened her eyes once more. She could no longer say anything. She signed to me to approach and put me on to her knees again. I do not understand what went on inside me. I was afraid, I trembled, my heart thumped, I had difficulty in breathing, I felt disturbed, oppressed, agitated; I was frightened. I felt that my strength was abandoning me and that I was going to swoon. But I cannot say that the experience was exactly painful. I went up close beside her; she signed to me with her hands to sit on her knees. I obeyed. She was as though dead and I as though about to die. We both remained a considerable time in this singular condition. Had some nun come in she would have been really frightened. She must have imagined either that we were ill or had fallen asleep. However, the good Superior (for one cannot have so much sensibility and not be good) seemed to come to herself. She remained collapsed in her chair: her eyes were still closed, but her face was animated by the liveliest colours. She took one of my hands and kissed it, while I said to her: "Mother, how you have frightened me!" She smiled softly without opening her eyes:

"But have you not been in pain?"

"No."

"But I thought you had. – Oh, the innocent! oh, the innocent darling! How I like her!"

As she said this she got up, sat down again in her chair, took me in her arms and kissed me violently on the cheeks; then she said:

"How old are you?"

"Not yet twenty."

"Impossible."

"It is absolutely true, Mother."

"I want to hear about your whole life. You will tell me?"

"Yes, Mother."

"Everything?"

"Everything."

"But someone might come in. Let us sit down at the clavicord. You shall give me a lesson."

We went to it. I do not know how it was but my hands trembled and the paper seemed only a confused mass of notes. I could not play at all. I told her so; she began to laugh, and took my place, but it was worse still. She could scarcely lift her arms.

"Child," she said, "I see you are scarcely in a state to teach or I to learn. I am a little tired and must rest. Good-bye; to-morrow without fail. I want to know everything that has happened to that dear little soul of yours. Good-bye."

Before, when I went away she had accompanied me as far as the door and followed me with her eyes all along the corridor to my own room. She would throw me a kiss with her hands and only go back into her room when I was in my own. This time she hardly got up: it was all she could do to reach the arm-chair, which was beside her bed. She sat, bent her head on the pillow, threw me a kiss with her hands, and I went off.

My cell was almost opposite that of Saint Theresa. Her door was open: she waited for me, stopped me, and said:

"Ah, Sister Susan, are you coming from our Mother's?"

"Yes," said I.

"You were there a long time."

"As long as she wanted me."

"That is not what you promised me."

"I did not promise you anything."

"Will you dare tell me what you did there?"

Although my conscience had nothing with which to reproach me I will admit, my lord, that her question embarrassed me. She perceived it, insisted, and I answered:

"Sister, if you will not believe me, perhaps you will believe our Mother. Go and find out from her."

"Sister Susan," she answered energetically, "take care what you are about. You do not want to make me unhappy. She would never forgive me! You do not know her. She is capable of passing in a moment from the greatest sensibility to complete ferocity. I do not know what would happen to me. Promise to say nothing about it to her."

"You want me to promise?"

"I implore you on my knees. I am in despair. I see clearly that I must resign myself, and resign myself I will. Promise me to say nothing about it to her. ..."

I raised her up and gave her my word of honour. She relied on it, and there she was right. Then we each shut ourselves up in our own cells. Once in my room, I became moody. I wished to pray and could not. I tried to busy myself with something, started one piece of work, which I dropped for another, and that for a third. My hands ceased functioning of themselves and I might have been imbecile. I had never felt anything like it before. My eyes closed of themselves, and I dropped off to sleep, although I never sleep during the day. On waking, I questioned myself on what had happened between the Superior and me, and looked into myself. On further examination I thought I half-perceived. But my notions were so vague, foolish, and ridiculous that I put them right away from me, and I finally came to the conclusion that it was perhaps illness to which she was subject; and then I thought that perhaps this illness was catching, that Saint Theresa had caught it and that I should catch it too.

Next day, after morning service, our Superior said to me: "To-day I hope I may hear your whole story. Come along ..."

I went with her. She made me sit down in her armchair beside her bed and sat herself in a rather lower chair. I dominated her a little because I am the taller and was in the taller chair. She was so near me that our knees intertwined and her elbows were on the bed. After a moment's silence I said:

"Though I am still quite young I have gone through a great deal. I shall soon be twenty, and I have been miserable for twenty years. I do not know if I can tell you everything, or if you will have the heart to listen to me. Sorrows with my parents, sorrows in the convent of Saint Mary, sorrows in the convent of Longchamps, sorrows everywhere. Mother, where shall I begin?"

"At the beginning."

"But, Mother," I said, "it will be a very long, sad story, and I should not like to depress you for so long."

"Do not be afraid. I enjoy crying. It is a delicious state of mind for a gentle nature, that of shedding tears. You must like weeping too. You will dry my tears and I will dry yours, and perhaps we shall be happy amid the recital of all your sufferings. Who knows how far emotion may not lead us? ..."

As she uttered these last words she scanned me from top to bottom with eyes already moist. She came still nearer to me, so that we were touching.

"Go on, my child, I am waiting, and feel quite ready

152

to get into the most emotional state. I do not think I have ever passed a more sympathizing and affectionate day."

So I began my story, much as I have written it to you. I cannot describe to you the effect it produced on her, the sighs she heaved, the tears she shed, the words of indignation she piled on my cruel parents and the terrible girls of Saint Mary's and Longchamps. I should be sorry to think they ever underwent the smallest part of the sufferings that she desired for them. I should not like to snatch a hair from the head of my cruellest enemy. From time to time she interrupted me, got up, walked about and then sat down again: at other times she raised her eyes to heaven, then hid her head between my knees. When I told of the dungeon, of the exorcism and the public confession she almost cried aloud. When I had finished she remained silent some time with her body bent over her bed, and I said to her:

"Mother, I am sorry for all the pain I have caused you. I warned you, but you would have it." She answered only with these words:

"The wicked creatures! the horrible creatures! Only in convents can all human feeling be extinguished so utterly. When hate works on a disposition naturally bad there is no length to which things may not go. Happily I am soft-hearted; I love all the nuns in a differing degree, they have taken on my character. They all love each other. But how can your feeble health have resisted all these tortures? Why have these little limbs not been broken? How has all this delicate machine escaped destruction? How comes it that the lustre of your eyes has not been dimmed with weeping?

The brutes! Fancy binding these arms with ropes ..."
She took my arms and kissed them. "Fancy drowning
these eyes in tears", and she kissed them, "or calling
forth from these lips complaints and groans", and she
kissed my lips, "or condemning this charming and
serene countenance to continual clouds of sorrow",
and she kissed my face, "or withering the roses on these
cheeks", and she stroked them with her hand and
kissed them, "or destroying the beauty of that head,
tearing that hair out, and lining that brow with care",
and she kissed my head, my brow, and my hair.
"Fancy daring to put a rope round that neck and tear
those shoulders with pointed nails!" She pushed aside
the covering of my neck and head and opened the top
of my dress. My hair fell scattered on my bare
shoulders: my breast was half-exposed, and she
covered with kisses my neck, bare shoulders, and half-
naked breast. I then perceived, from the trembling
that seized her, from her troubled speech, the wildness
of her eyes and hands, from the warmth with which she
hugged me, the violence with which her arms
embraced me, that her illness would not be long in
coming again. I do not know what was happening
inside me, but I was seized with a terror, a trembling,
and a desire to swoon which verified my suspicion that
her illness was contagious.

I said to her: "Mother, see you have disarranged me!
Suppose someone came in!"

"Stop! stop!" she replied in a suffocating voice. "No
one will come in."

However, I made an effort to get up and escape from
her, but I could not. I found I had no strength and that

my knees gave way under me. She was seated, I was standing up. She pulled me towards her. I was afraid of falling on her and hurting her. I sat on the edge of the bed and said to her:

"Mother, I do not know what it is, but I feel ill."

"And I too," she said, "but keep quiet a moment and it will pass. It will not be anything."

And, in fact, my Superior regained her calm and so did I. We were both overcome. My head was bent on her pillow, her head lay on one of my knees, her forehead was placed on one of my hands. We remained some time in this condition. I do not know what she was thinking about. For my own part I was not thinking at all – I could not, my weakness had obtained a complete hold of me. We both observed a silence which the Superior was the first to break. She said: "Susan, I think you said of your first Superior that she was very dear to you."

"Very."

"She did not love you more than I do, but you loved her better ... You do not answer."

"I was unhappy and she consoled me in my grief."

"But whence came your distaste for the religious life? Susan, you have not told me everything."

"But I have, Madam."

"What! But considering how charming you are (for you are very charming, child, you do not know how charming) you must have been told so."

"I have been told so."

"And the man who told you so was not unpleasing to you?"

"No."

"And you were attracted by him?"

"Not in the least."

"What! – your heart has never spoken?"

"Never."

"What! So it was not some passion, either kept a secret or disapproved by your parents, which has given you an aversion from convent life? Tell me that! I am not strict."

"Mother, I have nothing to confide on that point."

"But, once more, whence comes your distaste for the religious life?"

"From the life itself. I hate its duties, its occupations, the retreat, the constraint. I think I am meant for something else."

"But what makes you think that?"

"The crushing boredom. I am bored."

"Even here?"

"Yes, Mother, even here, despite all your kindness."

"But you do not feel in yourself any stirrings or desires?"

"None."

"I believe what you say. You seem to have a calm temperament."

"Fairly calm."

"Cold even."

"I don't know."

"You do not know the world."

"Hardly at all."

"Then what charm can it have for you?"

"That I cannot quite explain to myself. Still, it must have some."

"Is it your liberty which you regret?"

"That and perhaps many other things as well."

"And what other things? Talk to me openly, dear. Would you like to be married?"

"I would rather be married than what I am, that is certain."

"Why this preference?"

"I don't know."

"You don't know? But tell me, what impression does the presence of a man make on you?"

"None. If he is clever and talks well I like listening to him. If he is good-looking I notice it."

"And your heart is not stirred?"

"Till the present it has been unmoved."

"What! When they have turned lively glances on you, you have experienced no ...?"

"Embarrassment, sometimes. They make me lower my eyes."

"And without any distress?"

"Without any."

"And your senses said nothing to you?"

"I know nothing about the language of the senses."

"Such exists, however?"

"Perhaps."

"And you do not know it?"

"Not at all."

"What! You ... It is a pleasant language. Would you like to know it?"

"No, Mother, what use would it be to me?"

"It would dissipate your boredom."

"Or perhaps increase it. Besides, what can this language of the senses signify if it is addressed to no object?"

"When one talks it is always to somebody. It is certainly better than talking to oneself, though even that is not entirely without charm."

"I do not understand at all."

"If you liked, child, I would speak more clearly."

"No, Mother, I know nothing and would rather remain ignorant than acquire knowledge that would perhaps make me more to be pitied than I am already. I have no desires at present, and I do not the least wish to discover something I could never satisfy."

"And why could you not?"

"How could I?"

"As I do."

"As you do! But there is nobody in the House."

"There is you, dear, and I."

"But what am I? What are you?"

"How innocent you are!"

"Yes, you are right, Mother, I am very innocent, and would rather die than cease to be so."

I do not know why these words should have upset her ... but they made her entirely change countenance. She became grave and embarrassed. The hand which she had laid on one of my knees first ceased to press it, and was then withdrawn. She kept her eyes lowered. I said to her:

"Mother, what have I done? Have I let fall something which has offended you? Forgive me. I take advantage of the liberty you granted me and do not think out what I say to you, and even if I thought it out I should not say it any better, perhaps worse. The things we are discussing are so foreign to me. Forgive me!"

As I said these last words, I threw my arms round

her neck and laid my head on her shoulder. She threw her arms round me and clasped me tight. We remained some moments in this position; then, regaining her tenderness and serenity, she said to me:

"You sleep well, Susan?"

"Very well," I said; "particularly recently."

"You get to sleep at once?"

"Generally."

"When you don't get to sleep at once, what do you think about?"

"On my past life, or what is in store for me; or I pray; or I cry. I don't know."

"And in the morning, when you wake early?"

"I get up."

"At once?"

"Yes."

"You do not like dreaming then?"

"No."

"Or lying on your pillow?"

"No."

"Or enjoying the pleasant warmth of your bed?"

"No."

"Never?"

She paused here, and properly so, for what she was going to ask me was not right. And perhaps I am still more wrong to repeat it. But I have made up my mind to hide nothing.

"You have never been tempted to observe with satisfaction how handsome you are?"

"No, Mother; I am not sure I am as handsome as you say. And even if I were, one is handsome for others, not for oneself."

"You have never thought of running your hands over your lovely breast, over your body, your flesh, which is so firm, so soft, and so white."

"Good gracious, no! But that is a sin. And if I had done such a thing I cannot imagine how I should have been able to confess it."

I forget what we said after this, but then someone came and told the Superior that she was awaited in the parlour. The visit apparently annoyed her, and she would have preferred to go on talking to me, though what we said was hardly worth the trouble of regretting; so we separated.

The community had never been so happy as it was since my arrival. The Superior appeared to have lost her temperamental lack of balance. People said I had a settling effect on her. She even gave several days' recreation in my favour, and what are called feasts. On these days the food is better than usual, the services are shorter and all the time between them is given over to recreation. But these happy times were to pass for others and for me. The scene I have just described was followed by a number of similar ones, which I omit. Here is what then ensued.

My Superior began to fall a victim to nerves. She lost her gaiety, and her plumpness, and slept badly. The following night, when everybody was asleep and the House was silent, she got up. After having wandered for some time about the corridors, she came to my cell. I was sleeping lightly and thought I recognized her step. She stopped. Apparently she rested her head against the door, and in so doing made enough noise to wake me up if I were asleep. I remained quiet, and I thought

I heard a voice which wailed, somebody who sighed. I shivered slightly and determined to say *Ave*. Instead of answering, whoever it was withdrew. But she came back some time afterwards: the wails and sighs began again. I again said *Ave*, and the steps again withdrew. I reassured myself and fell asleep. While I slept, someone came in and sat down beside my bed. The curtains were partly withdrawn. She had a little candle, the light of which fell on my face, and she who carried it watched me sleeping: so I judged at least from her attitude when I opened my eyes. And this person was the Superior.

I sat up suddenly. She saw that I was frightened and said: "You need not be alarmed, Susan, it is I." I put my head back on my pillow and said: "Mother, what are you doing here at this hour? What can have brought you? Why are you not asleep?"

"I cannot sleep," she answered. "I shall not sleep for a long time yet. I am tortured by horrid dreams. No sooner are my eyes closed than I live in imagination through all the agonies you have experienced. When I picture you in the hands of those inhuman monsters I see your hair falling over your face, your feet bleeding, the torch in your hand, the rope round your neck: I feel they are going to take away your life: I shiver and tremble: my whole body breaks into a cold sweat: I want to run and help you: I wake up screaming and wait in vain for the return of sleep. This is what has happened to me to-night. I feared Heaven was announcing that some misfortune had come to my friend: I got up and came to your door and listened. You did not seem to be sleeping: you spoke and I withdrew: I came back, you spoke again and I withdrew again. I came back a third time, and when I thought you were asleep, I came in. I have been at your side some time and have been afraid to wake you. I hesitated at first to draw aside your curtains. I wanted to go away for fear of disturbing you. But I could not resist the desire to see if my dear Susan was well. I looked at you. How lovely you are even when you are asleep."

"How good you are, Mother."

"I am quite cold. But now I know that I need not worry about my child. I think I shall get to sleep. Give me your hand." I gave it to her.

"How calm your pulse is! How regular! Nothing disturbs it!"

"I sleep quietly."

"How lucky you are!"

"You will get colder than ever."

"You are quite right; good-bye, darling, good-bye. I am going away."

Still she did not go at all, but continued looking at me. Two tears rolled down her cheeks. "Mother," I said, "what is the matter? What has happened? You are crying. I am sorry I told you of my misfortunes!" At that moment she shut the door, blew out the candle, threw herself upon me. She held me in her arms. She was lying on the coverlet beside me. Her face was pressed to mine, her tears damped my cheeks. She sighed and said to me in a disturbed, choking voice: "Pity me, my darling."

"Mother," I said, "what is the matter? Are you ill? What can I do?"

"I am shivering and trembling," she said. "I have turned mortally cold."

"Would you like me to get up and give you my bed?"

"No," she said, "you need not get up. Just pull the coverlet aside a little and I may get near you. Then I shall get warm and be well."

"But that is forbidden, Mother dear! What would people say if they knew? I have seen nuns given penance for much less serious things than that. At Saint Mary's a nun happened to pass the night in another's cell; she was her particular friend, and I cannot tell how badly it was thought of. The Director asked me sometimes if nobody had ever suggested coming and sleeping by my side, and warned me gravely never to tolerate it. I even spoke to him of your caresses. I thought them quite innocent, but he did not think so at all. I do not know how I came to forget his advice. I had meant to speak to you of it."

"Everything round us is asleep, darling," she said. "Nobody will know anything about it. It is I who distribute rewards and penalties, and, whatever the Director may say, I cannot see what harm there can be in one friend taking in beside her another friend who has felt upset, woken up, and has come during the night, despite the rigour of the season, to see if her darling was in any danger. Susan, at your parents', have you ever shared a bed with your sisters?"

"No, never."

"If the occasion had arisen you would not have scrupled to do so? If your sister had come frightened and stiff with cold to ask for a place by your side, would you have refused her?"

"I think not."

"But am I not your Mother?"

"Yes, you are, but it is forbidden."

"Darling, it is for me to forbid it to others, to allow it to you and to ask it of you. Let me warm myself a moment and I will go away. Give me your hand. ...." I gave it her. ...

"Come," she said, "touch me and see. I am trembling, shivering, and like marble."

It was quite true.

"My poor Mother will be ill," I said. "See, I will go to the edge of the bed, and you can put yourself in the warm place."

I went to the edge, lifted up the coverlet, and she got into my place. How ill she was! She was trembling in every limb. She wanted to talk to me and came nearer. She could not articulate or move. She said in a low voice: "Susan dear, come a bit nearer ..." She stretched out her arms: I turned my back on her; she took me quietly and pulled me towards her. She passed her right arm under my body and the left over it, and said: "I am frozen; I am so cold that I am frightened to touch you, for fear of doing you some harm."

"Don't be afraid, Mother."

She immediately put one of her hands on my breast and another round my waist. Her feet were under mine and I pressed them to warm them, and she said: "See how quickly my feet have got warm, darling, now that nothing separates them from yours."

"But what prevents you warming yourself elsewhere in the same way?"

"Nothing, if you are willing. ..."

Suddenly there were two violent knocks on the door.

In terror I immediately threw myself out of the bed on one side and the Superior threw herself out on the other. We listened and heard someone gaining the neighbouring cell on tip-toe. "Oh," I said, "it is Sister Theresa. She must have seen you passing in the corridor and coming into me. She must have listened to us and overheard our conversation. What will she say?"

I was more dead than alive.

"Yes, it is she," said the Superior in an exasperated voice. "It is she: I have no doubt of it. But I hope she will not easily forget her rashness."

"Mother," I said, "do not do her any harm."

"Susan, good-bye, good night. Get into bed again and sleep well. I dispense you from prayers. I am now going to see this young fool. Give me your hand."

I stretched it to her from one side of the bed to the other. She pulled back the sleeve which covered my arms, and with a sigh kissed it all along from the end of my fingers to my shoulder; then she went out protesting that the rash girl who had dared disturb her should not forget it. Immediately I went to the other end of my bed near the door and listened. She went into Sister Theresa's cell. I was tempted to get up and go and interpose between them, supposing a violent scene occurred. But I was so upset, so ill at ease, that I preferred to remain in bed: I said nothing, however. I thought that I should become the talk of the House, and that this adventure in which there was nothing that could not be easily explained would be recounted in all its most unfavourable aspects: that it would be worse here than at Longchamps, where I was accused of I know not what: that our fault would come to the knowledge of our superiors: that our Mother would be deposed and both of us severely punished. Meanwhile I was all ears, and waited impatiently for the Mother to leave Sister Theresa's cell.

Apparently the matter was difficult to arrange, as she remained there nearly all night. How I pitied her. She was naked except for her shift, and stiff with rage and fright.

In the morning I should have been glad to profit by the permission she had given me and remain in bed. But it occurred to me that I ought not to do so. I dressed quickly and got to the choir first. The Superior and Sister Theresa did not put in an appearance, of which I was very glad; first because I should have found it difficult to meet her glance without embarrassment, secondly because the fact that she had had leave to absent herself from the service showed that she must have obtained from the Superior forgiveness, and forgiveness would only be bestowed on terms which would relieve me of anxiety. I had guessed correctly.

Scarcely was service finished, when the Superior sent for me. I went to see her. She was still in bed and appeared very exhausted. "I have been very unhappy: I have not slept a wink. Saint Theresa is mad: if it happens again I shall shut her up."

"Oh! Mother," said I, "do not ever shut her up."

"That depends on her conduct. She has promised me to improve, and I count on it. And how are you, dear Susan?"

"Very well, Mother."

"You have rested a little?"

"Very little."

"I was told that you were in the choir. Why did you not stay in bed?"

"I should have been uncomfortable there. And then I thought it was better ..."

"No, it would have been quite all right. But I feel I should like to have a sleep. You had better go and do the same in your cell, unless you like to accept a place beside me."

"I am extremely obliged to you, Mother, but I am accustomed to do so alone, and could not with anyone else."

"Very well. I shall not come to refectory for dinner. It will be served here. Perhaps I shall not get up the rest of the day. You will come with some others I have asked."

"And is Sister Theresa among them?"

"No."

"I am rather glad of that."

"Why?"

"I don't know, but I seem frightened of meeting her."

"Do not be nervous, child. I can assure you that she is more frightened of you than you need be of her."

I left her and went to lie down. In the afternoon I went to the Superior's room, where I found a largeish company of all the youngest and prettiest nuns. The others had already paid their visit and left. You are an authority on painting, my lord, and I can assure you it made a very pretty picture. Imagine a room containing ten to twelve people, of which the youngest might be fifteen and the oldest not more than twenty-three; a

Superior of about forty, white-skinned, fresh, rather
plump, half-sitting up in bed, with a double chin
which she carried off gracefully, arms as round as if
they had been turned on the lathe, dimpled fingers,
eyes dark and soft, hardly ever wide open, half-shut, as
if the owner found it tiring to open them, lips red as
roses, teeth white as milk, the prettiest cheeks in the
world, and an attractive head buried in a deep soft
pillow, her arms stretched languidly beside her, with
little cushions under the elbows for support. I was
seated on the edge of the bed, doing nothing; another
was in an arm-chair with a little embroidery frame on
her knees; others, near the window, were making lace.
Others were on the ground, sitting on cushions which
had been taken off the chairs, sewing, embroidering,
unpicking threads, or working at a small spinning-
wheel. Some were fair, others dark, no two were alike,
though all were good-looking. They differed as much
in character as in appearance. Some were serene, some
high-spirited, others grave, melancholy, or sad. Everybody, except myself, was working, as I have said. It
was not difficult to say which were friendly, which
were indifferent or hostile to each other. Friends had
got seats either side by side or opposite each other, and
while they worked they talked, asked each other
advice, looked at each other furtively, and squeezed
each other's fingers under the guise of handing a pin or
needle or a pair of scissors. The Superior ran over them
with her eyes: she reproached one with her industry,
another with her idleness, this one with her indifference, that one with her low spirits; she had the work
brought her and praised or blamed it. She altered the

cap of one. "Your veil is too far forward", "Your face is too much covered and your cheeks hidden", "The folds are all wrong." She distributed to everyone reproaches or caresses.

While they were thus occupied, I heard someone gently tapping at the door and went to it. The Superior said to me: "You will be coming back, Saint Susan?"

"Yes, Mother."

"Because I have something important to tell you. So do not fail me."

It was that unfortunate Sister Theresa. She said nothing for a moment, nor did I. And then I said: "You are wanting me, Sister?"

"Yes."

"How can I help you?"

"I will tell you. I have incurred the ill-favour of our Mother. I thought that she had forgiven me, and had some reason for supposing so. However, you are all assembled in her room without me, who am told to keep to my cell."

"You would like to come in?"

"Yes."

"You want me to ask leave for you?"

"Yes."

"Wait a moment, I will go and ask."

'You will really ask her for me?"

"Why should I not promise you to do so, and why should I not do so after having promised?"

"Oh," she said, looking at me tenderly, "I forgive her her love for you. You have all the graces, the loveliest soul, and the loveliest body."

I was enchanted to be able to do her this slight service. I came in. Another had, in my absence, taken my place on the edge of the Superior's bed and had leant over her, with her elbow propped up between the Superior's legs, as she showed her work. The Superior, her eyes nearly closed, said "Yes" and "No", almost without looking. I was standing by her side and she did not notice it. But she soon emerged from her small absent fit. The one who had taken my place gave it back to me. I sat down again, but then, bending slightly towards the Superior, who had risen a little on her pillow, I remained silent but looked as though I had a favour to ask her. "Well," she said, "what is it? Tell me what you want. How can I refuse you anything?"

"Sister Saint Theresa . . ."

"I understand. I am very dissatisfied with her. But Saint Susan intercedes for her and I forgive her. Go and tell her she can come in."

I ran off. The poor little Sister was waiting at the door. I told her to come along. She did so, trembling, and with lowered eyes. She was holding a long piece of muslin attached to a pattern which dropped from her hands at the first step. I picked it up. I took her by the arm and led her to the Superior. She fell at her knees and seized one of her hands with sighs and tears. Then she seized one of mine, which she joined to that of the Superior and kissed them both. The Superior signed to her to get up and sit wherever she liked. She obeyed. Refreshments were served. The Superior got up. She did not sit down with us, but walked round the table, laying her hand on one girl's head, pulling it gently back and kissing her forehead, lifting up the necker-chief of another, putting her hand over the neck and remaining propped up on the back of the chair; passing on to a third and letting a hand run over her, or putting it over her mouth, first putting the food to her own lips and then distributing it to this girl and to that. Having thus gone the round for a moment, she stopped oppo-site me and looked at me with very affectionate and tender glances, while the other girls lowered their eyes as though afraid to constrain or distract her, but especially Sister Saint Theresa. After taking our refreshment I sat down at the harpsichord and accom-panied two Sisters who sang without technique but in time and with a good voice and sure taste. I also sang, accompanying myself. The Superior was seated at the end of the harpsichord and appeared to take the greatest pleasure in hearing and watching me. The other Sisters stood up and listened without doing anything, or settled down to their work again. It was a delightful evening. Then everybody withdrew. I was going off with the others, but the Superior stopped me.

"What is the time?" she said.

"Close on six."

"Some of our advisers are coming. I have thought over what you said to me about your departure from Longchamps and have communicated my ideas to them. They have approved them, and we have a proposition to make to you. We cannot but succeed, and if we do succeed it will be something gained for the House and a comfort to you."

At six o'clock the advisers came in; this Council always consists of very old and decrepit women. I got up. They sat down, and the Superior said to me: "Sister Saint Susan, did you not tell me that you owed to the beneficence of M. Manouri the dowry which has been found for you here?"

"Yes, Mother."

"So I am not mistaken, and the Sisters at Long-champs have remained in possession of the dowry which you paid them on entry?"

"Yes, Mother."

"They gave you nothing at all back?"

"No, Mother."

"That is not right. I have communicated the facts to the Council and they think, as I do, that you have the right to appeal against them for the restitution of your dowry for the advantage of this House, or at any rate for the payment of the interest on it. What you possess as a result of the concern which M. Manouri felt about your future has nothing to do with what the Sisters of Longchamps owe you. He did not supply your dowry in order to pay off a debt to them."

"I do not think so. But to make quite sure, the quickest thing would be to write to him."

"No doubt. Then on the assumption that his answer is such as we wish, we have the following propositions to make you. We will undertake the action against Longchamps in your name. Our House will pay the costs, which will not be heavy because there is every likelihood that M. Manouri will be willing to take up the case himself; if we win, the House will share equally with you either the capital or the interest. What do you think of that, Sister? You do not answer. There is something on your mind."

"Yes, this. The Sisters of Longchamps treated me very badly and I should hate them to imagine that I was revenging myself on them."

"There is no question of revenge, but of asking for your own property back."

"But to make a spectacle of oneself again!"

"That is a mere trifle. You will hardly appear in the matter. And then our community is poor and Long-champs rich. You will be our benefactress, at least for as long as you live, though we do not need that motive to make us want to keep you. We all love you." And then all the Council in chorus ... "And who would not love her? She is perfect."

"I might die at any moment, another Superior might perhaps not share my feelings for you. No, she certainly would not. You might have some slight indisposition, some trifling wants. It is nice to have a little money of one's own to spend on one's own comforts or to enable one to help others."

"The fact that you have put forward these pro-posals proves, Mother," I said, "that there is much to be said for them. There are other considerations which affect me even more. But there is no personal feeling which I am not ready to abandon for you. The only favour I have to ask you, Mother, is to begin nothing without having conferred, in my presence, with M. Manouri."

"Nothing more proper. Would you like to write yourself?"

"As you like, Mother."

"Write to him then. And so that we may not have to return to this subject again, for I do not care about this sort of business, it bores me to death, write immediately."

I was given pen, ink, and paper, and on the spot I requested M. Manouri to be good enough to come to Arpajon as soon as his engagements allowed it as I still needed his assistance in a matter of some slight importance, etc. The assembled Council read this letter, approved of it, and it was sent.

M. Manouri came a few days later. The Superior explained the matter to him. He did not hesitate an instant before adopting her opinion. My scruples were treated as absurdities. It was agreed that the nuns of Longchamps should be summoned the very next day. They were. So despite everything, my name reappeared in reports, legal statements, and in court, and that with details, suppositions, and lies, and with every black slander which can prejudice a human creature in the mind of her judges and make her odious in the eyes of the people. But, my lord, are lawyers allowed to slander one as much as they like? Has one no redress against them? Had I been able to foresee all the bitterness this affair would bring along with it I protest that I should never have allowed its being begun. Care was taken to send several of our nuns the documents which were being published against me. At every moment they came and asked details about horrible incidents which had no shadow of existence in fact. The greater the ignorance I professed the guiltier they thought me. Because I explained nothing, admitted nothing, denied everything they thought everything was true. They smiled and spoke in a circumlocutory, but very wounding, fashion. They shrugged their shoulders at my supposed innocence. I wept and was miserable.

But troubles never come singly. The time for going to confession arrived. I had already accused myself of the first caresses the Superior had bestowed on me: the Director had very expressly forbidden me to go on accepting them. But how refuse things which afford the greatest satisfaction to the person on whom one is completely dependent, expecially when one can see no harm in them?

As this Director is going to play a great part in the rest of my Memoirs I think you ought to know about him.

He is a Franciscan called Father Lemoine, and not more than forty-five. He has one of the handsomest faces to be found anywhere. When he is not thinking it is gentle, serene, open, smiling, and agreeable. But on occasions his brow becomes wrinkled, his eyebrows frown, his eyes fall, and his bearing becomes austere. I know no two men more different than Father Lemoine at the altar and Father Lemoine in the parlour, alone or in company. But that is the characteristic of all monastic persons. And I have caught myself at it several times on the way to the grille and stopped to readjust my veil and head-band, to compose my countenance, my eyes, my mouth, my hands, my arms, my expression and my walk, and take on a borrowed bearing and reserve which would last more or less long according to the company in which I found myself. Father Lemoine was tall, well-built, gay, and very amiable in his moments of forgetfulness; he talks marvellously. He has in this House the reputation of a great theologian; in the world of a great preacher. His society is delicious. He is very well informed on an infinity of subjects foreign to his calling. He has a very fine voice, knows history, music, and languages well. He is a doctor of the Sorbonne. Though young, he has held all the chief dignities of his order. I think he is neither an intriguer nor ambitious. He had asked to be made head of Estamps because it was a quiet post, where he could give himself over without being disturbed to some studies which he had undertaken. The choice of a confessor is a great thing for a nunnery. It should be directed by a man of mark and position. Everything was done to get Father Lemoine, and we had him on special occasions at any rate.

When he was to come on the eve of the great feasts he was sent the carriage belonging to the House. You would have to see in order to believe the stir which waiting for him produced in the whole community. They would all be as happy as possible and shut themselves up to work away at their self-examination and get ready to take up as much of his time as possible.

It was the eve of Pentecost and he was expected. I was uncomfortable. The Superior perceived it and spoke to me about it. I did not hide from her the reason why I was worried. She appeared even more alarmed than me, though she did her best to conceal it. She talked of Father Lemoine as an absurdity, laughed at my scruples, asked me if Father Lemoine knew more about the innocence of her feelings and mine than did our own consciences, and if mine reproached me with anything. I answered, "No." "Very well," she said; "I am your Superior; you owe me obedience, and I order you not to speak to him about such stupid things. It is useless your going to confession if you have only got trifles of that sort to tell."

Meanwhile Father Lemoine arrived and I prepared myself for confession while those in more of a hurry had already got hold of him. My turn was approaching when the Superior came to me, pulled me aside, and said: "Saint Susan, I have been thinking over what you have said to me. Go back to your cell, I do not want you to go to confession to-day."

"And why not, Mother?" I answered. "To-morrow is a great day, a day of general Communion. What would you have people think of me if I am the only one not to approach the Holy Table?"

"No matter. People can say what they like, but you shall not go to confession."

"Mother," I said, "if you really love me, do not mortify me in this way. I ask it you as a favour."

"No, no; it is out of the question. You will get into difficulties with the man, and I do not want that to happen."

"No, Mother, I shall not."

"Promise me then ... it is quite unnecessary, you shall come to my room to-morrow and accuse yourself to me. You have done nothing for which I cannot reconcile you with God and absolve you, and you will communicate with the rest. Be off ..."

So I withdrew and remained unhappily in my cell, distressed and moody, not knowing what plan to adopt, whether I should go to Father Lemoine in spite of the Superior, whether I should be satisfied with to-morrow's absolution and make my devotions with the rest of the House, or whether I should abstain from the Sacraments, whatever people might say.

When she returned she had been confessed and Father Lemoine had asked why he had not seen me and if I were ill. I do not know what answer she had made, but the end of it all was that Father Lemoine was expecting me in the confessional.

"So go, if you must, but promise me that you will hold your tongue." I hesitated, and she insisted.

"You silly creature," she said, "what harm can you find in keeping quiet about something that is not wrong?"

"Then what is the harm in telling it?"

"No harm, only inconvenience. Who knows the importance that that man might attach to it? Now, promise me."

I still wavered, but finally I promised to say nothing about it if I was not directly asked, and went off. I confessed and said nothing about it, but when the Director interrogated me directly I hid nothing. He put me a thousand singular questions, which I still cannot understand as I recall them. He treated me indulgently, but expressed himself about the Superior in terms which made me tremble. He called her an unworthy libertine, a bad nun, a corrupted soul, and enjoined me on pain of mortal sin never to be alone with her or to tolerate any of her caresses.

"But, Father," I said, "she is my Superior, she can come into my room and call me into hers whenever she likes."

"I know, I know, and I am miserable about it. Dear

child, God be praised for having saved you up to now. I dare not explain myself more clearly for fear of becoming myself the accomplice of your Superior and of withering by the poisonous breath which would issue from my lips despite myself, a delicate flower which has only remained till your age fresh and spotless by the special protection of Providence. But I bid you fly from your Superior, repel her caresses, never go to her room alone, close your door to her, especially at night, leave your bed if she comes in despite your efforts, go into the corridor and call for help, if need be, descend naked to the foot of the altar, fill the House with your cries, and do everything that the love of God, the fear of crime, your Holy State and interest in your salvation would suggest to you if Satan himself came up to you and pursued you. Yes, my child, Satan. Such are the colours in which I am compelled to portray your Superior to you. She has sunk into the abyss of crime and is trying to pull you in after her. Perhaps you would be there already had your very innocence not filled her with terror and stayed her."

Then, raising his eyes to Heaven, he cried out:

"Oh! Lord, continue to protect this child ... Say after me: *Satana, vade retro, apage, Satana.* If the wretched woman questions you tell her everything, repeat what I have said to you. Tell her it were better that she had not been born, or that she should fall alone into hell by a violent death."

"But, Father," I replied, "you have heard her yourself an instant ago."

He made no reply, but, sighing deeply, he rested his

arms against one of the walls of the confessional and laid his head upon them as one overcome with grief. He remained some time in this state. I did not know what to think: my knees trembled. I was in an inconceivable state of distress and disorder. I was like a traveller walking in darkness between precipices he cannot see and attacked on all sides by subterranean voices crying: "It is all over with you!" Then looking at me with an expression calm but pitiful, he said:

"Is your health good?"

"Yes, Father."

"You would not be too much upset by a sleepless night?"

"No, Father."

"Very well. You shall not go to bed to-night. Immediately after you have had your food you will go into chapel and fall at the foot of the altar, where you will pass the night in prayer. You do not understand the danger which you have run. Thank God for having kept you safe. And to-morrow you will approach the Holy Table with the other nuns. Your only penance will be to keep away from the Superior and to repel her poisoned caresses. Go. For my part, I shall join my prayers to yours. I am aware of all the consequences of the advice I am giving you, but I owe it to you, and I owe it to myself. God is master and we have but one law."

I recall, my lord, but very imperfectly, everything he said to me. Now that I compare what he said as I have described it to you with the terrible impression it made on me, there can be no comparison. But this comes from the fact that it is broken up and disconnected. A great deal has been left out; I cannot remember it because I had no clear idea of it at the time and did not, and still do not, attach any importance to things against which he declaimed with the greatest violence. What, for instance, did he find so extraordinary in the scene with the harpsichord? Are there not people on whom music makes the most violent impression? I am told that certain tunes, certain variations and modulations used entirely to alter my expression, and that on these occasions I would be quite beside myself and hardly know what was happening to me. But I do not think I was the less innocent for that. Why should it not have been the same with the Superior, who was certainly, for all her foolishness and unreliable disposition, one of the most sensitive women in the world? She could not hear a story which was the least bit sad without bursting into tears. When I told her my own story the state to which I reduced her was pitiful. Why did he not make a crime out of her sympathy as well? And the scene at night, of which he awaited the issue with mortal terror ... Certainly the man is too severe.

However that may be, I executed his orders exactly, the immediate consequences of which he had no doubt foreseen. The moment I left the confessional I went and fell at the foot of the altar. My head was turned by terror. I remained there till supper. The Superior, anxious about what had happened to me, had sent for me, but she had been told that I was praying. She appeared several times at the door of the choir, but I pretended not to see her. The supper-bell sounded. I went back to the refectory and took my supper hastily. As soon as I had finished I returned to chapel. I did not appear at the evening recreation. At the hour for retiring and going to bed I did not go up. The Superior was well aware what had happened to me. The night was far advanced, everything was quiet in the House, when she came down to me. I retraced in my imagination the picture the confessor had drawn of her. I trembled all over and dared not look at her, thinking I should see her with hideous countenance and enveloped in flames. I said within myself: "*Satana, vade retro, apage, Satana*. Oh! Lord, save me and withdraw from me this demon."

She knelt down, and after praying for some time said: "Saint Susan, what are you doing here?"

"You can see, Madam."

"Do you know what time it is?"

"Yes, Madam."

"Why did you not go to your room at the retreat hour?"

"Because I was putting myself in the mood to celebrate the great day to-morrow."

"Then you intended to pass the night here?"

"Yes, Madam."

"And who gave you permission?"

"The Director ordered it."

"The Director can order nothing against the rule of the House, and I order you to go to bed."

"Madam, it is the penance imposed on me."

"You will replace it with other good works."

"It is not my choice."

"Now, child," she said, "come along. The coldness of the chapel at night will make you ill. You will pray in your cell."

Then she wished to take me by the hand, but I withdrew it quickly.

"You are avoiding me," she said.

"Yes, Madam, I am avoiding you."

Reassured by the sanctity of the place, the presence of the Divinity, and the innocence of my own heart, I dared to raise my eyes to her. But scarcely had I looked at her when I uttered a loud cry and began to rush about in the choir like a mad thing, crying: "Keep away from me, Satan." She did not follow me, but remained where she was, and said to me gently, stretching out her arms to me and in the most touching and gentle voice:

"What is the matter? Whence this terror? Stop. I am not Satan, but your Superior and your friend."

I stopped, turned my head towards her again, and saw that I had been frightened by an extraordinary atmospheric effect to which my imagination had given reality, and that she had been standing in relation to the chapel lamp in such a position that only her face and the ends of her hands were lighted and the rest was in shadow, all of which gave her a singular aspect. Having gained a little self-control, I dropped into a stall. She was coming up to sit in the next one when I rose and sat in the one below. So I went from stall to stall, and she also, till the last one. There I stopped and implored her to leave at least one stall empty between herself and me.

"Gladly," she said.

We both sat down, a stall separating us. Then the Superior broke the silence by saying:

"Might one know, Saint Susan, whence comes this terror which my presence causes you?"

"Mother," I said to her, "forgive me: it is not I, but Father Lemoine. He paints in the most awful colours your tenderness for me and your caresses, though I admit I see no harm in them. He told me to avoid you, never to go into your room alone, and to leave mine if you came in. He has portrayed you to my mind as the demon. I cannot tell what he did not say to me on the subject."

"So you spoke to him?"

"No, Mother, but I could not help answering his questions."

"So now I am revolting in your eyes?"

"No, Mother, I could never help loving you, and appreciating all the worth of your kindness, and asking you to continue it. But I shall obey my Director."

"So you will no longer come and see me?"

"No, Mother."

"Nor admit me to your room?"

"No, Mother."

"You will repel my caresses?"

"It will cost me a pang, for I have a tender nature and like to be caressed. But it must be so. I have made the promise to my Director, and I have sworn it at the foot of the altar. If only I could imitate the manner in which he explains his meaning! He is a pious man, an enlightened man. What interest could he have in pointing out dangers where none are, in alienating the heart of a nun from that of her Superior? But perhaps he sees in actions very innocent on both our parts a germ of secret corruption which he thinks developed in you and fears may develop in me. And I will not hide from you that in thinking over the sensations I have sometimes felt. . . . Whence comes it, Mother, that after leaving you and going to my own room I am agitated and moody? Whence comes it that I can neither pray nor settle down to anything? Whence comes a kind of boredom which I have never experienced before? Why do I feel sleepy, I who have never slept during the day? I thought you had some contagious disease which was beginning to operate in me. But Father Lemoine looks at it quite differently."

"And how does he look at it?"

"He sees everything black and criminal, your ruin consummated, mine projected. I do not know."

"Come, come," she said, "your Father Lemoine is a visionary. This is not the first onslaught of the kind which he has made on me. I have only got to get really fond of somebody for him to try and upset her. A little more and he would have driven poor Saint Theresa mad. I am beginning to be tired of it, and I shall get rid of the man. Besides, he lives thirty miles off; it is very inconvenient bringing him over, and then one can't have him when one wants. But we will talk of that at our leisure. So you will not go up?"

"No, Mother, I ask the favour of being allowed to pass the night here. If I failed in this duty, to-morrow I should not dare approach the sacraments with the rest of the community. But you, Mother, will you communicate?"

"Certainly."

"Then Father Lemoine has said nothing to you about it?"

"No."

"But how can that be?"

"Because he has not had occasion to talk to me of it. One only goes to confession to accuse oneself of one's sins; and I see none in my tender love for such a lovable girl as Saint Susan. If fault there were, it would be in concentrating on her alone a sentiment that should be distributed over all those who make up the community. But that does not depend on me. I cannot help seeing merit where it exists or feeling a preference for it. I ask forgiveness of God and cannot understand how your Father Lemoine can see my damnation sealed in a partiality so natural and so difficult to guard against. I try to make everybody happy, but there are some I love and esteem above the others, because they are more lovable and estimable. That is all my crime with you amounts to, Saint Susan. Do you think it a grave one?"

"No, Mother."

"Then, my dear child, let us each pray a little more and retire."

I besought her again to let me pass the night in chapel. She agreed on the condition that it did not happen again, and withdrew.

I thought over what she had said to me. I asked God to enlighten me. After reflecting, I came to the conclusion that, all things considered, even when people were of the same sex, there might be at least some indecency in the manner in which they showed their friendship: that Father Lemoine, who was an austere man, had perhaps exaggerated, but that his advice to show extreme reserve towards the excessive familiarity of my Superior might profitably be followed, and I promised myself to do so.

Two important incidents happened with but few days' interval. The first was that I won my case against the nuns of Longchamps. They were condemned to pay the nuns of Saint Eutropia, where I was, an income proportionate to my dowry. The other was that the Director was changed. The Superior herself informed me of this last event. However, I no longer went to her room unaccompanied. She no longer came alone to mine. She was always on the look-out for me, but I avoided her. She noticed it and reproached me for it. I do not know what was going on in her mind, but it must have been something extraordinary. She got up at night and walked about the corridors, particularly mine, and I heard her passing and repassing, stopping at my door, sighing and lamenting. I trembled and buried myself in my bed. By day, if I was walking or in the work- or recreation-room and placed in such a manner that I could not see her, she passed whole hours gazing at me. She spied on my slightest actions. If I went downstairs I found her at the bottom: she was waiting for me at the top when I went up again. One day she stopped me and began looking at me without saying a word. Tears flowed abundantly from her eyes; then suddenly falling on the ground and clasping my knees between her hands, she said:

"Cruel Sister, ask for my life and I will give it, but do not avoid me. I cannot live without you."

Her condition distressed me. Her eyes were dull. She had lost her plumpness and bright complexion. She was my Superior: she was at my feet, her head against my knees, which she held in her embrace. I held out my hands to her. She took them ardently, kissed them, and then looked at me again. I lifted her up. She swayed and could scarcely walk. I led her back to her cell. When the door was open she took me by the hand and pulled me gently to make me go in, but without speaking to me or looking at me.

"No," I said: "Mother, no, I have made a promise to myself. It is best for you and for me. I occupy too much place in your heart; and that is so much lost for God, to whom you owe it entirely."

"Is it that with which you reproach me?"

I tried, as I spoke, to free my hand.

"So you will not come in?" she said.

"No, Mother, no."

"You do not want to, Saint Susan. You do not know what may happen. No, you do not know. You will kill me."

These last words had on me an effect contrary to that which she had intended. I withdrew my hand hastily and retired. She returned, watched me for a few paces, then, going back into her cell, the door of which remained open, she began to utter the most piercing wails. I heard them and my heart melted. I was for a moment doubtful whether I should continue on my way or go back to her. Owing to some feeling of natural aversion, I went on, but not without grief for the state in which I left her. I have a sympathetic nature. I shut myself in, and felt extremely uncomfortable; I could settle down to nothing. I took several turns up and down my cell, distracted and worried. I went out and came back again. Finally I went and knocked at the door of my neighbour, Saint Theresa, whom I found in close conversation with another young nun who was a friend of hers. I said to her:

'Sister, I am sorry to interrupt you. But please listen to me for a moment; I have something to say to you."

She followed me back to my cell, and I said:

"I do not know what is the matter with our Mother Superior. She is so miserable. Perhaps if you went to see her you could cheer her up."

She made no answer, but left her friend where she was, shut the door, and ran off to the Superior.

But the state of the woman got daily worse. She became melancholy and grave. She suddenly lost her high spirits, which had been unfailing since my arrival. The discipline became extremely severe. The services were performed with befitting dignity, strangers almost entirely excluded from the parlour, the nuns forbidden to go into each other's cells, our exercises reinstituted with the most scrupulous exactness, no more assemblies with the Superior, no more refreshments, the smallest faults severely punished. I was still sometimes approached to obtain a pardon, but I absolutely refused to ask for it. The cause of this revolution was known to everyone. The old ones were rather pleased; the young people were in despair and looked at me with hostile eyes. But my conscience was at rest, and I paid no attention to their ill-humour and reproaches.

The Superior, whom I could neither console nor help pitying, passed successively from melancholy to piety, and from piety to raving. I will not follow her through these various stages. They would land me in unending details. I will only say that, in her first state, she sometimes sought me out and sometimes avoided me. Sometimes she treated us all with her accustomed gentleness; sometimes again she changed suddenly to an exaggerated strictness: she would call for us and then send us back again; announce recreation, and a moment later revoke her orders; summon us to the choir, and just as we were obeying her orders the bell would ring again for us to shut ourselves up. It is difficult to imagine the disturbed life we led. Our day passed in leaving our cells and going back again; in taking up our breviaries and putting them down; in going upstairs and downstairs; in raising and lowering our veils. Night was almost as much interrupted as day.

Some nuns addressed me and tried to make me understand that if I would show a little more complaisance and consideration for the Superior all would return to its accustomed order. They should have said disorder. I answered:

"I am sorry for you, but tell me clearly what I ought to do."

Some went away with bent heads, making no reply. Others gave me advice it was impossible to reconcile with that of the Director – I mean the one who had been removed, for we had not yet seen his successor.

The Superior no longer left her room at night, and passed whole weeks without showing herself at service, in the choir, in the refectory, or at recreation. She remained shut up in her room, wandered about the corridors, or went down to chapel. She would knock at the nuns' doors and say to them in a plaintive tone:

"Sister So-and-so, pray for me."

The rumour grew that she was preparing for a general confession.

One day, when I was the first to go down to chapel, I saw a paper attached to the veil of the grille. I went up to it and read:

"Sisters, you are asked to pray for a nun who has wandered from her duties and wishes to return to God." I was tempted to tear it down, but I left it there. Some days later there was another one on which was written:

"Sisters, you are asked to implore the pity of God for a nun who has recognized her aberrations. They are great."

Another day there was a third request:

"Sisters, you are asked to pray God to remove the despair of a nun who has lost all confidence in the divine pity."

All these requests, in which were pictured the cruel vicissitudes of a soul in pain, deeply grieved me. Once I remained a considerable time before one of these notices. I asked myself what these aberrations were with which she reproached herself: whence came the terrors of the woman, with what she had to blame herself? I went back to the exclamations of the Director, recalled his expressions, tried to find some sense in them, found none, and remained as it were absorbed. Some nuns who were looking at me were talking together, and, if I am not mistaken, looked on me as immediately threatened with the same terrors.

The poor Superior no longer appeared but with lowered veil; took no more part in the management of the House, spoke to nobody, and had frequent conferences with the new Director who had been given us. He was a young Benedictine. Perhaps it was he who imposed all the mortifications which she practised. She fasted three days a week, scourged herself, heard service in the lower stalls. One had to pass her door to go to chapel. We found her prostrated there, her face to the ground, and she only got up when there was no longer anyone there. At night she came down in her shift, with bare feet. If Saint Theresa or myself happened to meet her, she turned round and glued her face to the wall. One day as I was leaving my cell I found her prostrated, with arms stretched out and face to the ground, and she said to me:

"Come and trample me underfoot. I deserve no other treatment."

During the months which her illness lasted the rest of the community had time to get sorry for her and form an aversion for me. I will not dwell once more on the sad plight of a nun who is hated by the House: you ought to know all about it by now. I felt reviving in me, bit by bit, my old distaste for my condition. I brought this distaste and my sufferings before the new Director. He was called Dom Morel. He was a man of ardent temperament and about forty years old. He seemed to listen to me with attention and interest. He desired to know every incident of my life, and made me go into the minutest details of my family, my tastes, my character, the Houses in which I had been, that in which I was, and everything which had passed between the Superior and myself. I hid nothing from him. He did not seem to attach as much importance as did Father Lemoine to the conduct of the Superior

Checked out item summary for
GROSS, JOYCE
06-12 2019 9:32AM

BARCODE: 33420050086773
LOCATION: wn
TITLE: The immortal life of Henrietta La
DUE DATE: 06-20-2019

BARCODE: 33420007385405
LOCATION: wpn
TITLE: Reading Lolita in Tehran : a memo
DUE DATE: 06-20-2019

BARCODE: 33420007039856
LOCATION: wnb
TITLE: The Helen Forrester omnibus
DUE DATE: 07-04-2019

BARCODE: 33420003279691
LOCATION: wf
TITLE: Memoirs of a nun / Denis Diderot
DUE DATE: 07-24-2019

with me: he scarcely deigned to say a few words about it. He regarded the matter as finished. What interested him more were my secret feelings about the religious life. The more I opened myself to him, the more confidential he became in return. If I confessed to him, he confided in me. What he said of his sufferings was in complete conformity with what I had felt myself. He had entered into religion despite himself. He had the same distaste for his condition and was scarcely less to be pitied than I.

"But, Sister," he added, "what is to be done? We have but one resource, which is to make our position as little distressing as possible."

Then he advised me to follow the plans of life which he had adopted for himself. They were wise.

"With that," he added, "we do not avoid suffering; we merely bring ourselves to tolerate it. Truly religious people are happy only in so far as they make for themselves before God a virtue of their crosses. Then they rejoice and go to meet their mortifications half way. The bitterer and more frequent these mortifications are the more they rejoice. It is the exchange they make of present happiness for happiness to come. They assure themselves of one by the voluntary sacrifice of the other. When they have greatly suffered they say to God: '*Amplius Domine*, still more, O Lord'; and such a prayer God rarely fails to grant. But if these sufferings exist for you and me as for them, we cannot promise ourselves the same recompense: we have not got the one thing which might give them value, which is resignation. This is sad. Alas! How can I inspire you with the virtue you lack and which I do not possess myself? Yet without it we are in danger of being lost in the next world after having been wretched in this. In the midst of our penance we damn ourselves almost as surely as does the world amidst its pleasures. We deny ourselves, they enjoy themselves, and after this life the same tortures await us both. How painful is the position of a monk or nun without vocation! Such, however, is ours, and we cannot change it. We have been loaded with heavy chains which we shake unceasingly and cannot hope to break. Let us try, Sister, to draw them after us. Have no fear. I will come back and see you."

He returned some days later. I saw him in the parlour and examined him more nearly. Finally he had told me all about his life and I had told him all about mine, going into a mass of detail which served only to emphasize the similarity of our conditions. He had undergone almost the same domestic and religious persecution as I had. I did not perceive that the picture he drew of the distaste he felt for his life was hardly calculated to dissipate my own. But this was the effect it produced on me, and I think that the picture I drew produced the same effect on him. Thus it came about that the resemblance of character aiding resemblance of experience, the more we saw of each other the more we liked each other. The story of his trials was the story of mine; the story of his feelings was the story of mine; the story of his soul was the story of mine.

When we had talked at length about ourselves we also used to talk about other people, and particularly about the Superior. His position as Director made him very reserved. But still I deduced from what he said that her present condition would not be permanent, that she was struggling against herself, but uselessly; and that one of two things would happen. She would either return at once to her former proclivities or lose her reason. I was extremely curious to know more. He could have enlightened me on the questions I had put myself and been unable to answer, but I did not dare question him. I only summoned up courage to ask him if he knew Father Lemoine.

"Yes," he said, "I know him, he is a man of worth, of great worth."

"We suddenly stopped having him here."

"That is so."

"Could you not tell me how that happened?"

"I should be sorry if it were known."

"You can count on my discretion."

"They wrote to the Archbishop against him, I think."

"And what could they say?"

"That he lived too far off; could not come when he was wanted; was too austere a disciplinarian; that there was some reason to suspect him of innovating opinions; that he sowed division in the House and came between the nuns and their Superior."

"And how do you know that?"

"From himself."

"You see him, then?"

"Yes, I see him. He has more than once spoken of you to me."

"And what did he say about me?"

"That you were much to be pitied, that he did not understand how you could have held out against all the sufferings you have undergone; that he had only once or twice had occasion to speak to you; but that he did not think you could ever accommodate yourself to the religious life; that he had in mind ..."

There he stopped short, and I added:

"What did he have in mind?"

"The confidence is too strict a one for me to be able to say more."

I did not insist and merely added:

"It was certainly M. Lemoine who came between me and the Superior."

"He did well."

"And why?"

"Sister," he answered, taking on a grave expression, "follow his advice and try to be ignorant of the reasons for it as long as you live."

"But it seems to me that if I knew the danger I should be the more attentive to avoid it."

"The opposite might perhaps be the case."

"You must have a very poor opinion of me."

"I have the only possible opinion of your morals and your innocence. But believe me there is a terrible kind of knowledge that you could not acquire without ruin. It was your very innocence which impressed your Superior. Had you been better instructed she would have respected you less."

"I do not understand you."

"So much the better."

"But can the caresses and familiarities of one woman be dangerous to another?"

There was no answer from Dom Morel.

"Am I not the same as when I arrived here?"

There was no answer from Dom Morel.

"Should I not have continued to be the same? Where, then, is the harm of loving, of saying so, and testifying to it? It is so sweet."

"That is true," said Dom Morel, raising his eyes to me after having kept them lowered while I was speaking.

"Is sweetness then so common in religious houses? My poor Superior, to what a state has she fallen!"

"It is very bad, and I fear it may get worse. She is not made for her state. That is what happens sooner or later to those who run counter to the proclivities of their nature. Constraint diverts them to irregular passions, which are all the more violent for being ill-founded. It is a sort of madness."

"She is mad, then?"

"Yes, she is and will become more so."

"And do you think that such a fate awaits all those who find themselves in a state to which they were not called?"

"Not all. There are those who die first. There are those whose flexible character eventually yields. There are those whom vague hope sustains for a long time."

"And what hope can a nun have?"

"Why, first to break her vows."

"And when that hope is lost?"

"Then she hopes to find the doors open one day, and that men will abandon the absurdity of shutting lively young creatures in sepulchres and that convents will be abolished; or that the House will catch fire; that the walls of the cloister will collapse; or that someone will come to her help. All these suppositions revolve in her mind. The nuns talk it over among themselves. While walking in the gardens they unconsciously look to see if the walls are after all so high: in their cell, they absent-mindedly seize the bars of the grille and shake them gently. If the street is under the windows, they look out at it. If they hear anyone pass, their heart thumps and they sigh dimly for a liberator. If there is any noise which penetrates into the House, they are full of hope. They count on an illness which will put them in touch with a man or end in their being sent off to take the waters."

"True, true," I cried; "you are reading into the depths of my heart. I have built and still build up these illusions."

"And when reflection destroys them, for the health-ful vapours with which the heart endows the reason are from time to time dissipated, then they see all the depths of their misery. They detest themselves; they detest everyone else; they weep, cry out, and feel the approaches of despair. Then some rush to fall at the knees of the Superior and find consolation there. Others prostrate themselves in their cells or at the foot of the altar and call on Heaven to help them. Others tear their clothes or pull out their hair; some look for a deep pit, high windows, or a noose, and sometimes find it. Some, after long self-torture, fall into a sort of brutishness and remain idiots. Others, of a feeble and delicate constitution, are consumed by langour. The organization of others is disturbed and they become raving. Those are happiest in whom the same consol-ing illusions are reborn and flatter them almost to the tomb; their life is divided between error and despair."

"And the most unfortunate," I added, apparently with a deep sigh, "are those who experience all those states of mind in turn ... Oh, Father! how sorry I am that I have listened to you."

"And why?"

"I did not know myself, now I do. My illness will be less lasting. At moments ..."

I was going to continue when another nun came in, then a second and a third, then four, five, or six – I do not know how many. The conversation became general. Some looked at the Director, others listened silently with lowered eyes. Several questioned him at the same time, and all exclaimed at the wisdom of his answers. Meanwhile I had retired into a corner and given myself up to deep meditation. In the middle of this conversation, where each one tried to show off and attract to herself the preference of the holy man by appearing in the most favourable light, some one was heard slowly approaching, stopping at intervals and sighing. They listened and whispered: "It is she; it is our Superior." Then they all sat round in silence. And she, in fact, it was. She came in, her veil falling to her waist, her arms crossed over her chest, and her head drooping. I was the first one she saw. Immediately she withdrew from under her veil one of her hands with which she covered her eyes, and, turning a little to one side, she signed to us all to go out together. We went out silently, and she remained alone with Dom Morel.

I foresee, my lord, that you are going to form a bad opinion of me; but, since I was not ashamed of what I did, why should I blush to admit it? And then how suppress in this story an event which was not without important consequences? Let us say, then, that I have a peculiar turn of mind. When what I am describing is likely to excite your esteem or increase your sympathy, I write perhaps well, perhaps badly, but with an incredible swiftness and facility; my soul is cheerful, expression comes to me without difficulty, my tears flow gently; it seems to me that you are with me, that I see you and that you are listening to me. If, on the contrary, I am compelled to exhibit myself to you in an unfortunate light, I think with difficulty, I cannot express myself, my pen runs badly, the very nature of my handwriting changes, and I can only go on because I secretly flatter myself that you will not read these parts of my story. Here is one of them.

When all the Sisters had withdrawn, "Well, what did you do?" – Can't you guess? No, you are too high-minded for that. I went downstairs on tiptoe and took up my position at the parlour door to listen to what was being said there. "That is very bad," you will say. Well, yes it was, very bad; I said so to myself, and my agitation, the precautions I took not to be seen, the number of times I stopped, the voice of my conscience urging me at each step to go back, never allowed me to doubt it. But my curiosity was too strong and I went on. But if it is wrong to try and overhear the conversations of two people, is it not still worse to pass it on to you? This is one of those parts of my story which I can only write because I flatter myself that you will not read it, not that that is true, but I have to persuade myself.

The first word I heard after quite a long silence made me tremble all over. It was:

"Father, I am damned."[16]

I reassured myself and listened. The veil which had hidden from my eyes the dangers I had run was being torn off, when I was called away. I had to go, so I went. But alas! I had heard all too much. What a woman, my lord, what an abominable woman! ...

[Here the memoirs of Sister Susan stop. What follows is only a rough sketch of what she intended to say in the rest of her story. Apparently the Superior went mad, and the fragments which I am going to transcribe can only refer to her unfortunate state of mind.]

After this confession we had several days of peace. Joy returned to the community, and I received compliments which I angrily rejected. She no longer avoided me; she would look at me, but my presence no longer seemed to disturb her. I did my best to hide the horror which she inspired in me since by my fortunate or fatal curiosity I had got to know her better.

Soon she became silent and said nothing but "Yes" or "No". She walks about alone. She refuses food. Her blood is fired, fever attacks her, and delirium follows on fever.

Alone in bed, she sees me, talks to me, asks me to come and stand beside her, addresses me the tenderest remarks. If she hears steps round her room she cries: "It is she who is going by. I recognize her step. Let her be called in ... No, no, let her be."

The curious thing is that she never made a mistake, taking another for me.

She would laugh out loud and next moment burst into tears. The Sisters used to stand round her silently, and some wept with her.

Suddenly she would say: "I have not been to chapel. I have not said my prayers. I want to get out of bed. I want to dress. Let me dress." If her wishes were opposed she added: "At any rate, give me my prayer-book." She would be given it, open it, turn over the pages with her finger, and continue to do so when she had got to the end, while her eyes wandered.

One night she went down to chapel alone. Some of the Sisters followed her; she prostrated herself on the steps of the altar, began to groan, sigh, and pray out loud. She went out and came back again. She said: "Go and look for her. Such a pure soul! Such an innocent creature! If she would join her prayers with mine!" Then, addressing the whole community and turning towards the empty stalls, she cried: "Go away, go away, all of you. Let her remain alone with me! You are not worthy to come near her. If your voices mingled with hers your profane incense would corrupt the sweetness of hers in the sight of God. Withdraw! Withdraw!" Then she exhorted me to ask help and forgiveness of Heaven. She saw God. Heaven appeared to her furrowed with lightning, opening and thundering over her head, angels descended in anger, the looks of the Divinity made her tremble. She ran wildly round, buried herself in the darkest corners of the chapel, appealed for pity, glued her face to the ground, drowsiness overcame her, the cold damp of the place seized her, and she was carried into her cell like one dead.

She was quite ignorant next day of this terrible scene during the night. She said: "Where are the Sisters? I never see anyone now. I am left alone in this House.

They have all abandoned me, Saint Theresa as well. They are quite right. Since Saint Susan is no longer there I can go out, I shall not meet her ... Oh! if I could meet her. But she is no longer there, is she? She is no longer there? Happy the House which owns her! She will tell everything to the new Superior! What will be thought of me then? ... Is Saint Theresa dead? I have heard the death-knell tolling all night. Poor girl! She is lost for ever, and it's my fault, my fault! One day I shall be confronted with her. What shall I say to her? What shall I answer her? ... Woe to her! Woe to me!"

At another moment she said: "Have the Sisters come back? Tell them that I am very ill ... Lift up my pillows ... Unlace me ... I feel something oppressing me here. My head is burning. Take off my coifs ... I want to wash ... Bring me water ... Pour it out ... More ... They are white, but my soul is still soiled; I wish I were dead. I wish I had never been born, I should not have seen her."

One morning she was found barefooted, in her shift, with her hair undone, howling, foaming at the mouth, and rushing round her cell, with her eyes shut and her body pressed against the wall ... "Go away from this gulf. Do you hear those cries? They come from Hell. I see flames rising from that deep abyss. From amid those fires I hear confused voices calling me ... O Lord, have pity on me! Quick, ring the bell, summon the community. Tell them to pray for me. I shall pray as well ... But it is scarcely day, the Sisters are asleep ... I have not closed my eyes all night, I should like to close my eyes but cannot."

One of the Sisters said:

"Madam, you have some private grief. Confide it to me, that will console you, perhaps."

"Sister Agatha, listen to me. Come close up ... closer ... closer still ... No one must hear us. I am going to tell you everything, everything, but keep my secret for me ... You have seen her?"

"Whom, Madam?"

"Is it not true that no one is as sweet as she? Such a walk! Such reserve! Such nobility! Such modesty! Go to her ... Tell her ... No, say nothing, don't go ... You could not get near her. Heavenly angels guard her, they watch over her. I have seen them, you would see them, you would be frightened as I was. Stay here. Suppose you went, what could you say to her? Invent something at which she might not blush ..."

"But, Madam, if you consulted your Director ..."

"Yes, why yes ... No, no I know what he will tell me, I have heard it all already ... What should I talk to him about? ... If I could only lose my memory! If I could only return into nothingness, or be born again! Do not call the Director, I would rather be read the Passion of Our Lord Jesus Christ ... Read ... I am beginning to breathe again ... It only needs one drop of blood to purify me. Look, it gushes forth boiling from His Side. Incline the sacred wound above my head ... His blood flows over me, but does not rest there ... I am lost. Take down that crucifix. Bring it me."

It was brought to her. She clasped it in her arms, kissed it all over, and added: "Her eyes, her lips. When shall I see her again? Sister Agatha, tell her I love her. Describe my condition to her. Tell her I am dying ..."

She was bled and baths given her, but the remedies seemed to increase her ills. I dare not describe to you all the indecent gestures that she made or the dishonourable remarks that escaped her in her delirium. Continually she put her hand to her forehead as though to drive off evil thoughts and images. Heaven knows what images! She buried her head in her bed and covered her face with the sheets. "It is the Tempter!" she said. "It is he. What a strange form he has taken on! Get the Holy Water ... Throw the Holy Water over me! Stop! Stop! He has gone!"

She was soon sequestered. But her prison was not so well guarded that she did not succeed one day in escaping. She had torn her clothes to pieces and was running naked about the corridors, with but two ends of broken rope descending from her arms. She cried out: "I am your Superior. You have all taken your oath! You must obey me! You have imprisoned me, you wretches! This is the way you repay my kindness. You insult me because I am too kind-hearted. I shall not be so again ... Fire ... Murder ... Thieves ... Help ... Help, Sister Theresa; Help, Sister Susan ..." Meanwhile they had laid hands on her and she was led back to prison, and she said: "You are right, you are right. Alas! I have gone mad, I feel it."

Sometimes she seemed obsessed with the spectacle of different tortures. She saw women with ropes round their necks, or their hands tied behind their backs, and others with torches in their hands; she joined those who were making public confession. She thought she was being led off to death, and said to the executioner: "I have deserved my fate, I have deserved it. If only this torture were my last. But in eternity! An eternity of flames! ..."

I am saying nothing here which is not true. But I could add a great deal more which I have either forgotten or else blush to soil the paper with. After living several months in this deplorable condition she died. What a death, my lord! I saw her; I saw that terrible image of despair and crime at her last hour! She thought herself surrounded by infernal spirits. They were awaiting her soul to seize it. She said in a choking voice: "There they are! There they are!" – and as she warded them off on each side of her with a crucifix, which she held in her hand, she howled and cried: "God ... God!" Sister Theresa soon followed her, and we had another Superior, an old woman who was a mass of bad temper and superstition.

I am accused of having bewitched her predecessor; she believes it, and my troubles begin again. The new Director is similarly persecuted by his Superiors and persuades me to fly.

My flight is planned. I go into the garden between eleven and midnight. Cords are thrown me and I tie them round me. They break and I fall. My legs are torn and my loins bruised. A second and a third attempt and I am on the top of the wall. I descend. What is my astonishment when, instead of the post-chaise which I had hoped to find, I perceive a poor public conveyance. I am on the road to Paris with a young Benedictine. I was not slow to perceive from the indecent tone he adopted and the liberties he allowed himself that none of the stipulated conditions were being observed. Then I began to regret my cell and to feel all the horror of my situation. Here I shall describe the scene in the cab. What a scene! What a man! I scream. The cabman comes to my rescue. Violent quarrel between the cabman and the monk.

I reach Paris. The cab stops in a little street at a narrow door opening into an obscure and dirty alley. The mistress of the house comes to meet me and installs me on the top floor in a little room containing most of the furniture necessary. I receive the visits of the woman who occupies the first floor.

"You are young and must be bored; come down to my room. You will find a cheery company of men and women, not as charming but nearly as young as yourself. We are talking, playing, singing, and dancing – all sorts of amusements. And if you turn the heads of all our cavaliers the ladies will be neither jealous nor angry. Come along!"

The woman who talked to me like this had a gentle look, a soft voice, and a very insinuating manner of speech.

I passed a fortnight in this house exposed to all the solicitations of my perfidious ravisher and to all the tumultuous scenes of an ill-reputed house, every moment on the look-out for the chance of escape.

One day it came. Night was far advanced. Had I been near my convent I should have gone back. I run, without knowing where. Some men stop me. Terror seizes me. I fall fainting with exhaustion at the door of a tallow-chandler's shop. People come to my assistance. On regaining consciousness I find myself stretched out on a pallet, surrounded by several people. They asked me who I was, and I do not know what I said. I was given the servant of the house to take me back. I take her arm and we go off. We had already gone some distance when the girl said to me:

"I suppose you know where we are going?"

"No, child, to the workhouse, I suppose."

"The workhouse? Are you really homeless?"

"Alas yes."

"What have you done to be turned out at this hour? But here we are at the door of Saint Catherine's.[17] We will see if we can get anyone to open the door. In any case, do not be frightened; you shall not remain in the street, you shall sleep in my room."

I return to the tallow-chandler's. Horror of the servant when she sees that the skin has been torn off my legs by my fall when leaving the convent. I pass the night there. Next evening I return to Saint Catherine's. I stay three days, after which I am told I must either go to the general workhouse or take the first situation which offers.

Dangers I ran at Saint Catherine's at the hands of the men and women there. For it is there, I am told, that the rakes and procuresses go for girls. Thought I foresaw want, this lent no sort of charm to the gross seductions to which I was exposed. I sell my small possessions and choose others more suitable to my condition.

I go into service with a washerwoman, where I now am. I take in linen and iron it. It is hard work; I am ill-fed and ill-lodged, and have a bad bed. But on the other hand I am humanely treated. The husband drives a cab; his wife is rather rough, but a good-hearted woman. I should be quite contented with my condition if I could hope to enjoy it peacefully.

I have learnt that the police have got hold of my ravisher and returned him to his Superiors. Poor man, he is more to be pitied than I. His attempt has got abroad, and you cannot know how cruelly monks punish any crime that causes a scandal. He will pass the rest of his life in a dungeon. So shall I if I am caught. But he will live longer than I shall.

I am suffering from my fall. My legs are swollen and I cannot walk. I work sitting down, as I can hardly stand upright. Meanwhile I am apprehensive about what will happen when I am well. What excuse shall I then have for not going out? And how dangerous it will be to show myself! Fortunately, I have heaps of time before me. My relatives, who cannot doubt I am at Paris, are certainly making every possible enquiry. I had meant to summon M. Manouri into my loft. But he is dead.

I live in perpetual alarm at the least noise I hear in the house, on the staircase, or in the street. Terror seizes me, I tremble like a leaf, my knees give way under me, my work falls from my hands. I hardly ever close my eyes at night. And if I do get to sleep I wake up continually, speak, call out, and scream. I cannot imagine how those round me have not guessed my secret.

My escape is apparently abroad. I expected it. One of my companions mentioned it yesterday and added some odious circumstances and reflections of the kind that cause pain. Happily she was hanging the wet washing on the lines, with her back to the lamp, and so could not observe my agitation. Still, my mistress, who had observed I was crying, said to me:

"What is the matter Mary?"

"Nothing," I answered.

"Good gracious," she added, "are you silly enough to cry about a bad nun, without morals or religion, who falls in love with a nasty monk and runs off from her convent with him? You must indeed be soft-hearted. She had only got to eat and drink, say her prayers, and sleep. She was very well where she was, and had only to stay there. If she had had to go down to the river three or four times with the weather what it is now she would soon have learnt to put up with her position!"

To which I answered that we could not tell what she had gone through. I had better have remained silent and then she would not have added: "Come, come! she's a body that God will punish." On this I bent over the table and remained there till my mistress said:

"But, Mary, what are you dreaming about? While you sleep the work stands still!"

I never had the spirit of the cloister, as appears from my conduct. But I have grown accustomed in religion to certain practices which I repeat mechanically. For instance, if a bell rings, I make the sign of the cross or go down on my knees. If anyone knocks at the door, I say "*Ave*." If I am put a question, my answer always ends with "Yes or No, Mother, or Sister." If a stranger comes, my arms cross themselves over my chest, and, instead of curtsying, I bow. My companions burst out laughing and think it amuses me to imitate a nun. But their mistake cannot possibly last. My blunders will give me away and I shall be ruined.

My lord, help me quickly. Doubtless you will say to

me: "Tell me what I can do for you." This. I have no great ambitions and should like a place as lady's-maid or housekeeper, or even as an ordinary servant, provided I could live in retirement in the country, in the depths of the provinces, with worthy people who do not have a large number of visitors. Wages are of no importance. Safety, rest, bread, and water. You may be sure that I shall give satisfaction. In my father's house I learned to work and at the convent to obey. I am young and of a very mild disposition. When my legs are cured I shall have more than enough strength for my work. I can sew, spin, embroider, and wash clothes. When I was in the world I used to mend my own lace, and should soon get into it again. I am far from clumsy and should find nothing beneath me. I can sing, understand music, and can play the harpsichord sufficiently well to please any mother who had the taste for it. I could even give lessons to her children, but should fear to be betrayed by these signs of a careful upbringing. If I had to learn hairdressing I would find someone to teach me, and soon acquire this small accomplishment. My lord, a tolerable position if possible, or any sort of situation is all I need, and I ask for nothing more. You can answer for my morals, which are sound despite appearances. I am even religious. Ah, my lord, all my ills would be past and over, and I should no longer have anything to fear of men, had God not stayed my hand. That deep well at the end of the garden! How often have I visited it! – and only did not hurl myself in because I was allowed such complete liberty to do so. I know not what fate is in store for me. But if I must go back one day into a convent, of whatever kind, I answer for nothing. There are wells everywhere. But pity me, my lord, and save yourself in the future from long regrets.

PS. – I am crushed with fatigue, in continual terror, and cannot sleep. I have just reread, while lying down, these memoirs which were hurriedly written. I perceive that quite unintentionally I have been in each line truthful about my misfortunes but have greatly exaggerated my attractions. Can it be that we think men less moved by the picture of our sufferings than the image of our charms? Do we say to ourselves that it is easier to attract their fancy than to stir their hearts? I know them too little, and have studied myself too little, to say. Still, what would the noble lord, who is known as a man of exquisite tact, think if he were persuaded that I was appealing not to his benevolent but to his vicious instincts? This thought distresses me. Truly he would be wrong to impute to me personally an instinct common to all my sex. I am a woman, perhaps rather a coquette for all I know. But I am so naturally and without guile.

PREFACE
TO THE PRECEDING WORK,

TAKEN FROM THE
CORRESPONDANCE LITTÉRAIRE
OF M. GRIMM, 1770[18]

THIS charming Marquis had left at the beginning of the year 1759 to go and live on his estate in Normandy, near Caen. He had promised us to remain there only long enough to put his affairs in order; but his stay insensibly lengthened; he was with his children once more; he was fond of the local *curé*; he had become a gardening addict; and since an imagination as vivid as his required some object, he had suddenly become an ardent religious zealot. Despite this, he still loved us tenderly; but very likely we should never have seen him in Paris again, if he had not lost his two sons, one after the other. This event restored him to us about four years ago, after an absence of more than eight. His devotion has evaporated, as all things evaporate in Paris, and he is today more lovable than ever.

As we very much disliked losing him, we took counsel together, after having borne his absence for fifteen months, as to the best means of getting him back to Paris. The author of the preceding "Memoirs" recalled that just before his departure there had been much talk in society about a young nun at Longchamps who had made a legal appeal against her vows, into which she

213

had been forced by her relations. This poor recluse so excited the interest of M. de Croismare that, without having seen her, knowing her name, or even ascertaining if the facts were true, he solicited in her favour all the Counsellors of the Grand' Chambre of the Paris Parliament. Despite this generous intervention, by some accident Susan Simonin lost her case, and her vows were pronounced valid. M. Diderot resolved to re-open the affair to our advantage. He pretended that the nun in question had had the luck to escape from the convent, and in consequence wrote in her name to M. de Croismare to ask for help and protection. We had every hope of seeing him arrive as rapidly as possible to help his nun, or, if he saw through our plot at once, we were sure at any rate of a good subject for a laugh. But the matter took on a very different complexion, as you will see by the correspondence I am about to publish between M. Diderot or the pretended nun and the loyal and charming Marquis de Croismare, who never suspected our perfidy for an instant. It is this perfidy that has so long weighed upon our consciences. We passed supper-time reading out, amid shouts of laughter, letters intended to reduce our worthy Marquis to tears, and with the same shouts of laughter the answers of our worthy and generous friend. However, when we saw that the tender-hearted benefactor was getting too much interested in the fate of this unhappy friend, M. Diderot decided to let her die, preferring to cause the Marquis some distress rather than to risk tormenting him more cruelly by letting her live longer. On his return to Paris we confessed our iniquitous plot. He laughed at it, as you may well believe, and the misfortunes of the unhappy nun have served but to strengthen the ties uniting those who have survived her. But he never spoke of it to M. Diderot.

And now for a circumstance scarcely less singular. While this mystification went to the head of our friend in Normandy, the imagination of M. Diderot was similarly excited. He was persuaded that the Marquis would never admit a young person into his house without knowing her, and so began to write out in detail the story of our nun.

One day when he was entirely absorbed in his work one of our friends, D'Alainville,[19] went to call on him and found him plunged in grief, with his face bathed in tears.

"What on earth is the matter?" said M. D'Alainville; "what a state you are in!"

"What is the matter?" answered Diderot; "I am making myself miserable with a story I am writing ..."

It is certain that if he had completed that story, it would have become one of the truest, most interesting and most pathetic novels that we possess. One could not read a page of it without shedding tears; and yet there was no love-interest in it. It was a work of genius which at every point showed the strongest proof of the author's imagination: a work of public and general utility, for it was the cruellest satire ever written on our cloisters. It was all the more insidious in that the first part was all eulogy. His young nun possessed an angelic devotion and, in her simple and feeling heart, preserved the sincerest respect for everything she had been taught to venerate. But this novel only ever existed in fragments and remained so;[20] it is lost like an infinity of other productions of a rare man who would have immortalized himself by twenty masterpieces if, being a better husbander of his time, he had not squandered it on a thousand idlers, whom I shall cite at the Last Judgment, where they will have to answer before God for their crime.

(And I shall add, for I know M. Diderot a little myself, that he did in fact complete this novel and it is the very "Memoirs" you have just been reading, from which will be seen how important it is to distrust the eulogies of friends.)

This correspondence and repentance are all that we have left of our poor nun. You must remember that all these letters, and also those of the nun, were forged by this child of Belial, and that the letters of her generous protector are genuine and written in good faith, a truth of which we could hardly convince M. Diderot, who thought the Marquis and his friends must have been making fun of him.

From the nun to M. le Comte de Croixmar,
Governor of the Royal Military College

"A wretched woman, in whom M. le Marquis de Croixmar took some interest three years ago when he lived next door to the Royal Academy of Music, learns that he is at present residing at the Military College. She sends to find out if she can still count on his kindness, now that she is more to be pitied than ever. A word in reply, if possible: the situation is desperate. But it is important that the person who delivers this note should suspect nothing."

Answer

"A mistake has arisen. The Marquis de Croismare in question is at present living at Caen."

This note was written in the hand of a young person, whose services were employed throughout the correspondence. A messenger took it to the Military College and brought back the verbal answer. M. Diderot thought this first step necessary for several very good reasons. The nun appeared to mix up the two cousins and not to know exactly how to spell their name. Thus she learnt quite naturally that her protector was at Caen. Very likely the Governor of the Military College would quiz his cousin about the letter and send it on, which would give a very genuine air to our virtuous adventuress. The Governor, a most amiable man, like every one of his name, was as much distressed as we were by the absence of his cousin, and we hoped to make a conspirator of him. After getting his answer the nun wrote to Caen:

"Monsieur,
I do not know whom I am writing to. But in my present distress it is to you that I address myself, whoever you may be. If I have not been deceived at the Army College, and if you really are the generous Marquis whom I am seeking, I shall thank God. If you are not, I do not know what I shall do. But I shall take courage from the name you bear; I hope that you will succour an unhappy girl, for whom you, my lord, or another M. de Croismare, not of the Army College, used your influence in an attempt she made two years ago to

be quit of imprisonment for life, to which the cruelty of her parents had condemned her. Despair has just induced me to take a second step, of which you will doubtless have heard tell: I have escaped from my convent. I could no longer tolerate what I had to suffer there. And there remained to me only this method, or a greater crime still, by which to gain that liberty which I had sought from the fairness of the law. My lord, as you have been before my protector I hope my present situation will touch your heart and revive in you a feeling of pity. Perhaps you will think it is unbecoming of me to have recourse to an unknown man in circumstances like mine. Alas! my lord, if you but knew the state of friendlessness to which I am reduced, if you had any idea of the brutality with which all scandals are punished in religious houses, you would excuse me! But you have a feeling nature and you will be afraid of having on your conscience an innocent creature hurled into a dungeon for the rest of her life. Monsieur, do me the service I ask of you. It is a work of charity which you will remember with satisfaction as long as you live, and for which God will reward you in this world or the next. Above all, my lord, remember that I live in a state of perpetual alarm, and that I shall count the moments. My relations must suspect that I am at Paris. They are certainly making every possible effort to discover my whereabouts. Do not allow them the time to find me. I have brought away with me everything I possess. Up to now I have been living on my work and the kindness of a good woman, who is a friend of mine, and to whom you can address your answer. She is called Mme Madin, and lives at Versailles. This kind friend will provide me

with all I need for the journey, and, once placed, I shall
need nothing and shall no longer be an expense to her.
My lord, my conduct shall justify the protection you
may accord me. Whatever you reply, I shall blame
nothing but my hard lot.

Here is Mme Madin's address:

Madame Madin,
  at the Pavillon de Bourgogne,
   Rue d'Anjou,
 Versailles.

Be good enough to use two envelopes, the first for the
address, and with a cross on the second.

Oh, how I want to have your answer! I am in
continual anxiety.

   Your most humble and obedient servant,
      SUSAN SIMONIN."

This letter will be found in more extended form at the
end of the novel proper, where M. Diderot inserted it, at
the time when, the first rough draft having fallen into
his hands after twenty-one years of oblivion, he decided
to revise and put it into shape.

We needed an address to which answers might be
sent; we lit upon a certain Mme Madin,[21] wife of a
former infantry officer, who really lived at Versailles.
She knew nothing of our rascally behaviour, nor of the
letters we subsequently made her write to herself, and to
write which we made use of another young person.
Mme Madin only knew that she had to receive and
transmit to me all letters marked Caen. Chance had it
that M. de Croismare, on his return to Paris about eight

years after our crime, met Mme Madin in the house of one of our woman friends who had been in the plot.[22] This came as a thunderbolt. M. de Croismare was intending to inform himself thoroughly about the unfortunate girl who had interested him so much and about whom Mme Madin knew absolutely nothing. This was also the moment of our "general confession" and absolution.

Answer of the Marquis de Croismare

"Your letter has reached the very person that you were seeking. You are not mistaken as to my feelings. You can leave at once for Caen, if it suits you, to look after a young lady. Let the lady who is your friend send me word that she is despatching a lady's-maid of the kind I want, with such a recommendation of your capacities as she pleases, without going into any details. Let her also let me know the name you have chosen, the carriage you will be taking, and, if possible, the day of your departure. If you take the Caen coach, it leaves Paris early on Monday morning, arriving here Friday. It puts up at Paris in the Rue Saint Denis, at the Great Stag. If you find nobody to meet you on your arrival at Caen, go, while you are waiting, to M. Gassion's, opposite the Place Royale. As the strictest incognito is necessary on both sides, let your friend return this letter, in which you can have complete confidence, though it is not signed. Only keep the seal, which will enable the person to whom you will report yourself at Caen to identify you. Follow exactly and diligently the instructions in this letter, and for the sake of prudence bring neither letters, papers, nor anything else which might cause you to be recognized. They can easily come on at another time. Count confidently on the good intentions of your servant.

... near Caen, February 6th, 1760."

This letter was addressed to Mme Madin. There was a cross on the other envelope, according to the arrangement made. The seal represented a Cupid, holding a torch in one hand and two hearts in the other, with a motto which was illegible, because the seal had been broken when the letter was opened. It was natural that a young nun, who knew nothing about love, should take this representation for that of her guardian angel.

Answer of the nun to the Marquis de Croismare

"Monsieur,

I have received your letter. I think I have been very ill, very ill. I am very weak. If God takes me to Him I shall pray unceasingly for your salvation. If I recover I shall do whatever you tell me, my dear sir! You good man! I shall never forget your kindness. My kind friend ought to be coming from Versailles now. She will tell you everything.

I shall be careful to keep your seal. I see that it is the impress of a holy angel. It is you, my guardian angel."

M. Diderot, not having been able to come to the robbers' meeting, this answer was sent without being passed by him. He did not approve of it, and asserted that it would give our treachery away. He was mistaken and wrong, I think, in not liking our answer. However, in order to satisfy him we inserted in the books of our criminal committee the following answer, which was never sent. In any case, the news of her illness was essential in order to postpone the nun's departure for Caen.

FROM OUR RECORDS[23]

That is the letter that was sent, and here follows the one that Sister Susan ought to have written.

"Monsieur,
Thank you for all your kindness. It is unnecessary to think of anything further – everything is over with me. I shall appear in a moment before the God of Pity, and there I shall remember you. They are discussing whether they shall bleed me the third time. They will give what they think the proper orders. Good-bye, my dear sir. I hope my next dwelling-place will be happier than this one. We shall see each other there."

From Mme Madin to the Marquis de Croismare

"I am beside her bed, and she urges me to write to you. She was in the last extremity, and, as I cannot easily leave Versailles, I could not get to help her sooner. You may be sure, my lord, that she has gone through a great deal. She had a fall, which she hid from me. She was suddenly attacked with burning fever, which could be overcome only by bleeding. I think she is now out of danger. What disturbs her at the moment is the fear that

222

her convalescence must be a long one, and that she may
not be able to leave for a month or six weeks. She is
already very weak and will get weaker. Try then, my
lord, to gain time, and let us work together to save the
most unfortunate and interesting creature in the world.
I must describe the impression that your letter made on
her. She has wept much, and written the address of M.
Gassion at the back of a *Saint Susan* in her breviary.
Then she wanted to answer you, though so weak. She
had just passed through a crisis. I cannot tell what her
letter to you may have contained because she hardly
knew what she was doing. Excuse this letter, my lord,
but I am writing to you in a hurry. I am extremely
unhappy about her and do not at all want to leave her,
but it is quite impossible for me to remain here several
days in succession. Here is the letter that you wrote her.
I am despatching another along the lines you suggested.
In it I do not dwell on her social accomplishments. They
are unsuitable for the life she is going to live, and it
seems to me that she must give them up completely if
she wishes to remain unrecognized. Still, everything I
am saying about her is true. No, my lord, there is no
mother who would not be overjoyed at having such a
child. My first care, as you might imagine, has been to
assure her safety, and that is now done. I shall never
bring myself to let her go before her health is completely
restored, which cannot be before a month or six weeks,
as I had the honour of telling you before. And this is on
the assumption that there is no relapse. She is keeping
the seal of your letter. It is in her *Hours* and under her
pillow. I have not dared tell her that it was not yours. I
had broken it on opening your reply and replaced it

223

with my own. In her then dangerous state I could not risk sending her your letter without reading it first. I venture to ask you to send her a line, which will sustain her in her hopes, and I could not answer for her life if these hopes failed her. If you could be kind enough to give me a few details about the house to which she is going I would make use of them to keep quiet her fears. You may be quite sure about your letters. They will be sent back as regularly as the first one, and you should be reassured by the fact that my own self-interest will prevent my doing anything rash. We will conform in everything, unless you alter your arrangements. Farewell, my lord. The unfortunate darling prays for you whenever the state of her head permits it. I still expect your answer, my lord, as before, at the Pavillon de Bourgogne.

February 16th, 1760."

Letter of recommendation from Mme Madin, as requested by the Marquis de Croismare

"Monsieur,

The person in question is called Susan Simonin. I love her as my own child; but still you can take everything I am going to say literally, as I am not given to exaggeration. She has lost both her father and her mother; she is of good birth and education. She can do all those little things which one learns if one is capable and industrious. She talks not much, but quite well, and writes naturally. If the person for whom you intend her wishes to be read to, she reads magnificently; she is of medium height, and has a very good figure. I have rarely seen a more interesting face. She will perhaps be thought rather young, for I think she has hardly completed her seventeenth year.[24] But what she lacks in the experience born of years she quite makes up for in what is taught by suffering. She is very discreet and has more than usually good judgment. I can answer for the excellence of her character. She is religious, but not the least narrow-minded. She has a very simple nature, a quiet gaiety, and is never out of humour. I have two daughters, and, if her special circumstances did not prevent Mlle Simonin settling in Paris, I should ask for no other governess for them. I do not hope to find another one so good. I have known her since her childhood, and she has always lived under my eyes. She will leave here well set up. I will make myself responsible for her travelling expenses, and for those of the return journey, if she is sent back. This is the least I can do for her. She has never left Paris and does not know where she is going. She thinks herself lost, and I have had all the trouble in the world to reassure her. One word from you, my lord, as to the person for whom she is designed, the house which she will inhabit, and the duties which she will be expected to perform will have more effect on her than anything I can say. Surely it is not putting too great a strain on your good nature to ask you to do this. Her one fear is that she may not be a success. The poor child does not know of what she is capable.

I have the honour to be, my lord, with all the admiration you deserve,

Your very humble, obedient servant,

MOREAU MADIN.

Paris, February 16th, 1760."

LA RELIGIEUSE

Letter from the Marquis de Croismare to Mme Madin

"Madam,

Two days ago I got your note informing me of Mlle Simonin's illness. Her unhappy fate made me weep; her state of health alarms me. Could I ask you for the consolation of being told about her condition, and of what she intends to do, in a word an answer to the letter which I wrote her? I dare to hope everything from your kindness and from the interest you take in the matter.

Your very humble, obedient servant,

Caen, February 19th, 1760."

The same to the same

"I was in great suspense, Madam, and fortunately your letter has relieved my anxiety about the health of Mlle Simonin and her danger of being discovered. I am writing to her, and you can further reassure her as to the continuance of my interest in her. Her letter had impressed me; and, seeing her embarrassment, I could think of nothing better than to attach her to myself in getting her to look after my daughter, who has unfortunately lost her mother. This, Madam, is the house on which I have decided for her. I am sure of myself, and of my power to mitigate her sufferings without having to be indiscreet, which would perhaps be harder for other people. I shall always be unhappy about her lot and my own inability to do all that I should like, but we have to incline before the laws of necessity. I have a property seven miles from the nearest town, in a pleasant country district, where I live in retirement with my daughter and eldest son, a young man of good instincts and a religious turn of mind, whom I shall not, however, tell about her affairs. As for the servants, they have all been here with me a long time, so that we make up a very quiet and united household. I should add that I regard this proposition only as something to fall back upon. Should she find anything better, I do not intend to hold her by a contract. But she may rest assured that she will always find a sure resource in me. So now she must get well and not worry. I shall wait for her, and meanwhile should much like to have frequent news of her.

I have the honour to be, Madam, your very obedient, humble servant,

Caen, February 21st, 1760."

From the same to Sister Susan
(with a cross on the envelope)

"No one could be more distressed than I am at the condition in which you find yourself. I can become but more and more anxious to procure you some alleviation of the wretched fate which pursues you. Do not worry, get back your strength, and have complete confidence in me. You should think of nothing except regaining your health and keeping safely out of sight. If I could do more to make you comfortable I would do it; but I am handicapped by your position and can only bow to necessity. The person for whom I intend you is one of those whom I love most, and you will be chiefly responsible to me. Thus, as far as possible, I shall be careful to mitigate the little inconveniences inseparable from the way of life which you are adopting. You will owe me your confidence; I shall in turn have confidence in the way you set about your duties. This assurance ought to comfort you and assure you of my way of thinking and the genuine regard with which I am your very humble, obedient servant.

Caen, February 21st, 1760.

I am writing to Mme Madin, who will be able to tell you more."

From Mme Madin

"Marquis de Croismare.
Monsieur,
It is now certain that our dear invalid will recover. No more fever; no more headache: everything promises the promptest convalescence and the best of health. Her lips are still rather white, but her eyes are getting back their brightness. The colour is beginning to come back into her cheeks; her flesh is beginning to get clear again and will soon get back its firmness. Everything is all right, now that her mind is at peace. Now it is, my lord, that she appreciates your benevolence at its full worth; and nothing could be more touching than the way in which she talks of it. I wish I could describe to you all that passed between me and her when I took her your last letters. She took them with trembling hands and scarcely breathed as she read them; she stopped over each line; and, when she had finished, she said to me, as she threw herself on my neck and wept hot tears: 'So God has not abandoned me, Mme Madin, after all. So He wants me to be happy at last. Yes, it is God who

made me write to this good gentleman. Who else in the world would have taken pity on me? Let us thank God for this first promise, that others may be granted us.' Then she sat on her bed and began to pray. Then after this, as she went over some passages in your letter again she said: 'He is entrusting his daughter to me, Mamma; she will be like him, gentle, benevolent, sympathetic like him.' Then she stopped and said with genuine feeling: 'She has lost her mother. I am sorry that I have not got the necessary experience. I have no knowledge, but I will do my best. I shall be mindful day and night of what I owe her father. Gratitude must make up for a number of things. Shall I be ill long? When shall I be allowed to eat something? I no longer feel my fall in the least.' I send you these small details, my lord, hoping they may please you. She put so much innocence and enthusiasm into her speech and action that I was quite beside myself. I would have given everything for you to have seen and heard her. No, my lord, either I know nothing about life or you will have a unique creature who will be the blessing of your house. What you have had the goodness to tell me about yourself, your daughter, your son, and your situation, falls in exactly with her wishes. She persists in the first proposals she made you. She only asks for food and clothing, and you may take her at her word, if you will. Though not rich, I will take over the rest. I love the child; I have adopted her in my heart, and what little I have been able to do for her in her lifetime will be continued after my death. I cannot hide from you that the words, *something to fall back upon*, and *being free to find a better situation if occasion offers*, have caused her pain, and I was not sorry to observe this sign of delicate feeling. I shall not fail to keep you informed about the progress of her convalescence; but I have a great plan, in which I do not despair of succeeding during her convalescence if you could put me in touch with one of your friends. You must have many here. I should need a sensible, discreet, and tactful man, of not too great a station, who could himself, or by means of friends, speak to some people of lofty station whom I would name to him; such a person should have access to Court, though without a Court appointment. According to my way of envisaging the matter, he would not be admitted to our confidence, but would serve us without knowing how. Even should my effort be fruitless, it would be so much gained in that we should thus persuade people that she has left the country. If you can put me in touch with someone, please give me his name and tell me where he lives, and then write and tell him that Mme Madin, whom you have known for a long time, will be coming to ask him a favour, and will he kindly help her if the thing is possible. If you cannot suggest anybody we must not bother any more about it, but think the matter over, my lord. For the rest, you may count on the interest that I take in our unfortunate little friend and the prudence which I have acquired from experience. The pleasure your last letter caused her slightly affected her pulse. But it will not be anything.

I have the honour, my lord, to remain, with my respectful compliments,

Your very humble, obedient servant,

MOREAU MADIN.

Paris, March 3rd, 1760."

Mme Madin's idea of approaching one of Susan's generous protector's friends was a suggestion of Satan, by means of which her agents, in their cunning, hoped to prompt their friend in Normandy to approach me and to take me into his confidence over the whole affair. It succeeded perfectly, as you will see from the rest of the correspondence.

From Sister Susan to the Marquis de Croismare

"Monsieur,

Mother Madin has given me the two answers with which you have honoured me, and also shown me the letter which you have written her. I accept, oh, I accept! It is a hundred times more than I deserve, yes, a hundred times, a thousand times more! I have seen so few people, I am inexperienced, and I know so well all the qualities I ought to possess to be worthy of your confidence in me. My position will form me, and Mother Madin says that that is better than if I went into my position ready formed. But, oh dear! what a hurry I am in to be well, to go and throw myself at the feet of my benefactor, and to serve him by being useful to his daughter in every way I can. I am told that this will take a month at least. A month! What a long time! My dear lord, do not forget me! I am quite stunned with happiness; but they do not want me to write; they prevent my reading; keep me in bed; drown me in camomile; starve me to death; and all for my own good. Heaven be thanked! All the same I obey them greatly against my inclinations.

I am, my lord, with a grateful heart,
      Your very humble, respectful servant,
                  SUSAN SIMONIN.
Paris, March 3rd, 1760."

From the Marquis de Croismare to Mme Madin

"A slight indisposition from which I have been suffering for several days has prevented me, Madam, from answering you sooner, in order to express to you the pleasure which I experienced on hearing that Mlle Simonin was convalescent. I dare hope you will soon be good enough to inform me of her being completely cured, as I fervently desire. But I am deeply distressed that I cannot contribute to the execution of the plan which you contemplate on her behalf. As I do not know it, I can only suppose it excellent because of the prudence which you have always manifested and the interest you take in the subject. I lived a very retired life in Paris, and knew only a small number of persons, as retiring as myself, and acquaintances of the kind you need are not easy to come by. Pray continue to give me news of Mlle Simonin, whose interests are always dear to me.

    I have the honour to be, Madam,
        Your very humble, obedient servant.
March 31st, 1760."

From Mme Madin to the Marquis de Croismare

"Monsieur,
Perhaps I was wrong in not explaining my plan, but I was in such a hurry to put it into practice. This, then, is

what I had thought of. First you must know that the
Cardinal de T———[25] protected her family. They lost
everything by his death, especially my dear Susan, who
had been presented to him as a small child. The old
Cardinal was fond of pretty children: the charms of this
one had struck him, and he had promised to look after
her. But when he passed away, they disposed of her in
the way that you know of, and her protectors thought
they had done enough for the youngest by marrying off
her elder sisters. So it occurred to me that if anyone
could get to Mme la Marquise de T———[26] – who is said
to be, if not compassionate, at least very energetic (but
what does it matter by *whom* good is done?), and who
put herself to endless trouble over my child's law-suit –
and could describe to her the sad plight of a young
person exposed to all the dangers of poverty, in a remote
and alien land, we might by this means extract a small
pension from the two brothers-in-law, who have pock-
eted the whole inheritance and never dream of offering
us assistance. Really, sir, it would be well worth our
both thinking about this. You see, with this small
allowance, together with what I have left her, and what
she would receive from your kindness, she would be
quite comfortable for the present, not so badly off in the
future, and I should see her go off with less regret. But I
know neither the Marquise de T——— nor the secretary
of the late Cardinal,[27] who is said to be a man of letters,
nor anyone who knows them. And it was the child who
proposed I should write to you. For the rest I cannot say
that her convalescence goes quite as I should like. Her
loins were damaged internally, as I think I told you.
The pain from the fall, which had vanished, is making

itself felt again. It comes and goes and is accompanied by a slight internal shivering, but the pulse shows no fever. The doctor tosses his head, and I do not quite like his expression. She is going to Mass next Sunday. She wishes it, and I have just sent her a large hood, which will cover her to the tip of her nose, and under protection of which she will, I think, be able to spend half an hour in the dark little church near us without any danger. She sighs for the moment of her departure, and I am sure she will pray God for nothing more fervently than that He should hasten her recovery. If she felt able to start between Easter and the following Sunday I should not fail to let you know. For the rest, my lord, her absence would not prevent my acting, if I could discover among my acquaintances anyone who could do something with Mme de T—— and Dr. A——,[28] who has a lot of influence over her.

I am, my lord, with infinite gratitude on her behalf and my own,

Your very humble, obedient servant,

MOREAU MADIN.

Versailles, March 23rd, 1760.

P.S. I have forbidden her to write, lest she importune you: this consideration alone restrains her."

The Marquis de Croismare to Mme Madin

"Madam,

Your plan for Mlle Simonin appears excellent and pleases me all the more as I should be delighted to know her amid her misfortunes assured of a tolerable position. I do not despair of finding some friend who may put pressure on Mme de T—— or Dr. A—— or the secretary of the late Cardinal, but all this needs time and care, as much to prevent the secret coming out as to assure myself about the discretion of the people to whom I think I might address myself. I shall not forget this, and meanwhile, if Mlle Simonin persists in her present feelings and her health has sufficiently recovered, nothing need prevent her starting. She will find that my feelings are just the same as is my zeal to mitigate if possible the bitterness of her lot. The state of my affairs and the bad times compel me to live very quietly in the country with my children for reasons of economy: we live very simply. So Mlle Simonin need not put herself to any expense in buying smart clothes. Plain things are enough here. She will find me on my property, and in a simple united household, where I hope she will be able to find pleasure and enjoyment despite the tiresome precautions I shall be compelled to adopt with her. Be good enough to inform me of the day she leaves, and in case she has lost the address I sent her, it is:

At M. Gassion's, opposite the Place Royale, Caen. However, if I know the day of her arrival in time she will find someone there to bring her on here at once.

I have the honour to be, Madam,

Your very humble, obedient servant.

March 31st, 1760."

Mme Madin to the Marquis de Croismare

"Does she persist in her feelings, my lord? How can you doubt it?

What better fate can she have than to go and pass quiet, happy days with a man of position and in a decent family? And where would she lay her head if the retreat you have had the generosity to offer her were lacking? It is she, my lord, who speaks so. I have only to repeat to you what she says. She insisted on going to Mass on Easter Sunday, against my advice, and it did her no good. She came back feverish, and since that unlucky day she has not been well. My lord, I shall certainly not send her off till she is in good health. At present she suffers from inflammation of the loins in the place where she hurt herself when she fell. I have just looked, but can see nothing at all. But my doctor told me yesterday, as we came downstairs together, that he was afraid of vibration setting in and that we must wait and see how it develops. Meanwhile she has a good appetite, sleeps well, and does not lose weight. I only sometimes notice that her cheeks are redder and her eyes brighter than is natural with her. Then her impatience makes me desperate. She gets up and tries to walk, but the moment she leans on her bad side she screams enough to make your heart break. But I hope, despite everything, and have made use of the time to arrange her little trousseau.

There is a dress of English calamanco, which she can wear in one thickness during the warm weather and which she can double for the winter, and another of blue cotton, which she is wearing at present. Several white petticoats, of which two belong to me, of dimity, trimmed with muslin.

Two similar bodices, which I had had made for my youngest daughter and turned out to suit her perfectly. That will make up her summer dress.

Fifteen trimmed shifts, some of cambric, others of

muslin. Halfway through June I will send her the materials for making six others, with a piece of linen whitened for me at Senlis.

Some corsets, aprons, neckerchiefs.

Two dozen pocket handkerchiefs.

Some night-caps.

Six scalloped *dormeuses*,[28] with eight pairs of cuffs with one tuck and three with two.

Six pairs of fine cotton stockings.

This is all I have been able to do for her. I bought her the trousseau the day after the Easter feasts, and I cannot describe to you with what real feeling she accepted it. She looked at one thing, tried another, took me by my hands and kissed them. But she could never restrain her tears when she saw my daughter's bodices. 'Dear me! I said to her, 'what are you crying about? Have you not always been a daughter to me too?'

'*It is true*,' she answered. Then she added: 'I think I should hate to die now when I hope to be happy. Mamma, will the inflammation in my side never disappear? Suppose they put something there?'

I am delighted, my lord, that you do not disapprove of my plan and see how to make it come to something. I owe everything to your foresight. But I think I ought to warn you that the Marquise de T—— is leaving for the country, that Dr. A—— is inaccessible and crabbed, and that the secretary, proud of having been made an Academician after twenty years' canvassing, is returning to Brittany in three or four months from now, and then we shall be quite forgotten. Things lose their interest so quickly here. Even now people hardly refer to us; in a short time they will not do so at all.

Never fear that she will lose the address you sent her. She never opens her *Book of Hours* to pray without looking at it: she might sooner forget her own name of Simonin than that of M. Gassion. I asked her if she did not want to write to you, but she answered that she had begun you a long letter, which was to contain everything she would have to tell you, if God saw good to cure her and let her see you; but that she had a presentiment that this would never happen.

'It is going on too long, Mamma,' she added; 'I shall never profit from your kindness or his. Either his lordship will change his feelings or I shall not get well.'

'How absurd,' I said; 'you may be sure that if you encourage these gloomy thoughts, what you fear will happen.'

She said: '*Let God's will be done.*' I asked her to show me what she had written to you. I was horrified. It is a whole volume, a large volume. 'You are killing yourself with all that,' I said angrily.

'What would you have me do?' she answered. 'When I am not miserable I am bored.'

'And when have you found time to scribble all that down?'

'A little at one time, a little at another. Whether I live or die, I want all my sufferings to be known.'

I forbade her to continue, and her doctor did the same. But pray, my lord, add your authority to my prayers. She regards you as her dear master and will certainly obey you. But as I imagine she finds the hours long, and that she ought to have something to occupy her, were it only to prevent her going on writing, dreaming, and worrying herself, I had her brought an embroidery frame and I have suggested she should begin a waistcoat for you. She was delighted with the idea and has set to work at once. Pray Heaven she be not here long enough to finish it. One word, pray, to prevent her writing and working too much. I had meant to return to Versailles this evening; but I am not happy about her. This vibration beginning worries me, and I want to be with her when the doctor calls again to-morrow. Unfortunately I have some faith in the presentiments of invalids; they know their real condition. When I lost M. Madin, all the doctors assured me he would get over it. But he said himself that he would not; and the poor man spoke only too truly. So I shall stay here and have the honour of writing to you. If I have to lose her I do not think I shall ever get over it. You yourself, my lord, will then be fortunate in not having seen her. Now is the moment when those wretches who determined her to escape feel all they have lost. But it is too late.

I have the honour to be, my lord, with every feeling of respect and gratitude on her behalf and my own,

Your very humble, obedient servant,

MOREAU MADIN.

Paris, April 13th, 1760."

The Marquis de Croismare to Mme Madin

"I share, Madam, with genuine feeling your alarm about Mlle Simonin's illness. Her unfortunate state had always infinitely moved me. But the details into which you were good enough to enter as to her capacities and instincts prejudice me so much in her favour that it would be impossible for me not to take the liveliest interest in her. Thus far from altering in my feelings for her, pray repeat to her all I displayed in my letter to you, and which will undergo no change. I thought it wise not to write to her, so that she would have no occasion to worry herself with answers. There can be no doubt that all work is bad for her in her delicate condition, and, had I power over her, I would use it to check her. I can do no better than ask you to let her know my feelings in this matter. Certainly I should be delighted to have a letter from her personally, but I could not approve of an act of pure politeness on her part, which might help to delay her cure. The interest you take in her makes it unnecessary that I should ask you again to restrain her on this point. You may always be sure of my sincere affection for her and the particular and real regard with which I have the honour to be, Madam, your very humble servant.

April 25th, 1760.

P.S. I shall write at once to one of my friends whom you can approach about Mme de T——. He is called M. G——,[30] secretary to the Duke of Orléans. He lives in the rue Neuve de Luxemburg, near the rue Saint-Honoré: I shall warn him that you are going to call and make it clear that I am under a great obligation to you and ask for nothing better than an occasion to show it. He does not usually dine at home."

From Mme Madin to the Marquis de Croismare

"Monsieur,

How much I have gone through since I had the

honour of writing to you. I have never liked to make you share my sufferings, and I hope you will be grateful to me for not having put your feeling nature to such a severe trial. You know how dear she was to me. Conceive then, my lord, that for a whole fortnight I have seen her steadily slipping towards her end, in the acutest suffering. At last, I think, God has taken pity on herself and me. The unhappy girl is still alive, but it cannot, I think, be for long. Her strength is exhausted, she hardly speaks, and her eyes can barely open. Her patience is all she has left. Without that, what will become of us? My hopes for her recovery suddenly disappeared. An abscess had formed in her side, and had made steady progress ever since her fall. She did not wish it to be opened in time, and when she at last made up her mind to it, it was too late. She feels her last moment coming, and has sent me away, and I admit I am in no state to bear the sight. She received the Sacraments of the Church yesterday between ten and eleven in the evening. She asked for them herself. After this sad ceremony I remained alone by her bed. She heard me sigh, and felt for my hand, which I gave her. She took it and put it to her lips; then drawing me to her, said so low that I hardly heard her:

'Mamma, one favour more ...'

'What, child?'

'Bless me and go away.'

She added: 'His lordship ... do not fail to thank him.'

These must have been her last words. I gave my orders and went to a friend's, where I remained in immediate expectation. It is an hour past midnight. Perhaps at this moment we have a friend in Heaven.

I am with respect, my lord, your very humble and obedient servant,

MOREAU MADIN."

(This letter was written on May 7th, but is undated.)

Mme Madin to the Marquis de Croismare

"The dear child is no more: her sufferings are over; ours have perhaps still a long time to last. She passed from this world to that which awaits us all last Wednesday, between three and four in the morning. As her life was innocent, so her last hours were calm, despite all that had been done to disturb them. Allow me to thank you for the tender interest you took in her. It is the only duty which remains for me to do her. Here are all the letters with which you honoured us. I had kept some and have found the others among the papers which she handed me a few days before her death. They contained, she informed me, the story of her life with her parents, in the three religious Houses where she lived, and what happened to her after she left. I do not think I can read them now. I can see nothing which belonged to her, not even those things which in my love I had intended for her, without deep grief.

I am very glad, my lord, to have been useful to you, and I shall be flattered if you remember me.

I am, sir, with all those feelings of respect and gratitude which are due to men of heart and charity,

Your very humble, obedient servant,

MOREAU MADIN.

May 10th, 1760."

MEMOIRS OF A NUN

The Marquis de Croismare to Mme Madin

"I know, Madam, what it means to a tender-hearted benevolent woman to lose the object to which she is attached, as well as the pleasant opportunity of dispensing the favours so worthily earned both by misfortune and the amiable qualities which were those of the dear child, who is to-day the subject of your grief. I share them as heartily as possible. You knew her – which makes your separation the harder to bear. Though I had not had this advantage, her misfortunes had stirred me deeply and I was enjoying in advance the pleasure of being able to contribute to the peace of her days. If God has willed it otherwise and seen good to deprive me of the satisfaction, which I so greatly desired, I must thank Him for it; but I cannot remain insensible to it. You at any rate have the satisfaction of having acted towards her with the noblest sentiments and the most generous conduct. I admired all you did, and my ambition would have been to imitate you. There remains to me now but the ardent desire to have the honour of knowing you and to express to you in person how greatly I have been delighted by the grandeur of your soul and with what respectful consideration I have the honour to be, Madam, your very humble, obedient servant.

May 18th, 1760.

P.S. Everything relating to the memory of our unhappy friend has become very dear to me. Would it be asking you too much to communicate to me those little accounts which she drew up of her different sufferings? I ask this favour all the more confidently

243

because you told me I had some rights in them. I will be sure to send them back with all your letters at the earliest opportunity, if you think fit. Please send them by the Caen coach, which puts up at the Great Stag, Rue Saint Denis, Paris. It starts every Monday."

So ends the story of the unfortunate Sister Suzanne Saulier (called Simonin in his story and in this correspondence). It is very unfortunate that the memoirs of her life have not been put into order. They would have made very interesting reading. After all the Marquis de Croismare ought to be grateful to his perfidious friends for having offered him an opportunity to succour misfortune with a nobility, disinterestedness and simplicity really worthy of him. His rôle in this correspondence is not the least moving part of the novel.

We shall be blamed perhaps for having inhumanly hastened the end of Sister Susan, but this was made necessary by information received from the château of Lasson, that a room was being made ready to receive Mlle de Croismare, whom her father was going to remove from the convent where she had been since her mother's death. Our informant added that a lady's-maid was expected from Paris, who would also act as governess to the young person, and that M. de Croismare was incidentally trying to find a place for the nursery-maid who had been with his daughter up to now. This information allowed us no choice. Neither the youth, beauty or innocence of Sister Susan, nor her gentle, affectionate and tender nature, which might have touched the least compassionate heart, could save her from her inevitable death. But as we had come to share all the feelings of Mme Madin for this interesting creature, we were almost as much afflicted at her death as was her excellent protector.

If there are certain minor discrepancies between this account and the "Memoirs", it is because most of the letters are later in date than the novel itself; and it will be agreed that if ever there was a useful Preface it is the one you have just read and that it is perhaps the only one the reading of which has had to be postponed to the end of the work.

A QUESTION ADDRESSED TO MEN OF LETTERS

M. Diderot, having spent his mornings composing very eloquent, very cogent, very pathetic and romantic letters, employed later hours in spoiling them – suppressing, on the advice of his wife and his associates in crime, everything that was overdone or exaggerated in them and contrary to perfect simplicity and verisimilitude: with the result that if one had picked up the earlier ones in the street, one would have said: "That is beautiful, most beautiful ...", and if one had picked up the later ones, one would have said: "That is so true ..." Which are the good ones? Those which would have inspired admiration? Or those which were certain to create illusion?[31]

NOTES

1 Diderot is referring to a real establishment, the convent of the Visitation in the rue du Bac, in Paris.

2 It has been suggested that this is a slip for 'Alet', a town in the canton of Limoux.

3 A famous dancing-master of the period.

4 The monastery of the Feuillants lay between the rue Saint-Honoré and the terrace of the Tuileries.

5 The royal abbey of Longchamp, of the order of Sainte Claire, was founded in the thirteenth century, its nuns being known as Clarisses or Urbanistes. It was here that Marguerite Delamarre (see p. vii) took her vows in 1736. Originally austere, it had by the eighteenth century become worldly in tone. Its concerts of sacred music were a favourite attraction for the *beau monde*.

6 The famous aria sung by Télaire in Act I, Scene iii, of Rameau's *Castor et Pollux*.

7 It was the custom in many religious orders for a novice, on the occasion of taking vows, to be presented by her relations in her most elegant clothes, which she then exchanged for a religious habit, which had been blessed by the presiding Bishop.

8 The inference is that she sided with the campaign, enforced by the papal bull 'Unigenitus' of 1713, for the suppression of Jansenism. The Jesuit–Jansenist feud was a burning public issue throughout much of the century.

9 See Note 8.

10 'Qu'elle aille en paix', a euphemism to designate the dungeon, which was called *in pace*.

11 Louis Mannory was a well-known advocate in the Paris Parlement.

12 See Note 10.

13 The age at which a young woman could take religious vows was sixteen (as decreed by the Council of Trent), whereas, in France, she did not attain majority until the age of twenty-five.

14 The congregation of Saint [*sic*]-Eutrope-les-Arpajon, belonging to the order of Annonciades des Dix-Vertus de Notre-Dame (or 'Annonciades rouges'), was founded early in the sixteenth century. It was in reality a hospital order.

15 An historical implausibility, since the famous congregation of Port-Royal was dispersed in 1709.

16 Diderot consulted his friend Mme d'Holbach as to how the

Mother Superior should begin her confession and was impressed by her advice that there was only one phrase possible: 'Mon père, je suis damnée!'.

17 The Hôpital de Sainte-Catherine stood at the junction of the rue Saint-Denis and the rue des Lombards and was run by nuns of the order of Saint Augustine.

18 The Ms. reads '1760', but this would seem to be a simple error, since the Note by Grimm on which the Preface is based appeared in the pages of the *Correspondance littéraire* in 1770.

The opening of Grimm's Note, omitted by Diderot here, ran as follows:

The *Nun* of M. de la Harpe [the play *Mélanie, ou la Religieuse* by Jean-François de la Harpe] has reawakened my conscience, dormant these ten years, by reminding me of a horrible conspiracy of which I was the guiding spirit, in concert with M. Diderot and two or three other bandits of the same complexion among our circle. It is not too soon to confess it and to strive, in the holy time of Lent, to obtain pardon for it and for my other sins and to drown it all in the bottomless well of divine mercy.

The year 1760 is marked in the annals of Parisian gossips by the sudden and startling celebrity of Ramponeau [an author of street farces], and by the comedy of *The Philosophers* [a satire on Diderot and his friends by Charles Palissot], performed on instructions from high authority on the stage of the Comédie Française. All that remains of that business is a scornful recollection of the author of this fine rhapsody, named *Palissot*, which none of his protectors is willing to share; highly-placed persons, who supported his enterprise, feel obliged to disown it in public, as a stain on their honour. Whilst all Paris was enjoying this scandal, M. Diderot, whom this scoundrel of a French Aristophanes chose   his Socrates, was the only one to pay no attention. But what was our own occupation at this time? Please God that it were innocent! We had for long been attached with the tenderest friendship to the Marquis de Croismare, a sometime officer in the King's household regiment but now retired, and one of the most lovable men in the whole country. He is about the same age as Voltaire; and like that immortal man he preserves his youthful spirit with a grace, a gaiety and a piquant charm of manner which, for me, has never lost its savour. One might say that he was one of those 'amiable' men of which the style and pattern is not to be found outside France, for all that amiability and surliness are found the whole world over. I am not speaking of the qualities of his heart, the elevation of his sentiments, the delicate strictness of his probity; I am concerned merely with his intelligence. A vivid and cheerful imagination, an original turn

of mind, unrestrained opinions which he alternately adopts and condemns, a verve always curbed by grace, an incredible activity of mind,
combined with a leisured way of life and the endless resources of Paris,
make him invent needs for himself that have never occurred to anyone
before him, and equally strange ways of satisfying them, bringing him a
continual succession of new pleasures. Here are some of the elements
which make up the being of M. de Croismare, called by his friends 'the
charming Marquis' *par excellence*, as the *abbé* Galiani is for them 'the
charming *abbé*.' M. Diderot, comparing his own *bonhomie* with the
piquant turn of the Marquis, tells him sometimes: 'Your pleasantry is like
that of the flame of spirits of wine, gentle and light and running all over
my fleece without burning a hair.'

19 Henri-Louis d'Alainville (1732–1801), an actor.

20 This, of course, was not in fact the case.

21 Michelle Madin, *née* Moreau (1714–79), was a real person who, in
1758, having separated from her husband and daughter, was living in
Versailles, probably with some employment in the royal household. Not
much is known about Diderot's relations with her.

22 This would have been Mme d'Epinay (1725–83), mistress of
Grimm and a close friend of Diderot, in whose house the original plot had
been concerted.

23 The 'conspirators' evidently kept a detailed record of their
activities.

24 Diderot was several times forced to make adjustments to the age of
his heroine.

25 Cardinal de Tencin (1680–1758).

26 The Cardinal's sister, the Marquise de Tencin (1685?–1749), a
famous literary hostess.

27 The *abbé* Trublet, who became an Academician.

28 Dr Astruc, physician and friend of the Marquise de Tencin.

29 A sort of coif.

30 i.e. Melchior Grimm. It was an added twist to the plot to induce
Croismare to appeal to Grimm, a leading conspirator, for help.

31 The concluding two paragraphs are Diderot's addition.

OTHER TITLES IN
EVERYMAN'S LIBRARY

Everyman's Library, founded in 1906 and relaunched in 1991, aims to offer the most complete library in the English language of the world's classics. Each volume is printed in a classic typeface on acid-free, cream-wove paper with a sewn full cloth binding.